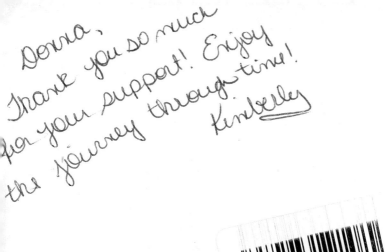

Donna,
Thank you so much
for your support! Enjoy
the journey through time!
Kimberly

A CIVIL AFFAIR
Kimberly Belfer

Kimberly
Belfer

Prologue

The American Civil War was a period of our history that time has never forgotten. For North and South, the survival of economic livelihood, the value of a human life, and the issue of creating a separatist nation, all played their parts in rocking the very foundation of our country's conscience and Constitution. This pre-Civil War story begins in 1860, where we are introduced to a small country town in Kentucky, a state that opted to remain neutral in its decision to secede the Union but bordered several Confederate states.

It is here we meet two young adults as the values and ways of life they were born and raised into are shaken down by the economic upheaval, a Presidential election, and the threat of governmental secession by southern states. Madeline is a woman who cares more about the survival of her family's bookstore than the survival of the state of affairs at the governmental office in Frankfort. Even though her brother is slated to take over the family business, his mind becomes more politically driven, causing Madeline to finally open her eyes to the troubled affairs of the state.

William is a man of little needs, since everything he has ever wanted has been provided for him by the wealth of his family's wheat plantation. As a young man who has been born and bred into high southern society, he knows his place has always been by his father's side and he is destined to become the next plantation master, even though they never quite see eye-to-eye on the politics of the business. His sister has been studying to be a nurse at one of the most elite universities in New York that money could buy. It is through his sister's letters that William realizes the true impact secession has not only on the survival of his family's plantation, but also on his family values.

As their worlds are torn asunder by the political divide of our nation, they are brought together by a common bond: their love for the written word. In this tumultuous tale of the destruction of a way of life and the value of the hard-working man, they find solace in each other. Can their love and their core ideals be saved as our nation and their families fight to survive?

Madeline

1

The summer of 1861 – that was when I had first met William. It had also been the summer that changed my life forever. That was a year ago, but I need to inform you of what had happened before then and how we got to where we are today. I'll begin back in the spring of 1860, shortly after my 18th birthday.

Daddy had just closed up the bookstore for the evening and Mama had already begun supper. My younger brother, Austin, had been seated in his usual chair by the fireplace, reading the weekly news. I had been seated opposite him, fiddling with a cross-stitch I just could not get right, waiting patiently for him to be done with some part of the paper so I could read it.

"You know this election is going to be a bad one," my brother had casually remarked.

"I really wish you'd let me have some of the paper so I can make a proper opinion about it," I had sighed helplessly.

Daddy had come into the room just then and kissed me on the head. "You don't need to have an opinion on it, Maddie. It's not proper for a young lady to dabble in politics." Sometimes, I hated when he had this view about me.

"And why not? Surely a lady could find herself entertaining without a clue what to say to the gentlemen talkin' 'bout politics." I always had to say my piece.

"Supper is ready," Mama had announced, breaking up our quarrel. "Make sure you wash up first!"

My brother had quickly thrown down the paper and ran out back to the wash-bin. Nothing was funnier than his race to the table and the boy sure had an enormous appetite. I had waited patiently again, this time for my turn to use the bin.

Once done, and on his way back to the house, he had turned around and shouted behind him, to me I assume, "I think Breckinridge has a shot!"

I had eyed him suspiciously but let the water run over my hands without saying a word. According to the papers, people had known how critical the election would be to the security of their jobs and their livelihood. With Breckinridge as the leading Southern Democratic Representative, splitting the Democratic party in two with his northern counterpart, Douglas, the divide in our country had begun on a political level, not just on an economic one. Daddy hadn't talked much about it, although my brother had insisted on stirring him up a bit now and again. Why Daddy had never allowed me to get involved in the conversations I'll never know, but he always repeated himself whenever I opened my mouth.

All politics and papers aside, when I had gotten to the dining table, everyone was already seated, food steaming at the center, smelling delicious as always. Mama had always created such feasts for us and we were very fortunate to have help in the kitchen, otherwise she'd be cooking almost the entire day. As I had seated myself and taken one of my brother's hands and one of my mother's, the pleasant smells had wafted around my head, before I bowed it for grace.

"Dear Lord, bless us this evening as we sit at your table..." My father's voice, barely above a whisper, had seemed to drown out in my ears until it was time for the Amen. When my brother had pulled his hand away and gathered food onto his plate, it had almost taken me by surprise. It truly amazed me how he could eat so much in just one sitting.

We hardly talked during the time we ate and we tended to save the conversations for evening tea by the fireplace. But that particular evening tea conversation had been anything but pleasant. Daddy had been the first to speak, while Mama had worked on her cross-stitch quietly.

"I've had a lot more gentlemen coming into the store than usual," he had begun, looking down at his tea as he spoke. "I've never seen so many, most of them scholars. I believe sales have been better than they've ever been."

"That's wonderful!" I believe I had shouted that.

"It's going to be a fine business for you to come into." He had been addressing my brother, who had taken up reading the paper again.

Austin had scrunched up his nose at the thought. Truth be told, my brother had not wanted the family business – the bookstore that had been built at the time of the first settlement in Kentucky. Austin had had his eye on a bigger prize and when he turned sixteen, two years from that time, he had wanted to enter into the world of politics. He had always believed in democracy but he also had a very good knack for getting people to listen – a fine quality in any politician.

"May I be excused from tea?" I had asked politely.

My mother had simply nodded and sighed, knowing she couldn't escape the way I could. I really had not wanted to get in the middle of yet another argument between them. Even though my brother was to inherit the bookstore, I had always found more of an interest in its bookkeeping and sales and atmosphere. The truth was I had secretly hoped my brother *would* go into politics so that *I* could learn the trade. I also always had a book between my fingers, sometimes just reveling in the feel of the spine or the pages. Books to me were like individual lives, waiting to tell their stories.

At that time of year, I believe I had been rereading Shakespeare's sonnets. I had always found myself reading certain ones on the most apropos days, so the words blended with the scene around me. If I remember correctly though, that had been the particular night I had chosen to read one of his tragedies instead. There's something to be said about the chills that run down your spine after reading a Shakespearean soliloquy.

Reading for me was something I always did. Daddy had sent me to a good school in the city so that I could learn to read and write and I never seemed to get enough of my literature classes. It was also probably due to the endless supply of books we had kept in the store. The shelves had seemed to blend together yet they were organized so eloquently.

Looking down at the book in my hand, as I sat in my bedroom, I had reread Hamlet's ode to his father's ghost. I had almost seen his petrified face as he realized the ghost is his father and I had practically felt the air in the room grow colder. Hamlet had just heard the truth of his father's murder by his uncle's hand and the hair on my neck had stood up. It had always pained me to see the characters unable to deal with their realities and I had often wished I could run to them, console them, and make them whole again. My brother would never understand the power of their words the way I did; just as I would never understand the political workings of his mind.

My thoughts had been interrupted though, as raised voices and angry words had come from the tea room. I had known it was inevitable. Austin had always wanted to talk politics and Daddy had always wanted to talk about the business. They had never seen eye-to-eye and it had been deafening to listen to them quarrel so. I had closed my first edition collection of Shakespeare, sighed, and squeezed my eyes shut, willing the noise to stop.

~~*

It had been late spring and the weather in our little town had gotten warmer – the promise of the summer to come. My brother had come home from school in a chipper mood, claiming that Breckinridge was to be making a stop here, in our town. My mother had been in the kitchen and my father had been in the tea room, reading the latest novel he had coveted from the bookstore. It had made me laugh to myself to see how upset he had gotten being interrupted from his book, a trait I no doubt inherited from him.

"And I suppose you want to go to the fanfare?" Daddy had asked him, pulling off his reading glasses and placing a marker between the pages.

"I'd be thrilled!" Austin had jumped up and down in place like a twelve-year-old instead of his fourteen years.

Daddy had looked him up and down then replaced his glasses. "I'd prefer you didn't waste your time with such nonsense."

"But it ain't nonsense! I just want to hear what he has to say!" Austin had protested strongly.

"I said no! I don't want you getting involved in the politics of this country!"

"Why not?" Austin had challenged. I tried so hard not to listen in, but I couldn't help it. It had been so easy with their raised voices.

"There's been talk," was Daddy's reply.

"What kind of talk?" Austin had pressed. I could almost hear the reluctance in my father's voice to answer his inquisitive son.

"There's been talk... around the bookstore. Gentlemen come in and talk politics. They say this election will hurt our economy, change our world."

"What do you mean? This election is exactly what we need! It'll give us a chance to boost our businesses and keep up with the high competition with them Yankee states!" The look of elation in Austin's eyes had been enough to put my father over the edge.

"Now listen here, boy! I will have no more talk of politics or this election in my house! You will not be going to that rally! I will not lose my bookstore because my son stuck his nose where it didn't belong! We work hard for our money and I'll be damned if some educated politician is going to take that away!"

"But that's what Breckinridge understands!" Austin had tried to protest. "There's no reason for us to lose our businesses while the North builds their super-factories!"

"There's been more talk than that, boy! You have no idea what a harsh world it is! There are whispered voices of the consequences of this here election!"

"But –"

"No more, Austin! Enough!"

Daddy had said his piece and Austin had lost the battle. I had known the truth of it though; I had read the papers. News could travel faster now that the railroad had come through our town. People talked and the media wrote it all down – again the power of the written word. There had been talk of a great rebellion – a stirring in the stomach of the South. We had looked at our northern brothers as outcasts, trading in their hard work for complex machinery. Large buildings had littered their cities and smoke had filled their air. It wasn't right, people had said, to make a living without putting your back into your work. They had countered, claiming working a machine was a lot harder than working manually.

Truth be told, I had been scared of them northern folk. Angry they were – bitter from the cold of their winters and smoldering from the heat of their coal-burning turbines. I had never met a Yankee before but I had heard the stories of how different their world was to ours. For one, no one owned another. To some it had been a release from bondage, but to me, it had been a necessity. If Mama had no help in her kitchen, she'd never have time for us, her family. And really, if those plantation owners didn't have their slaves, they'd have to make enough babies so their children could help in the fields. Our economy thrived because there were enough people to work the land; there was no need to build a factory and put those people out of work.

My thoughts had been interrupted yet again when there was a crash in the kitchen. Mama had shouted something and our servants scurried to fix the problem. I had rolled my eyes and my father chuckled, obviously noticing. I had met his eyes and he smiled at me before closing the book he had tried to go back to reading and coming over to me, a package in his hands.

"This is something I found at the bottom of one of the shipments from Raleigh."

I had ripped open the wrapping and gazed at a second edition copy of Wuthering Heights! "Thank you!" I had exclaimed, hugging the book to my chest.

"Now go put it in a safe place where your mama doesn't see it. She has no idea I bought it for you." His smile was the greatest gift a girl could ever have.

I had run up the stairs of our large two-story house and into my room. Carefully pulling a box out of my closet, I had placed the book in with the others. Every now and again my father would buy a special book just for me and include it with his orders to warehouses and bookstores elsewhere. How he had known my original Wuthering Heights had gotten wet on the way home from school one day, I'll never know, but it had been nice to know he thought of me this way. I don't recall him ever buying gifts like this for my brother.

Speaking of my brother, since his argument with Daddy, I hadn't seen him. He hadn't run upstairs to his room and he hadn't gone into the kitchen to bug Mama about supper. He might have slipped out the back door without any of us knowing. I had been putting the box back up on the shelf when he came whipping into my room, scaring me half to death, and causing me to drop the box, books flying everywhere.

"Austin!" I had screamed as I fell from the onslaught of books.

He had just stood there and laughed before helping me put the books away. One by one he had glanced at the titles and then cocked his eyebrow at me. "Does Daddy know you stole all these from the bookstore?"

I had yanked a book from his hands. "I didn't steal any of them. They were gifts."

"You have a secret admirer then?"

"No, they were gifts from Daddy. But, please don't tell Mama."

At supper that night, Austin had opened his big mouth and told Mama I had been stealing books from the bookstore. This had prompted Daddy to explain I hadn't stolen them but they had been gifts from him. This had then steamrolled into an argument about him buying me presents and spending valuable money. I had shot Austin an angry look, excused myself from supper, and ran upstairs to my room. Mama had come upstairs once the dishes were cleared by the servants.

"Madeline, honey, please talk to me. I don't want you to be upset."

"Mama, it's not what you think! I didn't ask him to buy me books!"

"I know but he should not be buying so many. Where are you keeping them all?"

"In a box," I had admitted.

"Please return them to the bookstore in the morning. Every book your father buys could be sold at a better price."

That night my heart had been crushed. Austin had just been himself, I knew. It had always been like him to feign jealousy when something wasn't going his way. Mama had known I had been spending too much time reading and not enough time learning how to run a proper kitchen. Even with my love of all things books, my father had still insisted on giving the bookstore to Austin in four years. I had known I had to give back the books but I had vowed to keep a few of my favorites – namely, Shakespeare, Austen, and a few bits of poetry. I also wouldn't dream of parting with Bronte, Dickens, Anderson, and Grimm. So needless to say, most of my books had not made it back to the bookstore.

William

2

The year was 1860 and I had been 20 years old, going on 21 later that year. For two years my father had been preparing me to take over the family business – our expansive wheat plantation on the outskirts of our small Kentucky town. In those years he had walked me through the fields testing my knowledge about the wheat plant – how the plant grows, when to harvest it, and how to manage over fifty slaves to make sure the crop didn't fail. For those years he had me join him as he brought the wheat to the grist mill, brought the wheat meal to the market, and our money to the bank. We were considered by many to be at the top of our class – high elite with no where else to go but further up (and my father preferred it at the top).

For two years my father, Jackson Lee Hutchinson, had continued to transition me into both the business and adulthood. At twenty, I had mastered the business but not adulthood. My entire life had been sheltered by the society I was raised into and I had no idea what to expect within the few short years to follow. Our world – plantation, slave, and South – would be turned upside down while the country split in two. It had also been during that time that I met a woman I will never forget. But I am getting ahead of myself, as I often do when the conversation veers towards the subject of women. My story begins here, in the late spring of 1860, where things in my adult life were beginning to change.

"Son, come here," Father had commanded from his study.

Sighing, I had followed the sound of his voice. "Yes, Father?"

"Son, I need to talk to you about my plans to expand the plantation. You have a high investment in its future and I value your opinions."

"How much were you planning on expanding? We already have five acres!"

"I was looking at doubling it to ten," my father had said.

"Ten?! But we would need to double our slaves! That's very costly," I had argued, always looking at cost versus profit.

"Son, I've heard around the poker table things are going to be changing. It's best to protect our interests and I feel expansion is best. Besides I also heard John's trying to purchase the adjacent plot. We should get to it first." He had smiled that day, proud of his investment choice.

"Is this about changing politics or chasing land, Father? You can't possibly feel expanding our plantation another five acres will be cost efficient! We'll have to get more workers and more hired help to maintain control on twice as much land!"

"Son, do you know what is going on out there?" he had pointed out the window.

"Yes, Father, you've made it a point to drill me on the wheat plant for several years now."

"No, I mean out there, beyond our small town or even Kentucky's borders?"

"Yes, sir, I've read the papers; I've heard the town talk. But I fail to understand how electing one person is going to ruin our plantation."

My father had gotten up from his chair and walked over to the window, strategically positioned so he could view the expanse of the plantation from his study. After staring outside for a few moments, he had instructed me to sit by a simple hand gesture towards the chair. As I sat down I had known this talk was not going to be like any of the others and that had not calmed my nerves. He had already turned back towards the window when he spoke to me again – I would never forget his words or the fear in his voice from that day.

"Son, this election could make or break our business. We can't possibly compete with the super-factories of the North and there is no way we'd be able to maintain our crop without supply and demand. But it's not just our livelihood that rides on this election. Your sister has written to us several times about Freemen of the North – men who were once slaves to plantation owners just like us, who were set free and who now earn a living in the local northern factories. Word has spread like wildfire and already there are slave revolts in Charleston, Savannah and Fredericksburg. We can't maintain a plantation and keep them in check under certain election results." He had finally turned away from the window, facing me with pain in his eyes. He had not waited for me to reply but instead continued to speak as he began to pace the room.

"Your sister is doing very well for herself in New York and I don't doubt the nursing education we are paying for is proving its worth. But you have to understand that there has been talk of a great divide of this nation when that election happens in November. I will not lose my family or my daughter to the North and the northern way of life if that secession happens!"

I had heard about it from the papers – how slaves that had escaped ran to the north and found work in the factories. Pay had been low but it had still been pay nonetheless. Those that didn't make it north had been killed or whipped into submission. Father had told me many times that slaves were whipped because they disobeyed, not because they were different. A plantation owner should never use the whip as a means to show superiority, just when necessary on account of misbehavior.

These revolts had begun as soon as men like Lincoln and Douglas began campaigning for the election. Trouble started brewing when fear of a "free" nation had set in. Although the skirmishes had been small, it had been enough to put any southern man on edge, believing at any time *his* slaves would be the next to try. And a plantation without slaves meant no crop harvested that year and an extreme drought in sales.

"Son, don't you see? With more land, there is more crop; with more crop there is more supply; and when this great nation decides to divide, we will have a surplus to see us through."

"What do you want me to do?" I had conceded, sighing heavily.

"I need you to draw up the paperwork for the sale of that property. We'll have to bring the papers to the bank for the official sale of the lot but we need to do it quickly."

"And workers? We'll need more."

"Patience, son. We won't be able to use the land this season, so we'll till the land next year when we start the new season."

"I still don't understand how this will help us, but fine. I'll draw up the papers."

I remember feeling defeated. I had wanted nothing more than to talk reason to him, but he had refused to listen. In my opinion it was a very costly move on our part and getting to the property before John was a very poor motive for the expansion. But that's how I am compared to him when it comes to running a business – I'm calculated, planning every move to the minute details. I try to look ahead to the results before making decisions. He has never worked that way.

~~*

During the summer of that year another surprise had come to me. After purchasing the extra five acres of property adjacent to ours, my father had decided to make a very risky move. Word had spread quickly through our town that he had *purchased* John's property, putting the man's tobacco farm out of business completely. I had walked into his study, prepared to argue with him further about his insane purchase.

"Father, how could you consciously put that man out of business?!" I had shouted at him. His back had been facing me as he stood by the window, a snifter of brandy in his hand.

"It was a very strategic move," he had replied calmly.

"Strategic?! That was the dumbest move you've ever made! Not to mention turning a neighbor into an enemy!"

"Don't worry yourself over it, son. The property will be converted." He had finally turned to face me.

"Converted to what? More wheat?" I had scolded. I remember how furious I had been with him; how much I had wanted to shout out how stupid he was.

"No. I'm cutting the tobacco crop by half and using the rest to build another property."

"You run the man off his land and then you build on his property? Are you mad?!"

"I haven't run him off his land. He still lives there."

"What are you doing then?" I had asked suspiciously.

"He needed help financially and the tobacco crop wasn't going to be enough. So I helped him out a bit." He had smirked at me then took a sip of his drink.

"What did you do?" I had raised my eyebrow at him.

"I told him I would take over half the tobacco crop and build him a second property for his daughter and his son-in-law. His son-in-law will work for me until he takes over the business sufficiently."

"What's the catch?" There's always a catch where my father is concerned.

"He needs only pay me back. I'm considering it a loan."

"So wait, whatever money the crop makes, you take?"

"I'm taking a cut of their pay as payment for my generosity. With interest."

"You're unbelievable!"

"And you need to trust my judgment, son. Things are changing in this world and we need to protect our assets."

"And what about John's assets? We took them all away from him!"

"Son, sit." I had done as I was told obediently. "John's son-in-law couldn't provide for his daughter as much as he wanted but she married him anyway. He wanted the young man in the business but couldn't afford to build a house for them. So I'm building the house for them, but in order to do that, I had to cut the crop in half. This way, his son-in-law can learn the business, live in his own house, and take over when the debt is paid."

"How long will they be indebted to us?"

"A few years."

"How many is a few?"

"Five to ten."

"You're putting them in debt for ten years?!"

"You act like I asked them to hand over their first born! It's just a loan."

"With interest!" I had argued.

"If you are going to argue every decision I make, how are you going to take over a business of your own?"

He had a point and I had hated him for the way he rationalized things. I had been making it hard for him to make any decision. His stern face had made me feel guilty and I hated how he could do that to me. In a matter of seconds the man could wipe my stature away, along with my inner pride. Being the son of a plantation owner had meant learning how to run the business but it had also meant never questioning his authority, or else.

~~*

The very next week, I had the opportunity to meet John and see first hand what had been going on with this loan my father had planned. My father had him sitting in the study, both men sipping their snifters of brandy. I swear sometimes my father couldn't have a meeting without a glass of liquor in his hand. Both men had been immersed in conversation when I entered the room but stopped as soon as I came in.

"I'm sorry to interrupt," I remember saying.

"No need to apologize, son. I'd like to introduce you to John White. John, this is my son, William."

"Nice to meet you, William," he had said politely, standing up to shake my hand.

"You as well, Mr. White," I had replied.

"Please, call me John. We're neighbors after all."

"All right, John," I had obliged, not wanting to offend him.

"Son, sit. We were just fleshing out the details for the loan I told you about."

I had groaned slightly, before taking a seat next to Mr. White. In front of both men had been a piece of paper with all the details written out in black and white. I had still been angry with him for cutting the poor man's crop in half, but as long as he had a house to provide for his daughter, son-in-law, and their eventual family, then it had sufficed. My father had attempted to offer me a drink but I had declined, preferring to do any and all business as sober as possible.

"I was explaining to John here that I don't want to change his ways of working the plantation. He will still be able to teach his son-in-law how to run the crop, but I will simply be taking over the bookkeeping."

I had looked up at him suspiciously, knowing how well my father dealt the cards. "How much of a cut are you expecting?"

"I was looking at a 40/60 cut where I would take the latter."

I could tell John had been uncomfortable about that share, so I quickly took control of the situation. "Father, may I speak with you in private please?" As soon as we were no longer in ear-shot of John, I had laced into him about his idea of giving the man less than he was worth. "I think 30/70 is better and we take the *former*."

"Son, that's going to leave him indebted longer," my father had growled.

"Actually, it will get him out of debt quicker since you will be giving him more of the shares of what the crop is worth and only taking a little for yourself to finance the construction of the house you intend to build," I had retaliated.

"You don't understand the principle here! We are trying to profit and survive in a world that is all about profit and survival! You can't make a profit when you are allowing someone to take his own share of the crop!"

"And you don't seem to understand that sometimes it is better to concede than cause neighborly problems in the future!"

"Why do you insist on undermining every financial move I make? You need to trust my decisions if you are going to have a business to run in the future!"

"If you want me to run the plantation in the future, then maybe you should trust my *own* judgment when it comes to its finances, assets, and expansion!" I defensively had argued my point and waltzed back into the study, determined to not leave John with too much overhang to worry himself sick over.

"John, does 30/70 in your favor work for you?" I had asked him politely.

"It certainly does!" he had exclaimed, appreciative that we reached a reasonable agreement for the contract.

"Good. Then our offer stands at 30/70 so you can still survive the winter and we can still receive our cut for the house."

I had quickly added the altered information to the paper already on the desk and had John look over the details. If my father insisted on doing things *his* way, I was going to make sure we still remained civil to our neighbors. John had signed the deal and we shook on it, sealing it as final. I had known already that my father would be lecturing me later, but I did not care. I had wanted John and his family to at least have some sense of pride left in them after we split their crop and built their house for them.

"Smart boy you've got here, Jackson," John had mused. "He's going to be great for your business."

My father had simply forced a smile and nodded, completely displeased with my negotiations and silently warning me of his anger and impending lecture. John had thanked us both again for helping him out in his situation and after finishing his drink, left us in the study. My father had poured himself another drink before even acknowledging me by silently asking me if I cared to join him, knowing full well what the answer would be. I had known he was going to lash out at me and I just sat back and waited for the verbal assault.

"We could have had him at 40/60 in our favor! That was a foolish and irrational business move! Never talk down your opponent unless *his* price is too high!"

"Forgive me if I don't wish to rob him blind or see his family starve!" I had shouted back. It had seemed as if most of our business disagreements became nothing more than arguments neither of us would be willing to lose.

"We need to think of ourselves and our own assets here! We would be able to better maintain our second acreage next year if we had gotten him to agree to 40/60! Now you'll be held personally responsible when our plantation goes under next year!"

"You exaggerate too much, old man! We are not going under simply because we gave him a chance to make a profit on his *own* crop!"

"You wait, son! This election will change everything!" Little did I know, he would be 100% correct in his assumptions.

Summer had flown by too quickly for us that year and the bookstore had flourished. Every summer between school years I had helped my father and brother in the store because it became our busiest time of year. That particular summer, my brother had been learning how to keep the records of sales accurate and how to order supplies, although he did it without care. I had been asked to organize some of the shelves and assist a few customers find something of interest, since my father was too busy teaching my brother how to handle the account. Most of my time though had been spent in the storeroom opening boxes, since it was customary for the owner and his *son* to tend to the customers.

As fall approached, the numbers of customers and shipments had dwindled and my brother had returned to school. This had given me the perfect opportunity to shadow my father and learn more about how to run the store, although he kept brushing it off as "only because your brother is still in school" and reiterated that when school was over, he'd be back in the store learning again. It had also been a time for me to interact with more of the townsfolk, since Daddy had reluctantly agreed to let me come out of the storeroom more often.

"Nice to see you, Miss Madeline," Mrs. Parker had replied, coming in one cool autumn day.

"Nice to see you as well, Mrs. Parker. Do you have an order to pick up?"

"No, dear; not today. Dr. Parker insists that this election has stopped anyone from coming in for their annual checkups, so we haven't been spending money on frivolous things," she had smiled politely.

It had bothered me how she could regard books as "frivolous things" and I had always wondered if her smiles were fake when she made conversation with me. In my young life, I had heard so many stories of the ways society wives acted – from the plantation owners to the doctors and lawyers – all prim and proper. While we lived comfortably, they tended to live extravagantly, buying expensive clothes and jewelry from Europe, mainly England. They also frequented our store. Sometimes the women would come in together, gossiping about the latest town scandal or plantation saga. At that time though, their tales had been truncated by comments about the election or slave revolts in other states. I had told my father that there was a reason to be up-to-date with politics but he never understood why.

"How are your parents and your brother, dear?" she had interrupted my thoughts.

"They are both well and my brother is back in school."

"Going to take over the business when he graduates, I presume? I'm sure your father is thrilled!" she had quipped.

"Actually, he's been considering getting into politics. I'm sure he could do wonders in Washington." Looking back, I wish I hadn't sounded so harsh but I really felt that she had been undermining my ability to run that store.

"Go heavens! Politics?! That's absurd! Only sons of politicians or lawyers need to go into politics! With the way your father runs this store, he's going to make an excellent bookkeeper!"

I had not meant for her comment to get me as upset as it did, but I countered her a bit too vehemently and I should have held my tongue. "Well I think if my brother wants to go into politics, he should. He'd make just as fine of a politician as he would a bookkeeper!"

"Miss Madeline, I never!" she had gasped, taken aback by my abrasive words. "You know it is not our choice what we are to become! Sons are to follow their fathers' line of work and daughters learn from their mothers! I'm quite surprised you are even working in the store, much less attempting to run it in your brother's absence!"

I had known I had overstepped my boundaries as a young lady by voicing my opinions the way I had done. I had no right to protest my brother taking over the business. With her taste for society standards, there had been no way I could have even tried to explain how much the bookstore meant to me. That day though, when my father had come out to the front of the store, instead of understanding my side of things, as he always had, society standards overshadowed my opinions of how things ought to be.

"Is everything all right, Mrs. Parker?"

"Your daughter here seems to believe her brother would make a better politician than a bookstore proprietor!" she had announced, the snide remark I knew had been meant to dispel any thoughts I might have had about becoming the next owner.

"She knows I am not going to let my son get involved in the nonsense in Washington and that he is just in school at the moment." He then lowered his voice but I had still heard him sharp as a pin. "Sibling rivalry."

"Of course," she had smiled that fake smile of hers. "I have one of each myself. Keep an eye on that boy of yours. He'll be great when he realizes his potential!"

Mrs. Parker had smirked again and walked out of our store. I had never felt so much anger towards her prim and proper ways as I had at that moment. I could not believe she had been so arrogant in her reaction about my brother being a bookkeeper and yet she had been so blind to the fact that I could *run* the business when he wasn't there. All my anger quickly changed to fear, when my father had turned around and approached me, the look in his eyes making me wish I could be in the storeroom instead of out in the open.

"Madeline Rose, what were you thinking? The Parkers are some of my best customers!" he had scolded me.

"You can't deny he doesn't want this! I was speaking the truth!" I had tried to protest.

"That's no excuse to speak about it outside of our house! Now I know you meant well, but Austin is well aware he is to take over the business when he turns 18. There's no reason to involve Mrs. Parker or any other customers in our affairs! The next thing we'll have going around town is whether or not I can keep my children in line!"

"I'm sorry if I offended you, but Mrs. Parker and her kind bother me!"

"*Her* kind? She is of southern blood just like you or me."

"Those ladies of society, coming in here and gossiping, always showing off their flashy jewelry! Every one of them uses their fake smiles while they look down on us, as if even we are inferior to them just because they have more money!"

"Madeline, they are good people and good for business and I will not tolerate you speaking about them that way! We are not here to discuss our family quarrels; leave that for the house! We are here to run a business!"

I had been too upset to see his reasoning and I still chose to act out. "I'm just tired of hearing about this stupid election and I'm tired of being told women shouldn't have an opinion about it while they come in here and talk about everything politics! Maybe if Austin *did* get into politics, there'd be changes instead of talk!"

"That's enough, Madeline! I've heard enough!"

"No, you haven't!" I had fought back even harder, trying to get him to really listen. "I'm tired of them coming in here and undermining my ability to run this store when Austin isn't here! I'm tired of them looking at me with their fake smiles, acting like they're better than me just because their husbands either own better businesses or plantations!"

"Those businesses and plantations are very important to our way of life, Maddie," my father had attempted to explain. "If we didn't have them, there'd be no one to buy our books and we'd be struggling to maintain our own livelihood."

"But do they have to come in here and flaunt it? Do they have to come in and make me feel like I don't know anything about anything?"

"You know that I appreciate everything you do for me here, right?"

"Yes, but it's only *temporary*." I had pouted like a child but my father did not give in.

"I'm sorry, Maddie, but that's the way things have to be. Your brother may be younger but he is going to take over the business when he comes of age. Now why don't you run along home and we'll talk more after supper."

I could not believe after voicing my anger and opinions, he was dismissing me! Making my point even clearer, I had grabbed a copy of Pride and Prejudice off of one the shelves and stormed out, the door slamming behind me. I had not gone straight home that day, though. I had stopped off at my favorite spot first – an old Yellowwood tree set back at the far end of a huge plantation.

~~*

The imminent election had been fast approaching and there was a heavy cloud of unrest that had set over the South, including our little town in Kentucky. Every one of our states had felt it, although everyone had tried to ignore it and go on with their busy lives. Breckinridge had fought hard to campaign, especially within his home state of Kentucky, and there had been worry that Lincoln's win would be catastrophic to us. At every chance they could get, more and more slaves had revolted against their owners, a costly measure for anyone. People had been afraid to spend money in town and local businesses began to suffer. It began with the saloons, dress-makers and smiths, quickly spreading to the general store, butcher, and our bookstore. The elite of society had invested their money in the banks and the only businesses not hurting seemed to be the mills, the lumber industry, and the plantations.

One day, in mid-fall, my brother had come barging into the bookstore after school. His eyes were bright, rounded orbs and his smile had spread from ear to ear. If I hadn't known Austin the way I did, I would have thought he had just met a girl. That had not been the case at all. Looking back, I'm quite glad my father had not been there to hear him that day.

"There's talk of secession!" he had exclaimed excitedly.

"Secession from what?" I had asked looking up from a book I had casually picked up reading – I don't actually recall what book it was because my usual reading for that time of year had been tucked away in a new hiding place so Mama wouldn't find it and force me to give it back to the store.

"The Union! There's been talk in Charleston, Baton Rouge, and Jackson! People are feeling the true weight of this election in their businesses and the South can't compete with the North anymore!"

"We can too compete with the North!" I had defended proudly, not fully understanding the extent of the political and economic world. "We have the ability to ship our goods and trade with Europe! They have whole countries over there waiting for what *we* can provide!"

"You think they will care about us when the northern factories begin producing five times as much as us?!" he had argued.

"They'll still buy from us!" I had vehemently protested, knowing that if England had not traded with us, our bookstore would not have half the books it carried.

"I've heard the talks! Kentucky isn't the only state who's hurting for business and for every revolt an owner loses more slaves and more money! Without money coming in as profit, he can't buy more slaves to replace the rebellious ones. As an owner loses more slave labor, he loses product and when supply and demand from Europe gets too great, they will search for a better replacement to the north!"

"You really think it will be that bad?"

"If Lincoln is elected it will! He's fighting us with a two-fold, double-edged sword! We'll lose our economy and our livelihood definitely!"

"Our business will be all right though? We won't lose everything will we?"

It was in that moment that I had begun to panic. Never before had I feared the election or what it would do to our lives. It had become all that anyone would talk about and the once-intellectual conversations had been replaced with political satire and disdain. In that moment, I realized that if we lost our bookstore, I would have nothing left to sustain my life. Our bookstore was all I had.

"If the North can build giant factories that can produce more for their businesses, what makes you think they couldn't produce warehouses full of the same books we have?" my brother had interrupted my mental breakdown.

"But, but..." I had attempted to form the right words for my fears.

Placing a protective hand on my shoulder, he had tried to calm me down. "We won't lose the store. Come on, it's almost time for supper and I'm famished!" As we locked up the store, I remember feeling a single tear slide down my cheek. There was no way I was going to allow anything or anyone to come between me and my bookstore, no one.

Right after supper that night, I had abruptly excused myself before Austin could engage Daddy in argument about the election. I had not been in the mood for more of the same conversation. Without answering Daddy's barrage of questions, I had thrown on my coat and walked out the door, allowing the crisp autumn night air to chill me. I had no idea where I was going to go but my feet had found their way to my old Yellowwood tree.

This particular tree had served many purposes over my eighteen years and I had practically grown up surrounded by its branches. Located at the far end of one of our town's plantations, it stood tall and broad and inviting, wrapping me up in security and comfort, something I had been lacking at that time. That tree knew my every emotion – from true happiness to heartbreak and everything in between. It was much better for me than keeping a journal of my thoughts.

As I sat down cradled by its exposed roots my mind had drifted back to past events and my body drifted to sleep. When I was a child, my father had fastened a wooden plank with two pieces of rope to act as a swing; as a teenager, I'd come out here to read when school let out or when my brother was working in the bookstore and I wasn't needed so much. All these thoughts I had considered "better times". In sleep, I subconsciously tried to will the thoughts away, but still they had flooded my mind, beginning when I was five years old.

> "Higher, Daddy, higher!"
> "If you go any higher you won't come back."
> "I'll come back, Daddy. I'll always come back!"
> "Eventually, you're going to learn how to push yourself and you won't need me anymore."
> "I'll always need you, Daddy!"
> "I hope so, baby, I hope so."
> "Silly Daddy. Higher!"

When I had been thirteen years old, only five years prior to that night, school had not been easy for me. I had started at a new school in the city and no one paid me any mind. When I had averted my attention to my books instead of attempting to socialize, not only did the teachers point me out but the students poked fun at my "obsession." They had taunted me relentlessly and my only solace had been that tree. Somehow, Daddy always knew where to find me.

"You didn't come into the store today after school. I had a feeling you'd be out here."

"I just needed to read for school and I wouldn't be able to concentrate at the store."

"Is everything all right, sweetheart? You hardly miss a day at the store and you were always able to do your work there."

"I'm fine. Just needed some quiet time I guess."

"Are you ill?"

"No, I just wanted to be alone with Heathcliff and collect my thoughts."

"You've named the tree?"

"It's a character from the new book I'm reading. I can't seem to put it down!"

"Just don't neglect your work on account of some fictitious boy."

"I won't."

As my body slumped back against the tree, a third image had come to me and I wrapped my coat tighter around me to keep warm. I had been sixteen at that time. My brother had been asked to come find me to question me about missing books from the store. I had never stolen anything in my life and there he was, accusing me of stealing from the very establishment that provided not only the money to buy food for us, but for Daddy to *purchase* specific books for me along with his shipments. What Austin had failed to realize was the fact that sometimes the shipment is wrong and we do not receive all of the books we ordered.

"Daddy wants to talk to you about missing books."

"I don't know anything about missing books. He knows I just borrowed a few. I will give them back when I'm done."

"We're not a library! We can't sell used books! Our customers will only purchase new books that haven't been opened by your prying hands! Now stop stealing from the store!"

"Our customers want books to look pretty on a shelf that will just collect dust! Do you actually think they *read* what they buy?"

"That gives you no right to take whatever you feel is worth reading! I should just have Mama go through your things and see where you're hiding them all!"

"I haven't stolen anything!"

"Why don't you ask our customers if you could *borrow* their copies? It will keep you happy that you get to read them and it will keep them happy to know that our books are not being read first before they get to purchase them!"

Before I knew it, the sun had begun to rise over the horizon and I woke up feeling groggy. Daddy would be so upset with me since I had not come home and Austin would most likely have received the brunt of his anger. Mama would have been worried sick that I had been kidnapped or worse. Slowly, I stood up to prepare myself for the inevitable and what I had been faced with was a very stern man, arms crossed and a furrow in his brow. His face had been shadowed by the rising sun over the trees, but I could tell by his stance that he was a man of wealth and stature, most likely the plantation owner making his rounds on his property. I hadn't known it at the time, but I would soon find out, that the man facing me was William's father and my poor Yellowwood tree had been a part of William's life all along.

"You are trespassing on *my* land," Jackson Hutchinson had spoken very aggressively towards me.

"I didn't realize this tree was part of the plantation property. I've been coming here since I was a little girl," I had politely replied.

"The property extends ten acres. Five of the acres have yet to be tilled. And you are still trespassing!"

"I'm sorry, sir, you don't seem to understand. This tree has been a part of my whole life. I can't simply abandon it because it is on a part of the property you have yet to use," I had stated boldly, not caring about the consequences.

"This is my property regardless! Now unless you remove yourself immediately, I will contact the authorities to have you arrested!"

"Tell me what happens to this tree once I leave?" I had demanded, ignoring his threat.

"It will stay. I have no use for it."

"If you intend to leave it be, may I have permission to come here and read beneath it? I have not bothered anyone in all the years I've been coming here and my father was the one who built that swing on it when I was younger."

His eyes had squinted as if he was considering my proposal. "As long as you do not venture into the plantation fields for any reason or speak with anyone while you are here," he had conceded reluctantly. "I don't need my slaves befriending a girl and neglecting their work!"

"I just want to sit by the tree and read, that's all."

"The minute you speak to *anyone*, your privilege of using this tree will be terminated! Do I make myself understood?"

"Very," I had sighed.

"Can I ask where your father works?"

I had known by the way he was asking that he had been hinting at what part of society I was from, especially since it was not customary for young girls to be out on their own so late at night or so early in the morning. Southern socialites definitely were not subtle by any means. It didn't matter to me because I had been proud of our bookstore and all it had provided for us over the years. I had puffed up my chest and stood taller before I answered him.

"McCall's Books, sir."

"I order from there all the time. I didn't know McCall had a daughter. I only know his son – a fine boy his is."

"Yes, I am his daughter and I work at the store as well."

"I've never seen you there when I come to pick up my orders. You must be taking care of the new shipments." His snide remark had pierced me.

"I've been able to assist customers some of the time," I had countered, trying to make him see that I was just as capable as my brother.

"Very well," he had dismissed me. "Since I refuse to stop purchasing from there, you may use the tree but if I find you anywhere else on my property, your father will be out one customer. My library is too valuable to deal with such nonsense!"

"Thank you, sir."

"Now go on and get! I'm sure you need to be getting home."

I had bowed my head slightly and turned to leave, just as I saw my father coming up the dirt path to find me. His coat collar had been turned up to ward off the morning chill and he kept his hands in his pockets to keep them warm. The man who had spoken to me was already halfway through his plantation by the time my father reached the tree and me.

"You're lucky I know your hiding place, Maddie. Let's get you home. Your mama is worried sick and I promised I'd bring you home alive and well."

The walk back had been silent and I did not receive the lecture I thought I would have. It was almost as if my father had known something had been bothering me – he knew exactly where to find me. For my careless and reckless behavior though, he had barred me from the bookstore for two weeks. At least I still had my tree to keep me out of trouble.

William

4

November had been the worst month for us. After the wheat was harvested and sent to the mill for processing, we all sat with baited breath for the election results. It would make or break our plantation for the following year. Word had spread like wildfire that states' rights would be taken away if Lincoln won and there had been rumors of secession the likes of which we had never known before. It had worried our family greatly since Gracie was still studying in the north. On one particular day, I had overheard my father speaking to Dr. Parker on my walk home from town. They were lingering around the plantation and Father had looked upset. I was afraid to find out what he knew.

"Any word from Grace, Jackson?"

"No; none. The last letter I received from her was this summer, speaking on general terms of how her studies were going."

"Do you think she'll come home if something happens in Washington?"

"She can stay up there and continue her studies if she chooses. We're paying top dollar to send her to nursing school in New York."

"Something else is troubling you, Jackson. What is it?"

"She's nearly twenty-three and I had hoped she'd be married by now. I know school was the best thing for her but I had wanted her to settle down here."

"Do you think she'll find –"

"I don't want to think about it, James. If this nation divides because of economic demands on the South, I will not lose my daughter in the process, especially to any young *northern* fellow!" he had spat venomously.

Gracie was smart, I noted to myself, walking briskly past them into the house. She would never risk being disowned by her family by marrying one of *them*. Her roots were in the south and southern blood ran thick through her veins. If the nation were to divide on unpleasant terms, she would be smart enough to come home.

I had paced through our mansion and finally allowed my feet to guide me upstairs to her old room. Gracie had left about three years prior to become a nurse in one of the best schools in the country. They were always taking new students and having money to pay for tuition had its advantages. What worried me was whether they'd send her back if our nation truly did divide.

I had peered into her room and saw that nothing had changed. Mother had left the room exactly the way she left it behind. On her vanity stood several small sketched drawings of us from over the years, perfume bottles, and a jewelry box Father had specially made for her with her name carved into it; on the shelf above her bed were her riding trophies before she broke her ankle and couldn't compete anymore. In a far corner stood a collection of dolls, all with porcelain faces and delicate features, which she had been given for Christmas over the years. And hanging from her bedpost were worn skates, stretched and fitted to her feet.

My sister and I were nothing alike. She was athletic and grew up competing in various local events – riding, skating, and when she was older, fencing. I could hold my own against her but my strength came from loading heavy bales of wheat into carts, lifting barrel after barrel of ale and spirits, and helping my father build and fix things around the house and plantation. Although we had slaves and servants to till the crop and work the kitchen, Father always told me it was a man's job to care for his home.

We were both smart, but because I had been destined to be the caretaker of the plantation, she had been allowed to pursue her own path. I often envied her this because she always knew she wanted to be a nurse. My father never hesitated to send her north to school and was proud of her choice. It was only now he had his doubts of her return to the south.

Our idea of society was another way we differed. She was very aristocratic, whereas I was more carefree. You would always find her entertaining the ladies and wives with Mother during afternoon tea, playing sweet music on our grand piano, but I never enjoyed the weekly or daily visits of my father's friends. You would never find me in the study discussing politics or worldly news while drinking brandy or smoking a cigar. I had little taste for society's posh behavior and as an adolescent I would run off outside and play soldier with my friends instead. As we got older, we'd go off to another part of the house on our own, and discuss the things that mattered most to teenage boys – women.

"Sweetheart, how long have you been back in the house?" my mother had interrupted my thoughts.

"About ten minutes or so. Why? Is something wrong?"

"Your father has news. He's called a family meeting."

"Shouldn't Gracie be here for that?" I had protested, not really sure I wanted to start this fight again.

"She is here in spirit and I'm sure your father will send her a letter," she had dismissed. That's what parents always do – they dismiss the concerns they don't want to deal with or argue about.

"She's not dead, Mother, and she's still a part of this family! Why didn't Father send for her to come home if the news was that important to call a family meeting?"

Sighing, she had answered me calmly. "If we made any decisions, we'll inform her and then she can choose to come home."

"*Choose*?! I'm forced to stay on this plantation while my sister chooses to come home?!"

"William, that's enough!" she had scolded. "Now come downstairs!"

She had turned on her heels and left me to take one last look at my sister's room before I had followed her downstairs and into the parlor room. Sitting there was my father as well as the head cook, the head of our servants, and our stable ward. Father had been nursing a snifter of brandy, per usual, and it angered me that my sister had not been here with us for any meeting. She was still a part of the family and she deserved to be a part of the decision-making process.

"Good, we are all here," my father had begun as I sat down. "I called you all here to bring you news from Washington." I had sensed the fear and anticipation growing quickly over the room before he continued. "It appears that Lincoln has indeed won the election."

Gasps were heard from every mouth in the room. My mother had been the first to speak, her words verbalizing what everyone was thinking. "What does that mean for us, Jackson?"

"Nothing yet but there is strong talk of secession now and we must be prepared for whatever happens." It had amazed me how calm he was and how much not having Gracie there didn't seem to bother him, especially after his conversation with Dr. Parker earlier. He hadn't even noticed my fists clenching around the arms of the chair I was sitting in.

"Should we send for Gracie?" That had been my mother, sounding as worried as I felt.

"I will write to her, but I don't want her to jeopardize her studies. There has been no word of Kentucky seceding from the Union so we are fine for now."

His nonchalant attitude had been what finally caused me to speak up and dispute him. "And when Kentucky realizes her southern roots and joins the secession, what will you do then? Do you think the North will gladly send her home? Or will they hold her hostage and force us to ransom her instead?"

"William, I will not be questioned and don't take that tone of voice with me!" he had shouted, all but smashing his snifter onto the table next to his chair. I had hoped he would do it, so he'd have one less glass to drink from.

"Gracie should be here, with us! She should be married to some plantation owner instead of in New York studying and you know it!" I really hated to be brushed off and I often found myself challenging rather than conceding to his decisions.

"That's quite enough! Now go to your room! I don't want to see your face until morning!"

"No, Father, face the truth! You sent my sister, your only daughter, away from her family and those she loves under the false hope she'd become a nurse! And what happens to her when this great nation divides? What happens when those in Washington force us to give up our livelihood for the promise of factories and large-scale cities like the one you sent Gracie to?" I had had to hold myself down so as not to jump up from my seat. My mother had placed her hand gently on my arm but I just shrugged her off, not wanting to be back down or be calmed down.

"Kentucky knows its rights and will keep to the code of the South, even if that means secession! But I will not jeopardize my daughter's future on the notion that the North will force our hand! William, it is only talk, hearsay. Nothing has been done and all that the southern states wait for is Lincoln's inauguration to know for sure. That gives us time to write to Grace and find out from her what is going on with our counterparts to the north." I truly despised how diplomatic and aristocratic he had sounded when it concerned Gracie. She was his daughter and he was treating her like another piece on his personal chessboard.

"So you'd use your own daughter as a spy before you make a decision to send for her to come back home?!" I had been outraged at this point, too blinded by anger to see any type of reason.

"I'd like to know what plans the North may be devising to take over my property, my land, and my plantation. If we have heard the cries of secession and slave revolts then so have they! They know we have been weakened by this election and it only gives them strength to build upon our sacred but breaking heritage!"

"This is disgraceful!" I had shouted, leaping from my chair and almost tipping it over.

"William!"

"No, I'm not going to listen to this anymore! Gracie shouldn't be up there while our country waits to divide in two! And what happens after we secede? Will the North let us go without a fight, without a war? Will you be able to live with yourself knowing she's away from home in time of war?!"

"Damn it, William, calm down! I will send for Gracie if that is what we agree on but I am still giving her a choice to stay there. Her studies are too important to –"

"To what? Too important to let go of because of your foolish pride? You wanted a son to take over the plantation and a daughter to study and be educated in a well-respected school up north. You want to plan your next move based on what our brothers to the north *might* do, meanwhile your daughter is going to be caught in the middle!"

"I will send for her! That's all I can do!"

"Fine!"

I had stormed out of the parlor room, leaving my father angry and my mother in tears. I wasn't sure where I was going to go but I couldn't breathe in that house. I knew I had heard correctly – all the rumors in town murmuring about Lincoln's win and impending secession – but there had been plenty of people in Kentucky who did not feel secession was necessary and that a compromise could be met. They did not want to break up a country because a select few from the north did not recognize the value of our states' rights. Now it had become very clear how fear would be the deciding factor for a divided country – the North feared a southern revolution to maintain our rights to bear arms, own men, and keep to our traditions, and the South feared their livelihood, values, and rights would be impeded upon and taken over.

~~*

In one month, it had erupted into a nightmare like I had never seen in all my life. Word had spread fast across the south that South Carolina had officially seceded from the Union. Soon to follow into the new year were Mississippi, Florida, Alabama, Georgia, Louisiana and Texas. One by one the South was breaking away, determined to hold onto its rights set by the Constitution and its long-implemented economic traditions that were passed from generation to generation.

Our town had been one of the fortunate ones. There had been no word at that time if and when Kentucky would join the fight for the South and our winter rations were plenty enough to see us through. Father and I had still been on coarse terms and we had yet to receive word that Gracie would be coming home. She had missed another Christmas and with the country in upheaval it had been even more difficult to get letters up to New York or to get her on a train to come south. Another argument between us had begun in his study and ended in the parlor room.

"What if we went up there to get her?" That had been my suggestion.

"We can't leave your mother alone to tend to the entire plantation for that long!" he had refuted, making a valid point. There was no way to leave my mother in charge of 65 men and women without both of us there.

"But how else are we going to bring her home?" I had demanded answers.

"We haven't even heard word from her that she *wants* to come home."

"What if they confiscated our letters and she never received them?" I had begun to panic, over exaggerating the situation again.

"Do you really believe that, William? Do you think they are that hateful that they would intercept our letters? Besides, they have nothing against Kentucky. We haven't joined the other states yet," he had argued.

"Anything is possible, correct? Father, I refuse to believe after everything that is going on, they wouldn't fight back! And I can't believe you are not fighting harder to bring her home!"

"I have heard just about enough from you, boy! I have tried to be reasonable and calm about bringing your sister home but nothing seems to be enough for you! William, just leave!"

My father had stood in the middle of the parlor room glaring at me, eyes wide with anger. He had said his final words so therefore the conversation was over. I had stomped out of the house, making sure to slam the door behind me for effect. I had no particular place to go at that moment so I ventured into town. Looking back I'd say it was not my brightest decision, but I headed for Sally's Saloon. I wasn't intentionally looking for a fight but one certainly found me.

After ordering a snifter of brandy (yes, I did drink it on very few occasions), I had taken a seat at the bar just to focus my attention on my drink. It had been a busy establishment, even with the economic troubles we had begun to have, and most of the seats around me had already been taken by men quite inebriated. I hadn't noticed the man who had joined me at the bar until the barkeep spoke to him.

"What can I get you friend?" he had asked.

"Cognac, please," he had replied. From the voice and the choice of drink I knew right away who it had been. I had turned to face him, still angry at Father and needing to release that energy with a confrontation.

"Hello, Rex."

"Well, if it isn't William Hutchinson! How the hell are ya?"

"I'm well, and you?"

"Could be better. My parents want to send me north to keep me away from the 'troubles of the South,' as they put it. I bet you anything they want to enroll me in medical school up there as well."

"Well, I'm surprised your father hasn't taken you under his wing here instead of thinking you should go up there for schooling. I'm sure it'll pass in time. Your folks have always been reasonable people."

"The Parkers may be society bred but they are anything but reasonable!" he had laughed. "By the way, your sister's still up north isn't she? I remember my mother mentioning something to that effect."

I had visibly cringed. "She's still in New York, yes. But we are trying to write to her to send her home. It's not safe for her to be there now."

Rex had placed his hand on my shoulder and the gleam that twinkled in his eyes I had seen before. "Well, if you'd like, I'd gladly go to New York and keep an eye on her for you – make sure she doesn't fall for one of them northern educated boys."

I had brushed his hand off and took another sip of my drink. "I believe bringing her home would be the better option."

"Are you saying I'm not fit for your sister?"

"I'm saying you're the same age as me and she is older by two years. What makes you think she'd want you?" That had been where I had gone wrong.

I believe Rex had thrown the first punch but before long, our fight was becoming a brawl and both of us were extricated from the saloon. Our fight had continued on out in the street until the authorities had been called and we were both nearly arrested for disorderly conduct. We were released on account that it was our first offense, but we were to remain separated by fifty feet at all times, including society events, walking in the town square, and even church services. Unfortunately, before the dreadfully embarrassing night had ended, Rex Parker had to have the last word.

"Grace Ann Parker does have a very nice ring to it, doesn't it?" he had smirked at me. The officer had to restrain me before I hit him again.

Christmas had been a somber holiday for us that year. There had been no festive songs and the melodeon that Mama usually played lay silent in the corner of the tea room; there were no large roasts or extravagant meals. We did not even go to church like we always had before. Daddy had hardly spoken to any of us when we all sat in the tea room because our store had lost a bit of money due in part because the election results closed our doors – Lincoln had won and Breckinridge came in third to Douglas, creating a chain reaction beginning with the plantation owners refusing to spend their money on our books. Mama had kept to herself and had retired early to bed almost every night, not wanting us to see her crying, even though I knew she had been. My brother had seemed to be the only one elated to ring in the new year. He had come racing into my room, which as we had grown older I was grateful to have, like a wild-man, eyes wide with excitement and discovery.

"Did you hear the news? *Seven* southern states have declared their secession from the Union!"

"I don't care!" I had shouted and it remains the truth to this day.

I had wanted this whole tragedy to end so our lives could find some sense of normalcy and the bookstore could function without everyone's panic of a Northern invasion. The longer we remained closed or did not place an order, the less money we would have for our invested future. My future especially had depended on its financial stability since I would be turning nineteen that year and had no prospects for a husband.

"You should care! If Kentucky is next, we will need to rethink the way we do business in this town!"

The sheer gleam in his eyes had been enough to frighten anyone. "And what about Daddy? Have you spoken to him about some of your strategies?"

"He won't speak to me at all. For someone who wants me to take over *his* business, he refuses to discuss anything but books and finances with me! It's like he's blind to what's really going on out there!"

"That bookstore is not just *his*!" I had been quick to defend. "Don't you care?"

"Why should I? It's perfectly clear you want it more than I do and you care about it more!"

"You should still have more pride in your family's business! It has given us everything we own!" I had argued.

"Once this state secedes I'm heading out to Frankfort, so there's no reason for me to care about it anymore."

"Frankfort? What could you possible do there?" I had instantly become suspicious and worried. Austin had sprung this on me and this was the first time I was hearing anything about going to our state's capital.

"I'm going to work for the Governor," he had smiled proudly.

"You are mad! Austin, this is completely senseless! Do you hear yourself?" I had protested, desperate for my brother to see fault in his idea.

"What is more senseless is that our delegates in Washington want to dissolve everything we have worked generations to perfect! What is outrageous is that our businesses are being taken away simply because the North feels they can manufacture more than us!" I had never seen the fire in his eyes burn as bright as it had in that moment.

"The very idea that you wish to challenge our government is

insane!" I had countered. "You are one boy, not even fifteen yet, and you want to confront all of Washington?!"

"Someone's got to *do* something, Maddie! I'm not going to accomplish anything sitting in a bookstore, tallying sales and organizing shelves!" he had complained.

"You make it sound like a chore!"

"If you want the store, it's yours! I don't want it! Enjoy your precious books, but when Washington decides to expand its northern factories and warehouses into our town, you won't have them either!"

"Our bookstore will make it through."

Even though I had spoken the words out loud, I had my doubts. My brother had huffed at my response and walked out of my room, determined to carve his own slice of destiny. To say I had been concerned for our little store would have been an understatement. With secession and the "Great Divide" already commencing, more and more townsfolk became restless with worry. Most people of the South, I had heard, were of sound mind that secession was unnecessary but inevitable. The people of Kentucky were no exception and readily leapt at the opportunity to compromise with the North rather than cause any further controversy.

I had worried for my family. If our business continued to fail, we had no other way to purchase food or supplies to sustain ourselves into the future. If it were allowed to continue to evolve in that direction, our house and property would have to be sold and that alone would break my father's soul. My mother would be just as heartbroken to know Austin was planning to leave for our state's capital.

I had also feared for our town. Should the North have the ability to subjugate Kentucky, our town would not survive. Since it was too small to sufficiently sustain itself on its own, we relied on major cities like Frankfort and Campbellsville to conduct our business. Our books were ordered from as far east as Raleigh,

North Carolina and as far south as Waverly, Tennessee, so if these major metropolises were transformed into the super-factory centers they had spoken about, there would be no need for our town's export and no need for us.

~~*

With the thaw of winter and the coming of spring, we had heard that skirmishes had begun throughout Virginia. Instead of secession being the term spoken, it was war that hung on the tongues of many southerners. War had meant armies and armies had meant townsfolk leaving their homes, families and businesses behind, possibly never to return. It was not even the South who spoke first of war, but the North, who had begun to worry themselves over the ramifications of a full Southern secession, which to us simply meant we were going to become our own government, separate from the North and their ways, yet undivided and true to the Constitution generations had abided by.

When spring had been in full bloom, word had reached our town that Fort Sumter had been attacked, causing a chain reaction of secession. Headlines in the local paper had announced that Virginia, Arkansas, North Carolina and even our sister state of Tennessee had joined the rebellion. At any moment we knew our own state could either be attacked by the North or forced to join the South's regime. This had been the perfect opportunity for my brother to come home from school and make an announcement that would shatter my entire family.

"I'm going to Frankfort when school closes for summer," he had stated so proudly.

"What did you just say, Austin?" Daddy had asked, casting an ominous look his way.

"I said that this summer I'm going to Frankfort," he had repeated, but did not cower at my father's glare, which surprised me. Then again, much of what Austin had proclaimed at that time had surprised, even frightened me, since he had never been known to be that outspoken.

"You are not getting involved in politics in any way!" Daddy sternly commanded.

"I won't be. I've decided to enlist in the newly formed Confederate Army!" Austin had announced without shame.

Mama had almost fainted right then and my father had been ready to beat his ideas out of him. "You most certainly will *not!*" he had bellowed, towering over Austin by a few inches.

"I am! They need strong men to lead and fight to protect the South's honor against the North's economic pressure. If I can't go to Frankfort to work in politics, then I will go to protect our Constitutional rights as citizens of the South as a soldier!"

"I will not allow it! You have three years before you are taking over the business and you are not going to foolishly let that go!"

My brother's emotions had become a combination of elation and anger but I could tell he could not decide which emotion to express at that exact moment. I had known he had wanted my father's approval for his choice but he was not going to get it. I had never seen my brother so passionate about something before and it rivaled my love of books. I could not stand them fighting over the business anymore, so I had finally decided it was time to interject.

"Austin, isn't there another way?" I had asked, hopeful that there was something else he could do from our town instead of Frankfort, which was so very far away.

"Don't you see what is happening out there? If we lose our state government to *them* we have nothing! I need to go and fight so the North doesn't destroy everything we live for as a southern family!"

"You've been conditioned to think this way!" my father stated, ignoring Mama, who had begun to fan herself on the sofa. "You can't possibly feel any type of violence will save us! You would do much better to stay in school and take over the business as we planned!"

"*You* planned this; I did not! I didn't want the business but you insisted on handing it over to me because I'm your son! Now I have the opportunity to do something bigger to save our business and you are not going to let me do it!"

"You will get yourself killed for no good reason!" Mama had finally chimed in.

"There *is* a reason! Our business is small, smaller than most bookstores in places like Raleigh and Charleston; that's why we order from them. If we let the North encroach on our bigger cities and allow them to build their super-factories and warehouses, we lose our bookstore whether I take over the business or not!"

"We can keep the business running if we sit down and plan better for the future. There's no reason to get involved in politics or even war for that matter!" Daddy had reasoned, practically begging Austin to sit and talk through his rash decision.

I had watched the dispute volley between them and all I could think about was our store – all those volumes that everyone was neglecting to care about during their argument of war and secession and a Northern takeover of our cities. Our store was at risk, our livelihood being taken away, and all my father cared about was having the *male* child take over the business. As much as I had not wanted Austin to leave, Daddy was not even listening to the reasons why Austin wanted or needed to go to Frankfort and I could not sit and listen to their argument wage on without an end in sight. I had blurted out the only thing that came to mind.

"What about allowing me to take over the business if Austin wishes to go to Frankfort?"

Both had glanced over at me but my father had spoken first. "Absolutely not! There is no way you will run that the bookstore when your brother is perfectly capable when he is of age! Besides, it is not proper to allow you to run a business and you know that! What would our neighbors think?"

"But he doesn't want it!" I had protested vehemently, becoming just as angry as both of them. "Please, let him go to Frankfort and fight for our business there! He's no good to the store if he doesn't care about the books inside!" I had begged on both Austin's and the store's behalf.

Mama had gotten up from where she was sitting, tears streaming from her eyes, and had tried to catch her breath. "I will not lose my baby or this family because our country cannot stay a country! Austin, Maddie, go to your rooms! This needs to be deliberated between your father and me and *we* will make the final decision without argument or discussion from either of you! Austin, if going to Frankfort is not in the best interest of the family or the business, you *will not* be going!"

My brother had stormed upstairs, stomping his feet on each step of the wooden staircase as he went. I had glanced over at my parents in turn and followed him. Before I had gotten to the top of the stairs, I had heard the door to his room slam shut, vibrating the banister I had been holding on to. When I had reached the landing, I had knocked lightly on the door, calling out to him to see if he would allow me to at least talk to him.

"Go away!" came the reply.

"Austin, let me in, please." I had heard the lock on the door being moved and then the door being opened. He had not looked at me nor talked to me but he had allowed me to walk further into the room.

"Austin, have you lost all your senses?" I had not meant to sound abrasive but that's how it had sounded at the time.

"Only in your eyes!" he had spat back.

"Austin, listen, what you're doing for the bookstore I understand, but putting your life in danger to make a statement to the North – that's asking for trouble!" I had tried to reason, a bit more sensibly and less abrasive this time. It was one thing to dabble in politics in our state's capital; it was another to join a war and fight in hand-to-hand combat.

"I don't need you to argue with me, Maddie! I'm helping you get what you want too! You want the store more than I do, so by me joining the Army, you can have it!"

"Joining the Army to fight in a war is crazy, Austin, and I'm not about to lose my brother over wanting to be in charge of our bookstore!"

"I'll be fine!" he had attempted to reassure me.

"Didn't you learn anything about the war our country was founded upon? Don't you remember the stories of casualties and death?!" I had reminded him of our history lessons.

"I also remember the stories of valor, glory and honor for one's country. Maddie, those men fought for their rights and beliefs as well! It's no different now than it was two generations ago!"

I could not argue with my brother anymore. I remember feeling so hurt that day that he had chosen his own selfish pride over the feelings of his family, but there was nothing any of us could do. I remember how determined he was to see his plan through and truly become a hero to the South. What I did not know then, was that a war with the North and a country divided in two, would pit families against each other, separate homes, and would leave its everlasting scar on our lives forever.

~~*

Spring was all but over, my nineteenth birthday had come and gone, and summer had been the season I had dreaded the most. Daddy had kept up his argument but Austin had kept to his word and at the end of his school term, he had packed a bag and left for Frankfort. Mama had been in tears for days (or perhaps it had been weeks) but my father had kept quiet, never letting anyone know how hurt he was that Austin had gone. The day after Austin had said goodbye, Daddy had reluctantly made me head bookkeeper and allowed me full access to our accounting and sales books. We had been able to open our store a few days a week, but we had only managed to make a few sales at most.

About two weeks after my brother had left and I had fully devoted my time to the store, the bell on the door had interrupted my daily reading time, signaling a customer. I was still set on continuing to read, hoping they were just browsing the shelves instead of actually there to pick up a book. No one had placed any orders since before the election and no one in our town had made any attempt to pick up the books that lay forgotten in the storeroom. Sneaking a glance before going back to my book, I had not recognized him and hoped he was not someone from a neighboring town or worse, a *Northerner*.

"Reading while at work is highly unprofessional to your customers," his voice had echoed before I had the chance to gaze up at a very handsome gentleman with eyes as dark as molasses.

"I work in a bookstore, sir. It would be more unprofessional to not be able to recommend a book to my customers. Besides, what else do you do in a bookstore but read books?" I had snidely replied back. I was not about to let this stranger come into *my* store and insult me.

"Does the owner of this establishment know that his hired hand has a wicked tongue to go along with her unprofessional notion for reading while customers are milling about?" His smirk had been laced with charm and I could tell right away from his accent and from his demeanor that he was of a higher class than my family – socialites were very easy to notice.

"My father is well aware I can hold my own against a worthy verbal adversary," I had retaliated, smirking back and catching him off-guard.

"A bookstore owner's daughter running his establishment with a tongue as vile as Katherina herself? Impressive."

I could not believe that this stranger had actually known literature well enough that he would dare to compare me to a character from a not-so-well-known Shakespearean play, even if it was Taming of the Shrew. "Better to be Katherina with her vile tongue than be sweet Ophelia, turned mad by a love she could not have," had been my witty retort.

"Or poor Juliet, who killed herself over her love-at-first-sight," he had countered. I had quickly become impressed that he could keep up with my quip.

"You seem to know your female Shakespearean characters, sir. Do you read his works often?"

"Sir sounds too formal after we have already exchanged such witty responses. Please, call me Will, and yes, Shakespeare happens to be my favorite writer to date."

"Well then, Will, are you a fan of his plays or his sonnets?"

"On days such as today, when faced with a *worthy* adversary, I prefer his plays," he had smiled again, mocking me with my own words and causing me to blush slightly. No one had ever had that affect on me before unless they were making me red with anger instead of pink with embarrassment.

"And on other days when an adversary is nowhere to be found? Do you sit by the fire and recite sonnets for your wife and children? Or a sweetheart perhaps?" I had been very bold in asking these questions but if he had dared to answer I'd know for sure if he had been married or taken, although I do not recall even glancing down at his fingers for a band.

"I neither sit by a fire nor do I have a wife, children, or sweetheart, if you must know. I prefer to read alone and I'm usually in my father's study or sitting by a tree when the weather is fair." He had kept his eyes locked on mine and I could not look away, I was so mesmerized by his presence.

"I've never seen you here before. Have tough times brought you into our town from elsewhere?" There had been the real question to ask that I am still amazed at myself for asking. If he had been from another town, then we would soon hear news about where this war was taking us.

"My father has lived in this town his whole life. He could not come into town today to pick up our order so I am picking it up for him." There had been a slight sense of pride in his voice and I had been ashamed at myself for thinking that this bitter time had only affected our livelihood and not everyone else's in town.

"Well I will not keep you waiting. What is the last name?" I had known I would be in the storeroom for a while as I retrieved his package, partly due to the fact that I was unsure where my father had placed all the old orders that were never picked up.

"Hutchinson," he had answered, standing taller than before as he spoke his last name, as if it had some standing in our store at all.

"I will be right back with your order," I had said to him, leaping down from my stool and heading into the storeroom. After rummaging through a few boxes, I had found a small package labeled 'Hutchinson' and hoped I had not kept him waiting too long.

"Here it is! That will be one dollar please." I had held out my hand, expecting him to pay me in full for the package I was handing him.

"Now wait just a minute. I need to inspect the book to make sure it is not damaged. Father doesn't like his books ruined before he receives them."

He had unwrapped the brown paper surrounding the book carefully, inspected it and then gently placed it down on the counter. After searching his pockets for money, he had handed me one dollar but our fingers lightly lingered. In that moment I had gone from the witty Katherina to the awe-struck Juliet. The mirrored look in his eyes had also told me that Petruchio had been reduced to Romeo.

William

6

I had lightly touched her hand as I handed her the money; anything just to have some physical contact. She was a beautiful girl and that day I had been thankful my father had given me the chore of picking up his book order he had neglected for months. She had challenged me with literary wit, something no other girl had ever done before, most too afraid to go against the grain of tradition. Naturally, they were all beautiful in their own way, but they were too close to my sister in personality – sophisticated ladies of society, without the ability or freedom to speak their own minds. This bookstore owner's daughter had shown me she had that freedom, at least when no one was around, which made her radiate more beauty than any of the society women my parents paraded in my direction over the years.

"Goodbye, Katherina," I had said to her as our hands slipped apart, deliberately enticing her Shakespearian love by calling her the shrew of prose.

"I do have a real name." Of course she did. Any fool would have known her parents were smart, educated folk and would dare not name her something so literary.

"Well," I had smiled at her, "you never told me what it was."

"Madeline." She all but whispered it but I did catch it before she lowered her eyes away from mine.

"Goodbye, Madeline." She had glanced up and as I caught her eyes, a lump formed in my throat.

"Goodbye," she had spoken softly as I tucked the book under my arm and headed out the door, the bells ringing after me.

On my way home I had felt as light as a feather and had decided to stop at Sally's Saloon, one of the few to remain open in such troubling times as they were. I had not stepped foot into that establishment since I had my argument with Rex Parker but no one seemed to recognize me as I came in. At that moment, I had needed something to settle my head from the unexpected literary battle and a nice snifter of brandy would most likely do the trick. I could have gone home for some, since we had an endless supply of it, but Father would have asked too many questions since he knew I had chosen not to drink around him at all. On that day, even the quiet chatter about the expanding Confederate Army was not enough to get Madeline out of my head.

"Something on your mind, sugar?" a female voice had cut into my thoughts and as I turned around, I had locked eyes with Savannah Parker, Rex's younger sister. I should have known better than to come to Sally's – it being the favorite place of the Parkers to have their liquor.

"Nothing you can help me with, I'm afraid." I had quickly turned back to my drink, afraid that a conversation with her would be trouble.

"Come on, handsome, talk to me."

Before taking another sip, I had glanced over at her, giving her a reason to join me. Cursing myself for even acknowledging her, I'm not quite sure what I had despised more – her smile that could melt a man's heart or her eyes that could pierce the soul. She had sat down next to me and ordered herself a drink, something women never did in saloons. It was always customary for a woman to sit at home and drink, unless she worked for the establishment of course. I had been doubly surprised to see her order the same drink as her brother, considering women mainly drank tea, or at most wine, in the privacy of their homes.

"Didn't know you drank Cognac," I had commented, not particularly sure why I started a conversation with her, knowing she'd never leave my side after.

"My brother introduced me to the drink. It's not my drink of choice with the ladies but I see you are drinking Brandy, so I needed something strong." Her green eyes were driving me insane and I had to look away and yank my mind back to my previous thoughts of Madeline in order to pay no heed to her presence next to me.

"What do you really want, Savannah?" My patience had begun to run thin.

"You already know," she had smirked, her eyes gleaming with the meaning behind her words.

"It was a mistake, you and me, and can't happen again." I had looked away again and taken a sip of my drink, allowing the warm liquid to take away the burning in my mind.

Before I knew what was happening, her hand was on my shoulder, pulling me around to face her. "You look like you could use something stronger and brandy isn't going to work." She nodded her head towards my glass instead of lifting her hand from my shoulder.

"Your mother would not approve if she found out about us," I had whispered, trying to convince her I had more power in this town than she. To a woman like Savannah, it would have been a fate worse than death for her family name to be tainted by the promiscuousness she had already committed. Women were to be pure before they were married and I knew first-hand that she was certainly anything but pure.

"My mother wants my brother to marry *your* sister, so why wouldn't she want me with you?"

"Because neither will ever be arranged, so get any thoughts of a union between our families out of your mind. Besides, I don't approve of the idea of my sister anywhere near your brother."

"I heard about your tussle. Will, you didn't need to prove how strong you were against my brother. I already knew," she had coyly replied, running her fingers down my collar. "And I'm sure my mother would be elated if she knew we were together."

I had yanked her hand away and gone back to my drink. "We're *not* together, Savannah!" I had growled.

"Is there someone else?" At first I could not answer but my mind immediately thought about Madeline and Savannah was close enough to notice the change in my expression. "There is someone else! Who is she? Do I know her?"

"There is no one else and I have to be getting home. My father is waiting for me." I had gotten up but she had stepped in front of me and would not let me pass. "Let me through, Savannah," I had growled at her again, not wanting to make a scene that people in this town would talk about for weeks.

"Not until I get a kiss goodbye."

"Not here."

"Somewhere else perhaps?" She had seemed too hopeful at the idea of meeting me in private.

"No."

I had gently pushed her aside and walked out of the saloon. There was no telling who would have said something if they had caught us in a compromising position and I had known from the minute she walked up to me at the bar that I needed to get away from her quickly. Savannah had been a mistake, just as I had told her, one that I will never make again, but I should have known that once she had gotten her claws into you, she did not let go so easily.

As I briskly walked home, hoping not to be followed, my mind wandered back to Madeline – her delicate features countered her aggressive tongue. Her dark eyes had captivated me even before she spoke a single word. I had been so caught up in my thoughts I hadn't even noticed that I had arrived at home. My mother had been sitting in the parlor room, leaning her head on my father's shoulder, her eyes wet with tears. My mind had immediately panicked and all thoughts of women left my head.

"William, please sit down," my father had instructed me, rather solemnly. "We received a letter from your sister."

All at once my eyes lit up and I had practically leaped out of my chair, unsure why my parents were so unhappy about receiving a letter from Gracie. "That's wonderful! When can we expect her home?" I may have been almost twenty-one but in that moment I was acting ten again.

"She's not coming home, William," Father had replied.

"What?!" I had shouted.

"She's decided to stay in New York and finish her studies. She will come home when she's finished with school." His calmness about Gracie's decision unnerved me.

"Doesn't she understand everything that has begun, that half the South has already rebelled and seceded, and we need her home?" My temper had begun to rise almost immediately and I could not stay in the chair any longer, leaping to my feet and glaring at his stubborn face.

"It is her choice to stay! I will not let this war hinder her from becoming a nurse!"

"Here's your book!" I had thrown it down on the table to further my point. "Don't speak to me until Gracie comes home!"

I had raced up to my room, slammed the door behind me, quickly changed out of my stifling business clothes that I wore every day, and grabbed a book off the shelf above my bed to read. When deeper reading was too much for me, I usually read Lord Tennyson's poetry and even with our differences, Tennyson was something both Gracie and I enjoyed reading, sometimes together under that large Yellowwood tree at the far end of our property. Reading it at that moment though had only caused more pain and more anger to surface and it had taken everything out of me not to throw the hard-covered book across the room.

My mind had soon wandered again back to Madeline. I knew I had to see her again; her alluring eyes had been begging me to see them once more. She was so different from Savannah and countless others I could not even bare to remember their names. There was something so beautiful about her that set her apart from all the women I had shown attention to in the past. I wanted to learn more about her, so I had made a decision to go back to the bookstore the very next day.

~~*

The following day, I had been woken up earlier than usual by my mother banging on my door and shouting at me to come outside immediately. I had raced to get dressed, hoping that Gracie had changed her mind and had decided to come home but I had been sadly mistaken. When I had reached the first level of our house I noticed chaos had ensued and I had to grab one of our servants to find out what was happening.

"The wheat, sir, it's on fire!" he had exclaimed as he ran past me out the back door, carrying a large bucket full of water.

I knew we had been having an exceptionally hot and dry summer but I never thought it would be severe enough to start a fire on our plantation. If we couldn't put it out fast enough and it spread too quickly, we'd lose half the crop for the season's harvest. Knowing that losing the crop would set my father back financially, I did not want to deal with his anger after the fact. Catching a glimpse of my mother out of the corner of my eye, I had stopped her from walking away too quickly so I could get some better answers from her.

"What can I do?" I had asked her.

"Your father has things under control with the slaves for now but we need more help to get water out there."

"How did it start?"

"Your father is investigating it. It might have been tobacco that started it."

"Do you think one of our...?" I had shuddered to think one of our own slaves had done this purposefully to add to all the rioting we had already heard about from other areas of the South.

"We're not sure who or what but rest assured, there will be a whipping when this is over!" she had announced rather annoyed.

Knowing we needed help and fast, I had made haste to the stables and saddled a horse as quickly as my hands could work the straps. We had little time to waste before the fire became uncontrollable again. As I galloped closer to town, there had been a part of me that wanted to veer off and head to the bookstore just to catch a glimpse of Madeline again, but time was of the essence and the plantation needed me more than my boyish whimsical desires. If I did not get the fire brigade out to our plantation in time, the fire would reach the soil and our crops would fail next season as well.

"William, what's the rush? What's wrong?" the chief of the brigade had asked as I leapt from the horse without allowing the steed time to fully come to a stop.

"There's a fire on the plantation! Our buckets aren't enough!"

"We're on our way!" he had stated, rounding as many firemen as he could.

I mounted my horse and was about to head back when I was stopped by Savannah standing in the middle of the road. "Hey handsome, where you headin' so fast?"

"I don't have time for this right now! I need to get back to the plantation!"

"Well, I'll come with you. It's almost tea time and I'd just love to talk with your mother again!"

"The plantation is on fire, Savannah! I really don't think she has time right now for tea!"

"Take me with you then!" she had demanded stubbornly. "I'd be happy to help any way I can."

"Have you ever done any hard labor in your life?" I had

questioned her incredulously.

"I've done some work," she had protested.

"Work like lifting buckets of water and being close enough to a fire you can feel it burning your skin?" I had pressed, really wishing she would leave me be.

"No, but I'm sure it's not so difficult."

"You're too delicate for that type of work and I don't want that responsibility over my head. I have to go!"

I had pulled hard on the reins and managed to push the horse into a gallop, leaving her in the dust its hooves left behind, but the crowded town square made it more difficult to maneuver around. When I had finally reached our plantation there were smoke clouds but no sign of fire, which meant the fire brigade had been more helpful than I. Leaving the horse still saddled in the stable, I had raced through the house and finally found my father in his study, his head buried in his hands and a drink on his desk. I luckily had remembered the rule to clear my throat before entering the room, announcing my presence.

"What was the outcome?" I had asked, afraid of the answer I would receive.

"One acre. We lost one whole acre," he had sighed, not lifting his head.

"Did it reach the soil?"

"Not sure. Have to wait for the ashes to cool before checking." He finally had lifted his head to acknowledge me. "Where were you, boy? Where were you when we needed your help? We lost three slaves from exhaustion and two from fire burns! The fire brigade got here after it was too late to save them and you weren't here to help!"

"I'm sorry. I got held up in town. Savannah cornered me and I couldn't get away!"

"Savannah? Savannah Parker?! Are you philandering around with Doc Parker's daughter? And don't lie to me, boy, I'll find out!"

he had shouted, pointing an angry and accusing finger towards me.

"I'm not doing anything with her! I never was! And *she* cornered *me*!"

"And you're not man enough to walk away?!"

"It wasn't like that!" I had defended uselessly.

"Boy, I'm warning you! Your responsibilities are here to this family and plantation! I'll not have you neglecting it for the sake of a girl like Savannah Parker or any other!"

"I wasn't *with* her! And I know where I belong!"

"Good! Now get out there, show your worth as scion master of this plantation, and find out if we are ruined for *two* seasons instead of just one!"

"Yes, sir."

I remember lowering my head like a scolded child and heading out to the field where I could already hear the wails of the families of slaves that had lost their loved ones. We only allow them one day of mourning before it is back to work and we have a small plot of land on the western edge of our plantation where we bury the dead of our slaves; our own family plot is part of the growing cemetery adjacent to the church in town. We do not allow our slaves more than this or they'd begin to expect more from us and their servitude and that would be enough to ruin us completely.

I had tried to appear authoritative like my father as I paraded through the fields of wheat. Every man, woman and child had hung their head guiltily, as if the fear of the whipping was more than they could handle. We did not whip often, as some plantation owners chose to do, but something like this would be just cause to use it. It was my duty as future master to question as many of them as possible to find out how it started, where it started, and who started it and if no response came, the whip would be the answer. As luck was going that day, nothing seemed to be in my favor.

"Does anyone know what happened?" I had been met with silence. "The faster someone tells me what went wrong, the faster this issue will be resolved." Still silence.

Impatience had been growing on me by the minute because all I really had wanted to do that day was go into town and see Madeline and my plans had been thwarted by this travesty. When the chief of the fire brigade had approached me, interrupting my useless interrogation and my wandering thoughts, I had hoped he would be able to give me a full report for my father. Placing his hand on my shoulder, I had known instantly it was not going to be good news. He had actually sighed before speaking.

"Half the acre's been scorched to the soil," he had reported solemnly.

"Thank you. I'll let my father know," was all I had been able to say.

"Does anyone know *how* it started?"

I had simply shrugged. "No one is talking."

"Well, I'd say it began at the far end, from the direction of the charred stalks. Didn't look like anything started on its own from the dryness of the air, so there must have been another catalyst."

"Any suggestions?"

"No. Any clues would have gone up with the flames. Don't fret, William, it could have been any passerby with lit tobacco or a match. It's much too dry out here for anything to be safe from fire."

"I'm too concerned with all the news of slave revolts to let this one slide as a passerby. They hear too much."

"I understand. We will stake out the charred half acre before we leave and good luck finding out what happened."

"Thank you, to all of you."

I remember feeling a mix of fear and anger when they had finally left our plantation. I had been woken up out of a surreal dream to learn that one full acre of our plantation had been burned, half of that down to the soil. No one seemed to know the cause of it and I could not humanely bring myself to whip them all for keeping silent. I had gone without breakfast and I really was in no mood for afternoon tea. I knew Father would be in a foul mood as well; something I had grown used to but certainly did not care for that day.

As it was my duty though, I had made my way back inside the house and told my father what had happened. Without a word, he had headed outside to the tool shed where he kept the whip, me following at his heels. I had cringed to think of the wrath he would be taking it out on them until someone was willing to talk. Wheat was a high commodity in the South and if we did not produce our crop, we failed a lot more than just ourselves. People would look for their wheat elsewhere and we'd be out of business entirely.

When my father had returned he growled angrily at me and threw the whip down at my feet. "Next time, find answers or start whipping! We don't keep control if we let them get away with keeping silent!"

I had picked up the tool and instantly felt sick to my stomach. I could not imagine using it on another human being, even if they were our property, a trait I had acquired from my mother I had assumed. Glancing down at my hands, the sight of blood on the whip has never been wiped away from my mind. Blood, human blood, had scarred me for life. I had quickly dropped the weapon of control and run out of the shed.

In the stables, I had wiped my hands on a towel, grabbed my horse that was still saddled, and rode off. I could not have stayed there one more minute longer without the nausea taking over. Riding out to the edge of the plantation and not stopping until I had reached the Yellowwood that stood there all by itself, I had all but leaped from the saddle just to breathe in the fresh air surrounding it. As the air filled my lungs, I had almost chocked back my surprise when I saw someone I did not expect sitting beneath the tree.

I had been slightly angered that someone would want to disturb me while I was reading and the horse's hooves approaching told me this person was determined to do so. I knew I had been caught and assumed whomever it was, was going to tell me to leave, but when I raised my head I had been shocked at who I saw racing towards me. Then I had heard his voice and confirmed that it had been him.

"We have to stop meeting like this." His words had had a slight chuckle to them and when I had looked up he had a smile on his face as he stepped down from his horse.

"I didn't know you knew this tree was here," had been my curt reply. I had still been upset that someone had interrupted my reading.

"It's on my father's property. Of course I knew it was here and I was gracious that someone had decided to put a swing on it – saved me a lot of trouble trying to impress the girls during my teenage years," he had chuckled again.

"This is *your* plantation?" I had exclaimed, not sure how to compartmentalize this new piece of information. More importantly, that meant that the man who had warned me of speaking to anyone had been Will's father and the *master* of the plantation!

I had wanted to cry but held myself back. I had quickly scanned the plantation for anyone who could run and say something to Mr. Hutchinson, but Will had stepped in front of me, blocking my view. It had frustrated me even more because any one of their slaves had the ability to disclose my whereabouts to the master of the plantation and then my relationship to my tree would be lost.

"Is something wrong? Were you expecting someone else?" He had seemed slightly bothered by the thought of someone else meeting me there but I had tried to ignore the guilt it implied.

"Your father told me I was not supposed to speak to anyone while I was here, so it's best if you leave before he catches us both." I had attempted to step away but he stepped closer, daring me to leave his presence, which under other circumstances I would not want to do.

"Why would he say such a thing? When was this?"

"Last fall, before the election," I had replied, suddenly realizing how every conversation now was using the election as a reference point.

"He never said anything to me about it. He knows I come out this way from time to time."

"Any other reason you come out here other than using my swing to woo a young girl's heart?" I had not meant for it to sound so harsh.

"To think, to read, to escape. Wait, did you say *your* swing?"

I had nodded my head slowly. "My father built that swing when I was younger. And it was my great grandfather who planted the tree here, before it was obviously part of your plantation."

"Why else do you come here?" he had asked me in return. His questions had made it difficult for me to concentrate on the dire need to leave the boundary of the plantation. I had wanted more than anything to sit with him and talk, possibly more simple conversation than we had had the day before.

"To read mostly," had been my weak reply.

"I'd be happy to share it with you," he had smiled, but I had frowned, knowing his father might see us out there together at any time.

"I really think you should leave. Your father gave me strict orders not to speak to anyone while I was here. If he finds us talking..." I had heard stories of plantation masters using whips on their slaves; I had shuddered to think what Mr. Hutchinson might do to me if he caught me so casually chatting with his son.

He had sighed heavily, seemingly dejected. "How often do you come here?" There had been hopefulness in his voice, as he too had not wanted our conversation to end so abruptly.

"I come back when I need to." I had tried not to smile but I could not help it. The thought of seeing Will again at *our* tree gave me butterflies.

"Well then I'll be seeing you, Madeline."

When he had said my name I had been drawn to the sound and gazed up into his eyes. "Please, can you call me Maddie?" I had finally let go of the insecurities and allowed myself to enjoy the intimate feeling between us.

He had smiled in return as he mounted his horse, finally heeding my warning about his father. Before riding away, he looked down at me again and I felt his gaze resonate through my entire body. "Goodbye, Maddie."

Truth be told, I had never made it to the store that morning, even though my father had specifically asked me to come in and help him reorganize our shelves. When news had reached our part of town that the wheat plantation had caught fire, my heart had almost stopped beating. I had been afraid the great Yellowwood had gone up in flames as well and I had to go and make sure it was still standing. I had sat by the tree and watched as they tried helplessly to extinguish the flames in the fields. I could have gone to get help but my feet seemed rooted at the spot, as if the tree was begging me not to leave. Now I know why.

I knew it had been childish of me to feel jealous of those unknown girls – it's just a tree after all – but I had sighed anyway, feeling a bit uneasy as he rode away. My concentration from my book had already been broken and I needed to get to the bookstore before my father came to find me again and scolded me for neglecting the business I had so wanted to be a part of. Taking a deep breath, I had begun to slowly move away from the tree when someone's footsteps approaching broke the silence in the air.

"It was you, wasn't it?" an angry voice had shouted at me.

"Excuse me, sir?"

"It was you who started the fire!" he had accused again. I had to blink at him a few times to realize it was Will's father. My heart had begun to beat faster, hoping beyond all hope that he had not seen me talking to his son.

"I did not start the fire!" I had defended, attempting to stand straighter than before. Ever since I was a little girl, whenever someone accused me of something, I had stood straighter and fixed them with a withering stare to defend myself. I could tell though, that my glare had not been working too well on Mr. Hutchinson.

"How long have you been sitting here while watching my crop burn at your hands?" he had not backed down.

"Why would I start a fire, here of all places? I love this tree and I only came out here when I heard that a fire had started to make sure the tree was still standing!" I had proclaimed loudly, hoping my raised voice would allow the truth to shine through.

"I just watched my son come from this area of the plantation. This is where they said the fire had started. If he knows you did something to my crop…"

"No! I don't even know your son!" I had lied terribly. "I arrived after he rode off!"

"I can tell when someone lies to me. You were here when my son rode by, which is against my rule I set for you and you watched my crop burn and never went for help!"

"I… I…" I had stammered, not knowing how to respond without continuing to lie.

"For both of those reasons you are not to return to this tree!" I had simply blinked my already forming tears away, not able to protest further. "Do I make myself understood?"

"Yes sir." I had solemnly bowed my head. He had stormed off, leaving me standing there with tears in my eyes, knowing I would never see Will again nor would I have my tree.

~~*

Halfway through that summer I had received an unexpected visit from Will to our bookstore, but this time he had been accompanied by a sassy young woman I did not recognize. My father had been in the front of the store rearranging bookcases, while I had been in the storeroom clearing off the shelves and making room for what my father had hoped would be new shipments. We had received a few sporadic personal orders from our devoted customers but with major cities like Raleigh and Memphis refusing to ship anything outside state borders, it had grown more difficult to bring in any new customers. It had felt like we were being cut off not only from within our own town, most people saving every penny they owned, but from the rest of the South as well.

"Maddie, please find the order for Hutchinson," my father had called into the storeroom. My heart began to race and a knot formed in my stomach, assuming the elder Hutchinson had come into our store, using a fake order, to address the situation about the fire on the plantation and the tree with my father.

Since the day Mr. Hutchinson chased me off of his property, he had stopped ordering books, just as he had threatened he would do. This was the first time we had an order from them since Will had come in the day we had met, and I had refused to go by the tree, too afraid of what Mr. Hutchinson would do if he had found me there. I had yet to find a way to tell my father about the incident by the tree and I would have hated for Mr. Hutchinson to make a fuss over something I did not do. Any time I had gone out to read, I had gone to the pond, but was always chased away by the birds.

My hands had been shaking as I took their order from a shelf in the storeroom and brought it out to where our customer had been waiting. "Your order, sir," I had barely whispered, head bowed and eyes down.

"Thank you, Miss Madeline." It had been Will's voice I heard and not Mr. Hutchinson's after all. My heart began to beat faster, not out of fear, but out of shear delight.

I had looked up then and caught his eye. "Hello, Will." I had attempted to hide my smile but failed miserably.

"I haven't seen you by the tree in a while," he had whispered close to my face as I handed him his book and our fingers lingered, my eyes never leaving his as he spoke.

"Your father told me never to return," I had spoken as low as I could until my father came by and interrupted us.

"Everything all right with the order, William?"

"Let me make sure it's the one my father ordered correctly."

"Of course. Have Maddie ring it up for you when you're done." My father had gone back to the bookcases and was showing the girl who had come in with Will a book or two.

"Who's she?" I had inquired, nodding my head towards her.

"That's Savannah Parker, Doc Parker's daughter." I had caught the slight way his eyes rolled at the mention of her name and I had to smile at his demeanor.

"You don't like her?"

"I can't talk to her about books!" he had sighed and I could tell he was frustrated with her very presence around him. "My folks even find her chatter incessant when she invites herself over for tea."

"Speaking of your parents, is this the book your father wanted?" I had pointed to the brown-paper wrapped book in his hand.

He had quickly unwrapped it and scrutinized its cover and pages. "It's not for him. It's something I decided I wanted for my own library."

I had taken the book from him and read its cover. It was an anthology of Shakespeare's tragedies. I couldn't help but smile, remembering our first encounter in the bookstore and how well he knew his Shakespearean female characters. I had handed it back to him just as Savannah came over and wrapped both her arms possessively around one of his, as if guarding him like a dog. She had not seen him roll his eyes at her as he peered up at me, but I had to stifle a laugh so he would not get caught.

"What did you order, handsome?" I had watched intently at their exchange of words, hoping he would not afford her the same attention as he did me.

Will had answered her dismissively. "Nothing you'd be interested in."

"Let me see. Shakespeare? Why would you read something as depressing as a tragedy?"

"He's one of the most brilliant English writers! And actually, some of his best plays were his tragedies," I had found myself entering into their conversation without being addressed. I had also caught Will smirking at my interjection, almost proud I had dared to say how I felt about the literary mastermind.

"I might have had to read something by him in school. I remember the language being too hard to understand!"

"Well, I for one find the language amazing. It baffles my mind how the words he uses are so profound and virtually roll off your tongue when you recite it out loud."

"Does she make any sense to you?" Savannah had asked Will. He had just shrugged but never lifted his gaze from me, which I had gladly returned.

"Why don't you wait outside while I pay for this? I'll only be a minute." Savannah had sighed dramatically and we had heard the bells ringing above the door but we had remained staring into each other's eyes.

"So, a book for your own library?" I had inquired, not able to stop the smile on my face.

He had shrugged again, never lifting his eyes from mine. "If I am to have a worthy adversary, I need to read up on my plays."

We both had laughed at the memory. "Even the mighty Caesar fell to a worthy opponent," I had begun to play our game.

"Et tu, Brute?" he had quoted, feigning shock.

I had chosen to ring up his order instead of continue our banter, lest my father catch wind of the conversation. "That will be one dollar and fifty cents and I prefer to be anyone but Brutus, preferably a female character. Besides, Caesar was too arrogant to rule an empire."

He had handed me the money and grabbed for my hand before I could pull it away. "Very true. You would make a much better Queen of Egypt than a Brutus." My cheeks had burned as I felt myself blush at his flirtatious words and actions.

I had been able to pull my hand away just as my father had come around a bookcase, carrying a pile of books to be relocated. He had said goodbye to Will and then disappeared around another bookcase. I had placed the money in a drawer behind the counter, locked it, and glanced back up again just in time to catch Will's eye as he was leaving the store. Walking over to my father, I had picked up a book that was on the floor next to him.

"I can do this if you want me to."

"I saw the way he was looking at you, Maddie," he had replied, ignoring my request. "How long has this been going on between you two?"

"There's nothing going on! I hardly know him!" I had exclaimed, shocked by his accusation.

"Did you know your favorite tree was incorporated into his father's plantation?" I had glanced down, but he picked up my chin with his hand. "Some people are saying they saw you by the tree when the fire started and that you were there speaking to William. Now tell me the truth – how long have things been going on?"

I had squared my shoulders the way I had always done and took a breath before answering him. "I had no idea until today that it was Will's plantation! When I heard about the fire, I went there to check on the tree, to make sure it was still standing! And I have only met him twice besides today, but nothing is going on between us."

My father had stiffened, dropping my chin and setting his jaw. "When?"

"Once here in the bookstore when his father sent him to pick up an order about two months ago and once the day of the fire.," I had lowered my voice as the shame took over me.

"What happened out there that day?" he had asked me without accusation this time.

"Will had come out to the tree after the fire had been put out. That's when I found out it had been *his* plantation all along. Mr. Hutchinson, he had told me once before that if I spoke to anyone while sitting there he had the right to make sure I never sat out there again, but I never talked to anyone... until today. After Will left the tree, his father came and began accusing *me* of starting the fire! .He then... he then told me I couldn't come to the tree anymore now that I've talked to his son and he refuses to buy anything from us anymore!"

"Maddie..."

"I know, I should have told you, but I couldn't! It hurt so much that I couldn't tell you but I swear I did not start that fire nor is there anything going on between Will and me."

"I can't believe Jackson would say such a thing to you! He knows better than to start trouble! He's also been one of my longtime customers!" he had growled, forgetting that he had been scolding me.

My father had handed me the remaining books he had been to putting away and started to walk towards the door. "What are you doing? Where are you going?" I had called after him.

"Please finish putting the books away and lock up. I will meet you at home."

With that he had left the store, slamming the door so hard the walls had vibrated. There had been no doubt in my mind he was heading for the Hutchinson plantation, which I would soon realize was not one of his best ideas. He had returned home with a bloody lip and a swollen eye. Mama had been furious with him and scolded him as if he was a child and that a grown man should not fight with another man. I myself felt a sense of pride that my father had gone out of his way to see justice be done on my behalf. That evening, after a very quiet supper, he had knocked on the door to my room to talk to me.

"May I come in?" he had asked cautiously, not wanting to intrude on my personal space. "I'm so sorry I didn't believe you from the beginning. And no matter what your mama thinks, I'm not sorry for what I did." I had glanced up at him as he took the liberty to sit on my bed. "Ever since your brother left I can't help but feel there are many who are waiting to see us fail. That tree was ours long before it was claimed by Jackson Hutchinson and his plantation. It wasn't even part of the plantation boundaries until he added it to his property line. I know you had nothing to do with that fire or his son but I still failed you." He had dropped his eyes and I had grabbed my hand in response. "I failed you just like I failed your brother."

"You didn't fail me and you didn't fail Austin. You went out there to prove to Mr. Hutchinson that your daughter is neither after his property nor after his son and I am proud of you for that. I can always find another tree."

"No!" he had shouted as he leapt from the bed. "Your great grandfather planted that sapling! That tree is a part of who you are, a part of your family, and I won't allow Jackson or anyone else to take that away from you!"

"What are you saying?"

"I'm saying I want you to continue going there as you always have! If he has a problem with it, he can answer to me!"

"But –"

"Don't worry about me. He has a strong right hook but for you, your brother, and your mama, it will take a lot more than one hit to knock me down!"

I had jumped up and into his arms, tears already falling from my eyes. He had held me tightly in a giant bear-sized hug and for a split second I felt like a child again. Before pulling away, I had whispered thank you into his ear. He had kissed my forehead and walked out of my room, leaving me beaming with pride. As soon as he had left, I went over to my desk and began to pen a letter to my brother, wanting so much to tell him everything that had happened and how proud I was of our father. I hadn't heard from Austin since he had left our town except for a short note to let us know where we could send our letters to. I had missed him so much and I thought about writing so many times but each time my words fell short. Now I finally had a reason and the words.

William

8

Madeline had been intoxicating and I did not know why. Savannah had even noticed that something had been different in the way I conducted myself around her and even she had decided the chase was not worth it. That day, when I had compared Madeline to Cleopatra, was the day I had decided that the wheat plantation and social engagements be damned. There was more to her, I knew; I could feel it. I had begun to order more books of my own, regardless of my father's expansive library, and I would take long rides out to the tree, using the excuse that I was going to check on the crop and the slaves, gaining respect from my father in eventually becoming the plantation's master. I had read there more often than usual, hoping, waiting, for the day she came to join me, but she did not.

I'm sure it had had something to do with Madeline's father, Mr. McCall, coming to call on us the very evening I had gone to pick up my first book order. Father had been furious at the interruption to his meal, as we had supper every evening at the same time, when light was still available to see our food. When Mr. McCall had argued about the tree being planted by his grandfather and my father retaliating about the tree being on *our* property, Mother had asked that they take their quarrel outside. I was then assigned the task of making sure the argument did not escalate to blows. As it was my father's custom, and most likely where I get my temper, he had instigated the tussle.

As it had gotten closer to the end of summer, what was left of the wheat crop would be harvested, and we still had not received any word from Gracie. I had read in the local papers that New York had been having its own political crisis, when earlier in the year Mayor Fernando Wood of Manhattan attempted to persuade the sovereign city-state to secede from the union as well. This had caused great outcries as far north as the capital in Albany, and I had feared that the state government would bar any southern travel out of the state until the matter had been resolved. What had worried me more was my father's lack of attempts to persuade my sister to return to us. Moreover, my mother had begun to ask more ladies over for tea, which under normal circumstances would not have bothered me, except that she insisted I entertain their daughters "as a gentleman should." This had included long walks out to the fields, dry and listless conversations, and unsuccessful attempts to thwart their societal charm. My mind had always wandered back to Madeline as their incessant chatter fell upon my deafened ears.

As the summer had come to a close, there had been a particular day I recall, where I had come back from riding out to the tree to find my mother entertaining her usual guests in the parlor room. The daughter that had been sitting beside her mother was a woman I'm sure would have made a perfect candidate for a wife in my parents' eyes, but to me, she had just been another girl, putting on airs to impress me.

"William, please join us," my mother had called out to me as I had come into the house. I had joined them in the parlor room, kissed my mother on the cheek, and waited for her to make the proper introductions. "I'd like you to meet Mrs. Marques and her daughter, Annabelle-Lynn."

"Pleased to meet you both," I had smiled, bowing my head slightly to address them in turn.

"Mr. Marques owns a vineyard outside of town." My mother had always seemed to identify people by their occupations. I had simply smiled at the inclination but I had not been in the mood that day to entertain. "Why don't you take Annabelle-Lynn for a walk and show her around the plantation," she had suggested, playing into the host role too well.

I had attempted not to roll my eyes or groan in displeasure as I gave her my hand to help her up. She had graciously thanked my mother for tea, waived goodbye to them both and we were off, setting a course towards the very fields I had just come from. There had been an awkward bit of silence as we began our walk but it gave me a chance to glance over at her without her noticing. With her long golden locks tied in braids and pulled back around the nape of her neck, her neckline had been exposed and elongated, causing my eyes to drift downward. With the fashion of the day creating a scoop line to their dresses, the sleeves had hung just below the shoulders, giving young gentlemen such as myself more than an eyeful. She was quite beautiful and I'm sure my mother thought she could have used that as defense against me when I reiterated the fact that I was not interested in marrying her friends' daughters.

"I do have a voice," she had sweetly smiled at me, attempting to begin an awkward conversation.

"I have one as well." I must have sounded like a fool to her and yet whenever I was around Madeline, I had always been able to speak my mind.

"Tell me more about yourself other than that you are the son of a plantation master," she had demanded of me. She had been more straightforward that some of the others, but I had been so used to their kind, speaking to them was virtually automatic.

Unfortunately, having been recently out to the Yellowwood and having Madeline still fresh on my mind, I said the fist thing that came to me. "I like to read." How much of a teenager I had sounded, especially to myself, but I did not care because I had not been purposefully trying to impress her.

"Well, an educated plantation master makes you that much more sought-after." I could tell she had been trying to goad me into a game of allure. "But I'm sure with running a plantation this expansive, you have little time for pleasure reading."

I had actually been offended by that insulting comment. Even with learning how to run the entire plantation and entertaining all the young ladies my parents constantly invited for tea and dinners, I still found time to be at that tree, reading and hopelessly waiting for a certain someone to join me. "I try to read as much as I can, actually. I've even started building my own library." I had smiled proudly at the confession.

"I'd like to see it some time – this collection of yours." By the look in her eyes, I had known her idea of seeing my collection had little to do with reading.

"Would you prefer to go for a ride instead of walking?" I had asked her, politely changing the subject and not engaging her flirtatious conversation.

"Oh, I don't ride. Father says it isn't proper for a lady to ride a stallion, since they were designed for men's legs."

I could not believe her father had said that to her. I had known plenty of women who rode horses, including my sister, who had won trophies and medals for riding! I had become quite annoyed with Miss Annabelle-Lynn and I wish I had suggested we go back to the house since I had not been feeling well. Instead, I had been changed off course when she asked me a very peculiar question and to this day, I have yet to understand why she had the audacity to ask it.

"How do you run your plantation?" she had inquired rather rudely.

"Pardon me?" I had practically choked out.

"How do you run your plantation?" she had repeated.

"My *father* runs this plantation very well."

"My father says you can learn a lot from a man by the way he runs his plantation."

"And if a gentleman didn't run a plantation?" I had challenged.

"We naturally don't associate with anyone who doesn't," she had smiled, pressing her lips tight together, as if it was beneath her to speak to anyone not of our class or status.

Placating her, I had sighed and answered her. "I make sure the crop is harvested properly each season; I see to it that every grain of wheat is accounted for."

"Do you use the whip daily?" she had interrupted.

"I haven't found a reason to," I had spoken softly, trying to forget the fire and the blood on my hands.

"You are a weak man," she had concluded rather rudely.

"I beg your pardon? I am far from weak," I had blinked, completely caught off guard by her forward comment.

"Father says a slave is bought property, just as a horse or house. In order to train it, you must use force; in order to keep it obedient, you must use force."

I had been stunned and stood there with wide eyes. "How does not using a whip on another human being make me weak?"

"They are below us, William. Any creature below us must be disciplined."

"What does your father say about speaking to your slaves?"

"No conversation, just commands. If you befriend one of them, they take advantage and revolt," she had continued without missing a beat.

"Does your father have any words of wisdom on marriage and family?"

"William, your family comes from the same breed as we do," she had laughed at my absurd question. "You know our marriages are simply alliances and every plantation owner has a mistress! It's highly common knowledge."

She had a point that I had been unwilling to agree with. My parents had had an arranged marriage but in time they grew to love each other and Mother had always confided in me that she had preferred me to marry for love, not for the dowry. I even had doubted my father could have had a mistress at all, but with Annabelle-Lynn, there was no arguing at all. As we reached our sunroom, towards the west end of the house, I had grown more impatient with our conversation and wished to be done with her. She had paused to look at the expansiveness of our wheat fields and I had found myself casting an eye out towards the tree.

"Have you any siblings?" I had asked politely, keeping the conversation as light as possible.

"An older brother. He's already married but there is little to like about her."

"Why is that?"

"She's got herself another lover," she had stated so matter-of-factly.

"How do you know?" Curiosity had gotten the better of me and I had wanted to know how she had been able to tell that her sister-in-law was an adulteress.

"She has this look in her eyes when I see her."

"And what look is that?"

"She never can fully look me in the eyes and she is constantly touching my brother, as if she is reassuring herself she still has a husband, despite her affair."

"That doesn't mean she has someone else," I had argued, thinking that if that were the case, I would never be with any of the women my parents threw at me, since my mind had always reverted back to thoughts of seeing Madeline again. In a way, I had felt guilty for even being there with Annabelle-Lynn outside the sunroom, wishing it were Madeline there instead, and instead of talking in circles about plantations and slaves, we were reading together or reciting poetry, the same poetry I used to read with Gracie.

~~*

How convenient it had been for my parents to coincide my twenty-first birthday celebration with the harvest that year. After what was left of the crop had been harvested by the slaves, my father and I took it to the grist mill to be processed, as we had done every year before that. This particular year though, my father had stepped back and allowed me to handle the transactions and the collection of the money, to better prepare me for my eventual duties as master of the plantation. Even in such troubling times as these, even with my sister still in New York, even with war beginning, he still had the audacity to groom me into the man he had wanted me to be. So it had been only natural that my parents invited several couples and their eligible daughters to a feast and gala not only in honor of the harvest but in honor of my reputation as the heir to the fortunes it reaped.

Father had interrupted everyone's chatter as he tapped his glass lightly with the ice tongs after he had refilled it with his favorite beverage. "I'd like to thank everyone for coming today. We are very proud of our son, William, not only because he is turning twenty-one, but because of the way in which he embraces his duty to the plantation. Even in these tumultuous times, he has shown his superiority in maintaining our crop and our livelihood. Now, please join us in the dining hall for the dinner portion of the evening's festivities."

I had found myself oddly not hungry but I assumed since I had been the reason for such an event, I could not have slipped away unnoticed. Mother had taken the liberty of seating me next to Annabelle-Lynn Marques and I had known why she had not seated me next to her and my father that day – an arrangement might be made, if I showed her more attention than the others. She had looked absolutely radiant, this I could not deny, with her flaxen curls tied loosely and cascading down, barely touching her shoulders. Her dress had been a powder blue with white lace accents and flowed to her ankles. As much as I had enjoyed gazing at her beauty, it was not until I had felt her brazen hand creep across my thigh under the table that I realized I should have slipped away when I had the chance. It was in that moment that I had felt utterly uncomfortable in Miss Annabelle-Lynn's presence.

"We should go for a walk," she had whispered softly into my ear. "It's quite stuffy in here."

I had not wanted to make a scene in front of all our guests, so I had simply nodded in agreement. When we had both excused ourselves and gotten up from the table, I took notice that several people smiled and nodded toward us, making it obvious that we would be the topic of conversation as soon as we vacated the room. Cursing myself for being too eager to leave, I had known it would be only a matter of time before an arrangement would be made, even though in our few brief encounters, I hardly knew her.

I had actually empathized with the other girls that had been subjected to the evening, knowing that my parents had deliberately seated me next to the one they had chosen for me. Unfortunately for all of them, my mind had never erased Madeline's face, her voice, or her smile, and at that time I would have rather risked calling on her than accepting the arrangement my parents had already made. In my own head, I had already made the decision to not agree to any arrangements before I had the opportunity to see Madeline again and be worthy of her courtship.

When we had reached the sunroom, I looked out the large full-length windows at the setting sun, knowing our time together would be brief, which eased my mind somewhat. Annabelle-Lynn's voice had interrupted my thoughts of arrangements and courtship and other women. "You do know they will arrange our marriage." It had been more of a statement than a question, but confirmed she knew it as well.

"I hardly know you." I had looked down at her shamefully as she had taken a seat on one side of the tête-à-tête chair, enticing me to join her on the other.

"What's to know? I'm the daughter of one of the largest vineyard masters this side of Kentucky. I am the younger of two children and I am a lady of the South. I play croquet and drink tea weekly with the other ladies in my town and I know my place in the home. It doesn't matter if you don't want this, I would still be aligned to marry you." It had been as if she had recited it since birth.

"Anything else I should know, before the arrangement is made?"

"I will run your home as any good wife should. I will bear your children and raise them according to the timeless Southern traditions. Mother has taught me well."

"Do you not care about companionship or love?"

"I am like a swan. I follow wherever you lead and take heed to your word."

I had finally joined her on the chair that is so eloquently designed for courting, yet I dared not court her that day. Pulling up her chin to look at her closely, I blatantly stated my case. "I can't marry you."

"That's not for you to decide," she had countered. "If our parents want our families to align, then we are betrothed."

"I can't and I won't marry someone who will simply obey my every command or raise my children the way they were taught by every generation of women down their family line."

"That's how our world works, William!" she had exclaimed, growing impatient with my inability to see reason. "This is the way things have to be and I have accepted it! You should too!"

"I can't!" I had argued, leaping up from the chair, trying to breathe within the confines of the sunroom.

"There's someone else," she had accused pointedly.

"There's no one else," I had lied, not just to her but to my parents and myself. There *had* been someone else, someone that would not leave the recesses of my mind.

"No, there is. I can see it in your eyes. My sister-in-law has that same look. Who is she?"

"No one," I had growled, stepping away from the chair completely and moving towards the windows once again. She had boldly come over and forced me to acknowledge her.

"Who is she – this girl who clearly keeps you from me?" she had tried again, this time in a softer tone and with more grace than aggression.

I had caught myself glancing out towards where I knew the Yellowwood stood at the far end of the plantation. I had known in that moment, there was something I needed to do. "I have to go."

"What? Why?"

"Please tell my mother I will be back shortly and not to worry. I'm sorry but there's something I have to do."

I had glanced at her then and caught a glimpse of the anger in her eyes, but there was no time to stand and argue with someone who would never understand. Hurrying to the stables, I had a stable hand saddle my horse and I took off, heading into town, hoping the now almost setting sun would not interfere with my plans. The need to see her had overpowered my senses completely and I knew what I was about to do was not only foolish but very unconventional. To my chagrin, the bookstore had been closed, most likely before the sun had begun to set. I had cursed myself for being so irrational, but I needed to see her again, just a quick glimpse to quiet the thoughts in my mind.

"Is there something I can help you with, William?"

I had turned my steed around and there stood Mr. McCall, casting an odd eye up at me, silently wondering why I had made the trip into town so late. "I... I would like to speak to Madeline, sir," I had stammered, unable to be more of a man in his presence.

"I'm sorry, William. Please understand, but your father has been one of my longest running customers and with the war at hand and winter approaching, I cannot afford any further conflict between me and Jackson."

"I can handle my father. Please sir, I just need to see her for a minute," I had found myself begging.

"I sent her to the General Store to pick up a few things before it closes. You will find her there. You say what you need to say to her and leave. Are we clear?"

I had nodded my head in reply, thanked him and whirled my horse around towards the General Store. She had just been exiting the building as I approached. Just the sight of her had caused me to catch my breath, something a girl had not done in a long time. Leaping down, I had casually stepped in her path to make sure she saw me.

"I have compared you to Katherina and Cleopatra, but I was wrong. You surpass them both in beauty, mind, and spirit."

She finally had glanced up and upon recognizing me, blushed. With a casual roll of her eyes, she had attempted to sidestep around me but I had been too quick and stood in her way each time. With a slight chuckle, I had finally seen her concede and look me square in the eyes. Those eyes had nearly taken my breath away.

"Who am I this time? There is no one else as witty as Katherina and no one as beautiful as the great Queen," she had replied, boldly challenging me again.

"I'm sure somewhere hidden in the great plays, there is another woman worthy of your comparison. Will you meet me to find out the answer?"

"Your boldness suits you, great Petruchio, and no. I will not risk being seen with you. My father has already taken a mighty blow on account of my foolishness. I'm sorry, but I have to get back to the store before he worries."

"Please," I had begged, grabbing her arm as she started to walk away. "I want to meet you somewhere. I want to talk to you, get to know you."

"You already know me, Will. I am the bookstore owner's daughter and my obsession with books and my stubbornness has gotten me into trouble more times than I would like to remember."

"But there is more to you than your obsession with the words on a page; I have seen it in your eyes!" I had attempted to be even bolder. "I'm fascinated with your love of literature and I would like nothing more than to indulge in daily literary battles, but you must understand that not seeing you at that tree has torn me apart this entire summer! You've captivated me like no other has ever been able to do and you have never left my mind. Please, meet with me and let me learn everything else there is to know about you!"

"I…"

"Meet me tomorrow at one by the tree. Don't worry about my father. He's put me in charge of the plantation for the afternoon."

"I really shouldn't," she had countered, but I could tell her protests had been waning.

I had saddled up on my horse and gazed down at her as she slowly lifted those eyes to mine. "Meet me by the tree. And bring one of your favorite books!"

I had pulled the horse away and at a fast gallop headed back to the plantation. My father would be furious that I had left my own gala but I did not care. Seeing her again only reaffirmed how much I had transformed over the years and how much arranged marriages and alliances meant nothing to me. Tradition or no, I had heeded my mother's words and refused to marry a woman that could not entice my inner being. I had wanted more for the rest of my life and if I was to carry on the family name as a wheat plantation master, I was also going to ensure that any woman I courted was capable of sustaining my every desire. On the day of my birth, at twenty-one years old, I had wanted nothing more than to be lost in any book, as long as Madeline McCall had been in my presence.

There had been a part of me that wanted so much to meet Will by the tree. There had been so much urgency in his voice and his words had made me blush, thinking of the emotions so many of the women in the stories I had read about had felt when a gentleman came to call or paid them any mind. The main reason I could not have gone to see him was because my father needed me in the store more than ever. With Austin still determined to play the hero for the South and my father left with no other children, it had been forfeited to me to make sure our bookstore remained stable in our small town. As much as I had wanted to see Will again, I had an obligation to my father and to our family.

It had been late fall of 1861 when my father had come into the store, the bells ringing above the door as he entered, his face drawn. He spoke not a word as he had busied himself with tidying up the storefront, moving books to different locations and taking a rag to the bookcases to clean off some of the older volumes and the shelves. When he had finished, he came over to the counter, where I had busied myself with another book.

"We received a letter from your brother," he had mumbled, looking down at the counter instead of my eyes. I had leapt from the chair I had been sitting on and moved around the counter, forcing him to look at me.

"When? What did he say?" I had asked impatiently. A letter from Austin meant news about the war. It had also meant we'd know if the larger cities were willing to barter with us again.

"A few days ago."

"A few days?! Why didn't you tell me? What did he say? Is he all right?" I hadn't been able to stop the questions from coming.

"Calm down; he's fine; nothing's happened to him. He's been living out of a tent outside of La Fayette in Tennessee. He couldn't tell us much more than that. He would like to be home for Christmas though."

You could see the hurt in his eyes that day. I had gently touched his arm but he pulled it back and turned away from me again. The bells on the door interrupted and he quietly slipped into the storeroom, leaving me to help the customer. I had glanced over at the door and was taken aback to see Will standing there staring back at me. I had been so concerned about my father and the letter from Austin that the thought never crossed my mind that Will could come into the store at any time. Glancing back nervously towards the storeroom, I had made sure my father was not going to come out before I walked up to him and pulled him behind one of the bookcases.

"Have you gone mad? What are you doing here?" I had half whispered.

"I came to pick up a book order... and to see you," he had stated, smiling at me in his usual charming way.

"You can't be here right now!" I had practically exclaimed too loudly.

"Why not? I told you, I have to pick up an order."

I had glanced anxiously towards the storeroom again. "Come back in an hour. We'll be closing up then and I'm sure my father will want to get home. I can excuse myself by telling him I need to pick something up from the General Store first."

He had nodded graciously, accepting my arrangement and turning to leave. With the door open, he had turned his head to face me. "I make you my queen. Whatever happens out there, here, you will always be my queen," he had quoted word-for-word before closing the door behind him.

I had been stunned, my mouth hanging ajar and my breathing shallower. Will had just quoted from one of my favorite books, Wuthering Heights! At that time, I had understood him to only read Shakespeare – the books he had been ordering had been pre-wrapped and my father had always taken the liberty of dealing with the sales. It never had occurred to me that he would be reading more than simple plays and sonnets.

"Maddie," my father's voice had cut into my thoughts and caused me to jump where I stood. "I'm going home. I'm not feeling well. Please stay here at the store until it is time to close and I will see you at home."

My heart had sunk immediately when I caught a glimpse of his reddened eyes and knew his heart was still hurting for Austin. I knew it had pained him to teach me everything he had already taught my brother and inside it had embarrassed him to know that his daughter had taken over the family business instead of his son. Part of the reason I had not made an effort to be out at the tree more often that summer was because I had secretly wanted to prove to my father that I had been just as capable of running the store as my brother. As much as I loved that tree, it had served its purpose and now my brother's decisions were determining my future.

I had been confused and befuddled by Will's actions and words. Had he someone else and I was just a girl he had wanted as a mistress? Or had he been trying to court me only to have another woman waiting in the wing? I had little time to think things through as the bells on the door rang out again, signaling another customer. I had no time to react and could not believe that an hour had already passed since he had left my presence, but there he stood, unwilling to walk away, unwilling to explain himself.

"Maddie, what's wrong?" he had asked, genuine concern in his voice.

"Why do you compare me to a shrew and adulteress?" I had demanded, clearly more outspoken than I had ever been since we had met, but I had needed answers.

He had only smiled at my feeble attempt at being upset with him. "Katherina was no damsel. She could hold her own intellectually and even when she had met her match with Petruchio, they fell in love *because* of their way with words. From the moment I met you, you challenged me with wit and words, something no other girl has ever been able to accomplish. Cleopatra, although her flaw was her affairs, was one of the most beautiful women in all of Egypt, of all of the Roman Empire, which was what attracted the likes of Caesar and Antony to her. You dress far different from the way I'm used to seeing women dress but even in your plain clothes and drab colors your beauty radiates from within. The others I have met over the years try too much to impress me with their frills and lace and make-up and it only hides the dowdiness of their personalities."

Stunned into silence, I had blinked a few tears away, not even realizing my eyes had shed them. I had wanted an explanation for why he had compared me to those vile women and now I had it. What made it worse was that he had completely turned my anger around and I no longer could hate him for his literary comparisons. His words had shocked me and yet sent a warm feeling throughout my entire body. No one had ever said such powerful things to me in all my nineteen years. It was a wonder I hadn't fainted on the spot, but instead I had been rooted to the floor, unable to move, unable to speak, unable to do anything but blush.

"You flatter me with words I have never heard before. You are all too well accustomed to say such things under false pretenses of flattery." I had wanted his words to be true, but I had known even then that they were just words. Courting in all of the books I had read always ended when the one courting revealed that he had only been baiting the woman and nothing more.

Lifting my chin so our eyes met, he had practically whispered his reply. "I swear to you, on every book in this store, that I have never driven myself to madness over a girl. When you stand here in front of me, you take my breath away; when you are no where to be found, my mind wonders where you are and what you are doing. I have gone out to that tree more times in the past two months that I have been out there in the last five or ten years of my life. I had asked you join me there so that I could learn everything there is to know about you."

"We shouldn't meet like that, especially there," I had quickly protested, interrupting his speech.

"Why not?"

"People talk, Will! My father does not need any more problems than he already has. Do you not know what they say about him now that his son has gone to join the new Confederate Army? They say he is not fit to be a father because he has allowed his son to fight in a war without purpose! What do you think they'd say if his daughter was found being courted by a man that they feel has no business with her?"

"Your brother has joined the Army?" he had quickly changed the subject. I had thought that news would have traveled quickly in our town, as small as it was, but I had assumed the things that happened to us folks in the center of town meant nothing to those with larger houses and many more servants living on the outskirts of town.

"Yes, and Daddy has put me in charge of the store. It's unconventional, I know, but I don't have any other siblings and there are no other sons. So tradition has been forfeited to save our family legacy."

"I'm sorry. I didn't know."

"Will, you ask me to risk so much just to spend time with you. You ask me to meet you at a tree that we have both had in our entire lives and never once crossed paths. Right now my family is torn apart by this war and you ask me to take myself away from my responsibilities just so you can learn more about me. I'm not going to be this great literary love affair you want me to be and I'm sorry to disappoint you."

He then cupped my cheek in his hand. "You are anything but a disappointment to me. And my family is cursed by this war as well. While my father attempts to ignore that it affects our crop, my sister continues to study at nursing school in New York. Every day I walk the fields wondering whether today will be the day our slaves decide to revolt and free themselves. My parents have vowed to see me married before my twenty-second birthday and insist on my undivided attention to these girls that have no personality at all! The only solace I seem to have these days is going to the tree and hoping you'll be there to join me, reading in the still silence while the rest of the forsaken world goes on around us!"

I hadn't wanted to, but I knew I needed to pull away. "Do you have an order to pick up? The sun is setting quickly and I need to be getting home before my father comes to get me."

Ignoring his perplexed and saddened look at the breaking of the spell between us, I had quickly walked back to the storeroom to search for what I had hoped was an order for Hutchinson. Since my father had taken the liberty of labeling a hutch with letters to better organize our orders, it was easy to see a brown-paper wrapped book in the cubby for H. Deliberately and curiously, I had opened the wrapping just to peak at what he had chosen to purchase this time. After his quote from Wuthering Heights, there had been no telling of what Mr. William Hutchinson would dare to read. The cover was all gray and the title had been imbedded into it with white letters spelling the words *North and South*. The author, Elizabeth Gaskell, was a fairly well-known English writer and adversary to Charles Dickens not ten years prior and this particular title had proven to be very controversial in his eyes.

Walking back to the storefront, I had noticed that Will had taken notice of the book that had been lying on the counter, open to where I had stopped reading it about two hours prior. He had looked up and smiled upon hearing my footsteps creak on the wooden floor. I could not help but smile back.

"I see you have a knack for prying," I had replied, attempting to be snide but the laughter in my voice had come through.

"It appears we both have similar tastes in our authors and in prying. I heard somewhere that Charlotte Bronte had been a very close friend of the author you hold in your hand now." I had glanced down at the book, now unwrapped completely, and blushed. I had been caught. Without waiting for my reply, he had continued. "Perhaps we can become close friends as well."

~~*

The air had grown cooler as the weeks had passed on and winter was soon upon us. I had attempted to read by the tree three times but each time there had been quandaries. The first two attempts, I had seen Will there with a beautiful girl swinging on *my* swing. She was quite the opposite of me, with her long satin dress and wavy blonde curls. I remember feeling inadequate on both occasions and had quickly turned around and walked right back to where I had come from, completely unnoticed by them.

The last attempt, I had seen him sitting there with his back against the tree, a book in his hands. I hadn't wanted to disturb him so I simply walked away. Several occasions, he had come into the bookstore and although I knew he had ordered books, my father had ushered me into the storeroom and made several attempts at thwarting Will's advances. Each time though I had heard him sigh with disappointment.

As soon as the winter's chill had hit our town, Will had stopped coming to the store altogether and it had gotten too cold to even attempt the long walk out to the tree. That had also been when I received a personal letter from the post. There had been no return address so I automatically assumed Will would be trying to get in touch with me via letter instead. I had been in shock when I started to read it and realized who it was from instead.

Dear Maddie,

I am writing this letter in confidence since I didn't want Daddy and Mama to worry about me. It's been several months since we've begun our journey into Tennessee and our rations are small. I'm afraid we may not make it through the winter if we don't receive our supplies soon. We haven't seen any action yet and the men are getting restless.

I thought this was going to give us a chance to make history and march on Washington and take a stand for our rights as citizens of the South. But it isn't anywhere near what I expected. The saddest part is most of the men are mere boys – all around my age – waiting for their own personal glory.

I want to say it was worth it and come home but until I see for myself what the war is really about, I have to stay. If I come home for Christmas, I will be considered a deserter and they don't arrest deserters; they shoot them.

I am sending a separate letter to Mama and Daddy only to tell them that I am okay and alive. But please, don't speak of this to anyone. If I am caught writing about the frontline, I could be considered a spy and who knows what they might do to me then. I miss you.

As Always,
Austin

I had heard some talk in town about the Confederate Army leading troops into several states to "safeguard" against an assault from the North, but I hadn't heard anything else about the war itself. Here my brother had been giving me first-hand accounts and I had been asked not to tell anyone about it. When my father had come into our tea room, I had quickly shoved the letter and envelope into my book, using them as a bookmark so no one would notice who it had been from. He had seemed in much better spirits than he had been the few weeks prior to that day. I wished I had shared in his higher spirit.

"We received a letter from Austin!" he had exclaimed, smiling. As much as he had hated that Austin deserted his family, he had still been anxious to hear from him and went to the post station every day to see if there was a letter waiting there for him.

"What does it say?" Mama had asked, putting down her needlepoint, something I had long since forgotten to try to learn again.

"Just that he is all right and he will try to come home for Christmas."

I had swallowed hard, knowing I held the truth in the letter hiding in my book – the truth I would never tell. I had been about to ask him another question when there was a knock at the front door. All three of us had exchanged panicked looks. Although we had just received letters from Austin, he could have written those weeks ago, knowing how long it takes for the Post Service to send a letter, especially over state lines. If he had been wounded or worse, the news might reach us before his letters did.

We had heard the postman on the opposite side of the door address my father as he opened the door. "Mr. McCall?"

"Yes?"

"I have a letter for you from Mr. Hutchinson."

"Thank you," he had replied dryly, looking back at me to see if I had heard who the letter was from.

I had done nothing in recent weeks to anger Mr. Hutchinson, so I could not understand why my father would receive a formal letter from him.   My first instinct had been that it was a formal announcement for Will's wedding to the girl I had seen him with at the tree and my breath had caught in my throat. Ripping open the letter my father had read it to himself until his eyes had grown wide and he had scowled up at me. He had handed me the letter and walked away, not speaking one word to me until I had read the letter completely.

> Dear Mr. McCall,
>
> I would like to formally ask your permission to allow your daughter to meet with me outside of our chance meetings in town. It pains me that Madeline has not come to the tree at the far end of our plantation, knowing that is has been a part of your family for many generations.   My father has no business controlling something that does not belong to him. I will look for her tomorrow afternoon. Thank you.
>
> William Jacob Hutchinson

I had followed my father into the kitchen, where he had been searching the cabinets for liquor. Since none of us drank anything but champagne on special occasions, I had walked over to him and pulled his arms down, closing the cabinets one by one. He had quickly engulfed me into his arms and I felt him sigh against me. I had hated seeing my father this way – defeated and upset. When he had pulled back to look at me, I could tell he was at a loss for words, but he still whispered his concern.

"I don't want to lose you too."

"You are not going to lose me. The bookstore means more to me than anything else." I had hated lying to him, but to see him that way, broken, I just couldn't tell him the truth. I did not have it in my heart to tell him that I had been flattered by Will's forwardness and determination to see me again. What I did not understand was why Will had insisted on taking other girls out to the tree when he had wanted me there all along.

"Maddie, this family is all I have," Daddy had interrupted my thoughts. "I will not lose my children to better men than me."

"How can you say that? No man is better than you!"

"Austin has gone off to war, to take command under a general of an army of men, instead of taking heed to my demands for him to take over the store. And you, you are being courted by a man whose name means more in this town that mine. His father has influence over whether them rich folks decide to buy my books or not!"

"I'm not, I swear! I have no idea why he would do such a thing! Let me go see him and I will talk to him on your behalf!" He had sighed heavily but I could tell he was conceding.

"It is better if I go and face his father myself. No need for either of you to be involved in our quarrel."

"We are already involved because Will sent that letter. Please, let me go and speak to him on my own."

I had known the letter to my father had said tomorrow afternoon, but something had compelled me to see if he would be there that evening. As soon as he had silently nodded his head, I left him and the house behind, practically running to the edge of town, pulling the collar on my coat up around my neck tighter, as the temperature began to drop with the setting sun. The closer I had gotten to the tree though, the angrier at Will I had become, outraged that he could court another girl using *my* swing and then have the audacity to send that letter to my father. When I had arrived, my instincts had been correct and he had been sitting there against the trunk, reading by the last light of day.

My footsteps on the ground had caused him to look up at who was approaching. He had quickly jumped to his feet and closed his book without bothering to put a marker in to remember his place. "What are you doing here?" he had asked. I was unsure whether his voice had been sincere or upset by the interruption.

"Your letter to my father was unnecessary," I had replied, still angry with thoughts of another girl at that very spot swirling around my head.

"My letter was needed to prove how serious I am about you."

"I saw you! I saw you here with *her*! How serious are you really about anything when you are here countless times courting another girl?" I had gritted through my teeth.

"My father threatened to cut down this tree if I didn't comply with his rules!" he had argued back.

"What are you talking about?"

"My father claimed I was neglecting my duties being conditioned as master of the plantation, when in fact I have been spending too much time out here hoping you would return to the tree! He told me that he would cut it down if I didn't comply and that meant courting a girl my parents want me to marry!"

"I... I saw you with her and you looked... happy! Your father threatening to cut it down is just an excuse!" I had surmised.

"I wanted you here, not her! There were so many times I was here by myself but you never returned! Why didn't you come back?"

"I *did* come back! Countless times but every time I was here I saw you with *her*! I will not be the great Queen Cleopatra to your Julius Caesar!"

"What is wrong with being Cleopatra?" he had asked, smiling at the reference I had made.

"Cleopatra was an adulteress! Caesar was married and had children when he met and fell in love with her! Their love affair was probably the greatest in all of history and it was what eventually caused both Rome and Egypt to fall! I will not be your Cleopatra if you are destined to marry someone else!" I had finally taken a breath.

Glancing around us, I had needed to reassure myself that no one had either followed me there or had been watching. When I had turned my head around to face him again, he had been looking up at the stars. "Do you ever come outside at night and wish on a star?"

I had been caught off-guard by his question and stared at him blankly while he continued. "I have come out here almost every night wishing on the same star. Do you know what I wish for? I wish that my sister would come home so my father would stop pushing his life on me; I wish that this whole idea of war would be resolved before any real fighting can occur; I wish that I had the choice that my sister has, to be anyone I choose to be instead of being conditioned into being what *they* want me to be!"

I could tell all of this had been too much for him to bear and I had gently touched his arm. He had looked down at me then and I had seen the tiredness in his eyes. "I'm sorry that I yelled about the reference to Cleopatra. I just... I don't want and I can't be a second thought to you. I don't want my father to lose his business over the fact that *your* father has been threatening to take down this tree. Maybe it would be better for all of us if he did!"

"Maddie, no!" he had exclaimed. "This tree belongs to you. My father has no right to use his money or power in this town to stop you from coming here!"

"I won't come here if you are going to use *my* swing to court other girls! It *is* my swing and I have every right to say what happens here or not!"

"I agree with you! Maddie, if I have offended you by bringing her here then I wholeheartedly apologize. If I have wronged you by comparing you to Cleopatra, not realizing how strongly you felt about her, I would gladly search my entire library to find one single character to compare and compete with how beautiful and strong and confident you are!"

I had been stunned into silence. No one had ever come close to saying something so poetic and causing me to blush at the same time. To my surprise, he had boldly taken a step closer to where I stood and gently placed his arm around my back, pulling me into him, the warmth of his body radiating between us. I had no longer needed confirmation of the way that I felt inside whenever Will was near to me, because my knees had instantly felt weak and I had to grab a hold of his arm to keep from toppling over. Glancing up into his eyes and seeing the same feeling resonating back at me, I had closed my eyes just as his lips came down on mine.

William

10

Our town had succumbed to the war as soon as the winter had begun. Most of the smaller shops had closed, crops that hadn't yielded enough at the harvest had brought about a decline in supply, and those families with sons or brothers in the Army had begun to fear every knock at their doors, thinking they would receive a letter from the Secretary of the Confederacy. We had finally received word from Gracie that she would be coming home for Christmas, much to the delight of my parents. To me though, something had not been right as I had revisited her letter in my room by candlelight one evening in early December. Her words were too methodical and it bothered me greatly since her original letters to us were so delicately penned with details and description of her life studying to be a nurse.

"Son, are you all right?" Mother had pulled me out of my trance, standing in the open doorway.

"I'm fine. I just miss her." She had come over and kissed my forehead, a bit of understanding in her actions.

"She'll be home in a few weeks. Your father and I are going to host a welcome home party for her. I'd like to invite the Marques. You seem to be getting along well with their daughter," she had hinted.

I had sighed heavily. "It's a welcome home party for Gracie. You shouldn't be arranging any engagements on *her* day." I had known this was going to be a battle I would not win.

"I don't want to arrange your marriage before you've had time to get to know her, you know that. I've told you that before. But you know how your father is with celebrations and such. Occasions need to be large enough to surpass everyone else's, which means a welcome home party for your sister will not be enough. He'll want to announce an engagement if he can."

"I don't understand your hypocrisy in this! You were the one who insisted that I don't marry until I am in love with the girl and now you're telling me that Father wants to announce an engagement between two people that hardly know each other, let alone are in love! Besides, Gracie is coming home, finally, to be with us for the holidays and you are pushing this with me! This will be Gracie's day and if and when I'm ready to be engaged, I'll allow you to throw a party for just me and my fiancée!"

"Your father still wants to invite them and I'd like to introduce you to everyone as exclusive at least," she had pressed.

"Fine. But do not push any engagement announcements while they're here!" I had exclaimed, unnerved by the efforts of my father to persuade my mother against her better judgment.

My mother had left my room and again I was there with only my angered thoughts and Gracie's letter. Something had not been right but I could not put my finger on exactly what it was. Glancing out the window that faced the plantation, I had spotted a faint glow way off in the distance. All the slaves and servants had retired for the evening so I knew it couldn't possible be them. Fear of another fire had gripped me, causing me to quickly pocket the letter, grab my coat and lantern, and head out towards the beacon of light.

When I had found her, she had been sitting against the base of the tree, her head bent and eyes reddened from tears. I had no idea what had happened or why she had been there but I hated seeing her reduced to this, since I had grown accustomed to her smile. I had placed my lantern down on the ground and knelt near her. Touching her arms lightly, I had spoken as softly as I could.

"Maddie? What's wrong?"

She had sniffed and slowly lifted her head. "We can't be seen here like this."

"I have every right to be here and so do you. Tell me what's wrong. Did my father say something to you again? I know I've been careful meeting you out here."

She had shaken her head and wiped her eyes with the back of her hand. "No. I... I got a letter from Austin," she had squeaked out.

"Your brother?" She had nodded her answer, giving me a signal to continue. "That's good, right? You were worried about him –"

"He's not coming home for Christmas and the weather is forcing them to move northeast into Virginia to avoid the frost," she had interrupted me, her eyes telling of the pain she felt.

I had sat down next to her and swept her up into my arms, kissing her temple lightly. In that moment, I had felt so guilty for being the slightest bit relieved that Gracie was coming home from the north. She had responded by quickly burying her head in my chest and sobbing again.

"Shhh," I had tried to soothe, "it'll be all right."

"How do you know?" she had asked meekly.

"They're just moving east to avoid bad weather. When winter's ove,r he'll come home, you'll see." I had tried everything to reassure her but with my own doubts about the war still lingering it was difficult to comfort her.

"Did you hear from your sister?" She had peered up at me through such hopeful eyes and I had to shift my weight under their scrutiny and avert my eyes away from her.

"She's coming home for Christmas," I had replied without expression.

"You're not happy about it?"

"It's just that... I've read one or two of her other letters and this one doesn't sound right. I'm afraid she's being forced to write to us this way."

"What way? You think she's being forced to lie to her own family?" Quickly her voice had changed to one of concern.

"I feel like they're going to keep her there now that the war has begun. Her letters used to be more detailed and colorful, talking about the city of New York and the University she's studying at, and the people she's meeting. Now they are short and without explanation!"

She had reached up and with gentle fingers caressed my cheek. "She'll be okay," she had soothed.

I had simply nodded but my fear would not subside. There had been more I had to tell her and I knew she would be upset once she heard the words. "My parents would like to introduce Annabelle-Lynn and me together at Gracie's welcome home celebration."

"But –"

I had quickly silenced her with a finger to her lips. "They have no idea I've been meeting you here practically every day. I only see her once a week when our mothers decide to have tea."

"But the slaves – they'll talk!" she had protested, but I shook my head.

"I've already threatened them for their silence."

"I knew coming here more often was a terrible idea! My father said that I should keep coming here even after your father took away my rights. As soon as you wrote that letter, he changed his mind! Your father has threatened to cut down this tree just so you'd swear your allegiance and follow his rules! We've defied both our fathers ever since, just to see each other here!"

I had tightened my grip around her small waist. "My father is still under the impression that I continue to check on the crop and plantation. He has no idea we've been out here together and no one would dare say anything if they happened to see us."

"I hate being so secretive like this! If I had been someone else's daughter, your father would have no objection with me or us! My father is still a man of dignity and pride for his business and we live comfortably enough!" she had argued, leaning backwards in my arms so she could see my face directly. "Are you ashamed of me?"

"What? No!" I had shouted, instinctively cupping her face with my hand. "I would never be ashamed of you! If I had learned another trade, perhaps I would have ownership of a store like yours! But instead I have had wheat stuffed into my head and proper etiquette forced down my throat! My father treats even my relationships as business transactions with no regard for the emotional turmoil it creates!"

She had smiled, something I had missed among the tears. "This celebration for your sister – you have to be introduced with Annabelle-Lynn?"

"I don't have a choice. I wish there was something I could do."

She had scrambled to her feet, offering me her hands so I could follow suit. When she had looked up into my eyes, I saw the same twinkle that I had always seen whenever she combated me with literary references. "I'd like to go as your date to your sister's homecoming," she had announced, not averting her eyes at all.

"What?"

"The look on your father's face if he saw me enter your house as your guest would be enough to keep him quiet about this whole Annabelle-Lynn arrangement he has! I don't want to let him win!" Her words had been commanding, almost as if she had been declaring it to my heart.

"I don't want him to win either, but I do think we need to keep this a secret for the time being, at least until my sister is home and settled. I promise I will thwart any of their advances to proclaim me exclusive to Annabelle-Lynn as long as I possibly can," I had made clear my intentions.

My father had been ridiculous in his demands to teach me everything I needed to know about the plantation and the crop, but

I had refused to allow him to make demands on my heart. With my mother partially on my side and her willingness to understand that forced marriages were becoming a thing of the past, I had hoped to keep them all at bay as long as I possibly could. My mind had already been made up as to my feelings for Madeline and the more time I had spent with her, as fleeting as it had been, the more I knew that I needed to remain cautious as to how to officially introduce her to my family. Gracie's homecoming gala was not the right time.

I had been about to lean down and seal my promise with a kiss, when footsteps and another lantern could be heard and seen coming towards us. I had felt her stiffen in my arms and I held onto her protectively, as I too had been worried we were about to get caught. When the person had finally come into view, I had almost sighed with relief when I saw it was *her* father and not my own. My relief had been short-lived though, when I had seen how upset he had been.

"Maddie?" he had demanded her attention, causing her to pull out of my arms abruptly.

"Yes?" she had replied with her head bent.

"It's time to go home. Please don't make me come out here again. Your mama was worried sick when you took off after supper."

"I'm sorry."

"I'm going to assume William here was not the reason you ran out of the house." His tone had been stern and I could tell he too had not known of our secret meetings.

"No!" She had shouted in reply. "He... he found me out here and had just come to see why I had come here after the sun had gone down."

"Please sir, she was upset and I could not leave her out here alone," I had sidled up next to her and intervened on her behalf.

"There's no reason to come out here in these cold temperatures just because you were upset. You can always talk to your mama or me. Now let's get you back to the house. I don't want to have to come out here again to retrieve you when your mama starts to worry about you being out after the sun has gone down."

"Yes sir," had been her weak reply.

I had no choice but to let her slip away that evening. When her father had turned around and started heading down the dirt path towards the road, I had grabbed for her hand to reassure her that it would be okay. As her hand had slipped from mine, the full effect of the chill in the air had taken over and I had felt it in my entire body. I had waited until their lantern lights were far enough away before I myself headed home. I still could not shake the feeling that something had not been right with my sister's letters and that this war was going to bring more heartache to both our families before the winter was over.

~~*

The week before the Christmas holiday that winter, I had received a personal letter from my sister. There had been no formal address on the envelope. I had not been sure how she was able to get it to me this way, but it found its way into my hands when I had gone to the post station to pick up a package my father had ordered. The postman had almost forgotten it had been there, but he handed me the tattered and worn envelope with a confused look in his eyes. I had thanked him for it and raced home, hoping my sister was not in any sort of trouble in the North. Without paying any attention to my parents, I had raced up to my room, closing the door and ripping open the envelope.

Dear Brother,

I am writing to you only, with the hope that it finds you safely. I will not be coming home for Christmas. The races won't stop this winter and I need to continue to ride and train. Perfection is the key to winning.

They've changed the location of the next race and I'll be riding in Delaware soon. I've heard the horses there are less tame and I'm afraid to try to ride them. There's been talk of setting up a racing track near a port city such as Baltimore and we will be practicing everything we have learned there. I will try to write again but riding takes a lot of time and they monitor our progress closely. Our parents will receive another letter letting them know the trains have stopped running for the winter. I love and miss you.

                    Always,
                    Grace Ann

My heart sank as I re-read the letter I had received. She was not coming home and the fact that she wrote it in our old childhood riding code so no one would understand what she had really been talking about, meant that someone from the North had been watching the letters already. I had refused to look at my parents, angry at them for not trying harder to bring her home before the war had started. Bitterly I had to play the devil's advocate because in their defense, they had no idea war was even going to happen. It had been speculation until that time. After they received their own letter, our meals had become silent and our late afternoons had been filled with my father comforting my mother's tears.

To attempt to save face and ignore the pain, they had planned an elaborate Christmas Eve party and decided to introduce Annabelle-Lynn and me as a couple to the rest of their society friends. I had been even angrier with them – substituting me for my sister so they could feel happy about something. Meanwhile, I had spent the entire time in torment, wishing for my sister's return and wanting so much to have Maddie there by my side instead of a woman who looked ridiculously pleased to be on my arm.

"Everyone is so happy for us," Annabelle-Lynn had whispered into my ear as we sat at the table in our dining hall.

"Yes, they do seem to approve of the match," I had commented dryly, taking a sip of the drink that I had made sure I had that day.

"Something's bothering you. What is it?" As sweet as she had been, it was not concern in her eyes that I saw, at least not the concern I had seen in Maddie's eyes when I told her about my sister.

"Nothing. It's nothing," I had brushed off. "Care to dance?" There had been a sense of urgency in my voice that to this day I'm sure was because I needed something to distract my mind or because I had wanted her to stop prying for the truth.

She had accepted the offer graciously and we made our way to the dance floor as a new song was played by the strummers my mother had hired for the afternoon. A few others joined us for a traditional dance we had learned in our earlier years – a dance passed down from generations ago with the first settlers of England. It had been good to dance and smile and let go of what had ailed me, but I had known I was only putting up a front for anyone who wanted to doubt my affections for Annabelle-Lynn that day.

When the song had ended, we bowed to one another cordially and I had led her back to our table for something to quench our thirst. More women had joined us and I had found myself searching the room for the gentlemen's corner, needing to retreat from their stifling glances and fake smiles. When my view had been completely obscured by the ladies, I had sat back in my chair and allowed the women's catty chatter to thrum in my ears, drowning out the violins and wind instruments playing in the background.

I had obviously not been listening because a gentle hand on my arm had shaken me from my thoughts. "What? I'm sorry, ladies."

"It's quite all right, William. We were just wondering if you heard the latest news from town?"

"And what news is that?" I had tried to keep my eye roll to a minimum when they had begun their usual gossip.

"McCall's Books is another store closing for the remainder of winter," Annabelle-Lynn had declared. She had known I was an avid reader, but could she have known that I had secretly been meeting Maddie by the tree? Could she see in my eyes that there had been someone else all along?

I had sat straighter in my chair, in need of further clarification. "Do you know why?"

"I heard that his wife was sick and he needed to be home," I had heard one lady explain.

"That's not right. I heard it was his daughter," another lady had chimed in.

"I didn't even know he had a daughter," a third had responded.

As a knot had formed in my stomach, I knew I had to keep asking questions to get the correct answers. "Did anyone say what was wrong with her?" If something had happened to Maddie, I would have been devastated.

"There's speculation of a heart condition," Annabelle-Lynn had announced.

"Or heartbreak," someone in the group had interrupted rather rudely. "Poor dear's got a son in the Army."

"I heard the daughter got herself in quite the predicament with a young gentleman in town. Big disgrace to her family." I had narrowed my eyes towards the woman who had felt the need to speak of Maddie that way but secretly prayed the gossip was not true.

"I also heard it could be because Mr. McCall had no more books to sell," Annabelle-Lynn had interjected. I had been only able to stare at her. "Without us buying his books, he would have to sell them to the cities to make any sort of profit." She had actually smirked at her own comment.

"You're absolutely right, sweetie," one woman had spoken proudly to her. "It's up to us and our farms to keep those small businesses in town open. You have a smart one there, William. Hold onto her."

I could only smile weakly at best. Their conversation had been dangerously close to scandalous and I had not wanted to be associated with such gossipers. To my surprise, Annabelle-Lynn kept the conversation going. "Preferably, I'd rather be buying a new gown with the silks they import from France than a book that will just collect dust on a shelf! You can definitely get more use out of a dress than a book you read once and discard after!"

I had felt like she had been purposefully stabbing me with her words, much the opposite of how I had felt whenever I had been verbally assaulted by Maddie; her words had made me feel alive and wanting more. I had taken my glass, politely excused myself from the table, and walked out of the dining hall. Turning around slightly to see the party continuing on without me without anyone caring I had left the room, I had grabbed my coat and gloves and headed outside for some fresh cold air. As soon as the air hit my skin, I had shivered, not able to calm my nerves or keep my body warm. Angrily, I had thrown my glass against the side of the house, liquor splattering and glass shattering everywhere. I knew I had to see her for myself and find out the truth from her own lips. If her father *had* sold the books to other bookstores in the cities, there would be no more ordering books from the store and no more time at the tree.

Checking my watch and glancing up at the sky, I had known that the setting sun meant they had probably gone to church for the Eve service and would be heading home soon. Without a second thought, I had saddled a horse and quickly galloped towards the church. Much to my chagrin, the service had ended and the crowd had dispersed. Searching to my right and left, I had caught a glimpse of what I had hoped was Maddie and her parents. I had decided to come around them and meet them head-on, instead of startling them from behind, so I had pulled hard on the reins and galloped in another direction. My jaw had dropped when I saw her – a long cream-colored dress peaking from the bottom of her winter long-coat; her hands covered in a white muff. Her hair fell loosely around her shoulders, dark curls surrounding her face.

"William, this is a surprise," I had heard her father say, interrupting my thoughts.

"I... well, I wanted to wish you all a Merry Christmas," I had sputtered and cursed myself for not having a plan or some other reason for being there, again foolishly going after something without thinking ahead.

"You came here, this late in the evening, to wish us a Merry Christmas?"

I had known I had been caught, so I had to at least be a man and ask permission first. "I'd like to speak to Maddie, if it's all right with you." I had hoped he wouldn't mind. After all, it had been Christmas.

"Five minutes; that's all you may have," and her parents shut the door behind them as they entered the house that I hadn't even realized we had reached.

Leaping down from the horse, I had to step back slightly to take in her full beauty. There had been nothing about her that had screamed unworthy and it unnerved me that she had so often spoke of herself so. Gazing into her eyes, the real reason I had come there to see her that evening and the only reason to be standing in front of her in that moment, had become all too clear.

I hadn't expected him to show up at my house at all, let alone that late in the evening on Christmas Eve, but something in his eyes had told me he was not there to wish my family well on the holiday. When he had wrapped his arms around me and pulled me into a fierce kiss that had left me breathless, I knew it certainly had not been to see my parents. I had to blink a few times to compose myself but once I saw the look in his eyes, I knew something was wrong. He had continued to keep me in his arms even as I attempted to pull back, afraid to let me go.

"Did something happen?" I had asked, full of concern, as I gently touched his cheek.

"Gracie didn't come home and there was nothing I could do to stop it from happening!"

"Stop what?" I had finally taken notice to his long frock coat and pants.

"They announced us together tonight," he had blurted out, finding his shoes somehow interesting enough not to look at me.

"But you said –"

"They had another party anyway!" he had interrupted. "It's like she's not even alive!"

All I could do was embrace him; let him know I was there for him. "I'm sorry," I had whispered into the air between us.

His grip around my waist had tightened as he held on. "They talked about your father and the store tonight."

"Who did?" I had glanced up into his eyes.

"The women!" he had exclaimed, holding me at a distance so he could see my face clearer. "Please tell me the store isn't closed," he had begged.

I had taken a step out of his embrace and looked down shamefully. "It's true."

"What happened?" I could hear the concern in his voice. "Maddie, tell me," he had pleaded, lifting my chin with his fingers.

"They stopped buying our books!" I had cried into the night air.

"Who?"

"Everyone! They just stopped ordering, stopped coming in to browse or purchase, stopped all our sales! Even *you* stopped coming in!"

"My father forbade me to go!" I had scoffed at his reply. "So none of what they are saying is true?"

I had cocked my brow at him in confusion. "What else did they say?"

"Is your mother sick?" he had asked suddenly, catching me by surprise.

"No, she's perfectly healthy." I had continued to give him a puzzled look.

"Have you heard from your brother?"

"Not since he wrote to me about his march to Virginia."

"And you're not having a child?"

"What? No!"

"Then I can sleep better tonight," he had sighed, pulling me back into his arms. I had snaked mine up around his back and rested my head against his chest, content to stay that way for as long as possible.

"You came all the way here to confirm all those horrible rumors?"

"I wanted to make sure everything was all right and I needed to see you. I've missed you." He had sounded genuinely sincere and I wanted to believe him but knowing he had allowed his father to overpower him, I could feel the hurt building up inside of me.

"You haven't been distracted by someone else?"

I had felt him intake his breath and then slowly let it out. "I had no choice. You know that."

"I'm sure your family likes her," I had stately flatly, trying not to give away the hurt in my voice. The reality of the situation was hitting me fast.

"It doesn't matter who they like, not when I choose you." I could feel myself blush and it had not been from the cold. In fact, in his arms, I had felt very warm.

"I want to come to the next ball," I had stated bravely, lifting my head so he knew I had been serious.

Before he could challenge me though, my father had opened our front door and caught us in our embrace. "Madeline, go inside. It's too cold out here."

I had gazed up at Will with sadness in my eyes. "Go, I'll handle your father," he had whispered.

"Madeline Rose, I am not going to tell you again, go inside!" Daddy had bellowed sternly.

"Can I at least say goodbye to him?"

"Go!" I had sighed and then I felt Will's breath in my ear.

"Don't worry about me. I'll be okay. And I will see you again."

Nodding my head and letting go of his arms, I had walked steadily inside the house and shut the door behind me. My father had suspected there was something between us but he had turned a blind eye – until that evening. When he had come up to my room to bid me goodnight, he had finally decided to be open about his concerns.

"I know that you are no longer a little girl and I can't protect you the way I used to."

"But –"

He had put his hand up to stop me from interrupting him.

"May I?" he had gestured towards the bed I was sitting on. I simply nodded and he had seated himself next to me before continuing.

"I know that William cares a lot about you and I appreciate his honesty with me, but whatever is going on with him has to stop. I have told him that he is to stay away from you for at least the rest of the winter, if not longer."

"No!" I had shouted into the room, unable to keep my emotions at bay.

"Madeline, please. I will not argue about this anymore. It is bad enough your brother isn't here. I need you here, to help with the store, not sneaking around with a plantation owner's son."

"But the store is closed," I had tried to argue, as if that one factor would be enough to justify what had been transpiring.

"If we can't open it within the next two months we will either starve or be forced to move!"

I had gasped in surprise, not realizing the magnitude of the situation. "But what does any of that have to do with Will and me?"

"I've asked William to buy our store," he had announced solemnly.

"What?!" I had exclaimed, leaping from the bed.

"I had no choice. It had to be done."

"But what? How? Why?" I had stuttered not understanding his reasoning for what he had just done.

"His father's plantation brings in more than half the money for this town. You know that his father also happens to be one of my longest running customers. I asked William to draw up the paperwork for a sale of half the bookstore. This will give us enough money to survive the winter."

"No! You can't!" I had argued more aggressively as he stood from the bed, taller and broader than I had remembered my father to ever be.

"I can and it's already done! Now why are you so upset about this?"

I couldn't speak. I had glanced out the window into the dark winter night. I could only whisper my answer. "It was supposed to be mine."

"What was that, my dear?"

Clearing my throat and looking at him again, I had allowed the tears to finally flow freely down my cheeks. "The bookstore should be mine, not theirs. They have no right to it!"

"They have every right if they give us money to keep this family alive!"

"But I'm your daughter! I have more of a right to the business than they do!"

"You are my daughter and I'm hoping in the future you will meet a man you can call your husband that can provide for you. As for now, their money can provide us with a means to get through the winter long enough for your brother to return."

"So that's it then? Use me as a mere substitute for my brother in his absence and then sell it to the highest bidder until he returns?"

"You listen to me, young lady, we are through with this discussion! You have no ownership to that store! Your brother *will* return and he *will* take over the business the way he is intended! And you are not to see William again because it is now not a suitable relationship for business!"

When he had left my room, my heart sank as my body crumpled to the floor. I had felt claustrophobic in my large bedroom, gasping for air that I couldn't breathe. I had felt like I had lost everything that Christmas and I had nothing left. I had poured my heart and soul into our store, for my father to go and sell half of it away, to the very family he had once told me to defy! The more time I had spent among its volumes, the more I had wanted it to be my life and no one else's. When he had told me not to see William anymore, I knew that winter I had lost everything that had been dear to my heart.

~~*

The winter months had seemed to go on forever but just as the year turned, a great twist of events happened in my life. Upon hearing of the sale of half our store to Mr. Hutchinson, some of the elder ladies had begun coming in more frequently, causing us to stay open and not close for the winter after all, as if it were *he* who had changed their minds. My father had even placed some of the more popular women's novels on a special table to entice them to spend more money. It had become more difficult for me to assist my father with the accounting or to learn anything new when they came clambering into the store in groups discussing the latest war news or town scandal. It had been on a particular day in late January of 1862 that I was graced by the presence of one woman I will never forget.

"Do you happen to have anything in the realm of Nathaniel Hawthorne? I'm attempting to rid my beau of his incessant chatter about Shakespeare," she had smiled, although it did not reach her ears, automatically registering with me as fake.

"We have several of his novels as well as his short story collections. Was there anything in particular you were looking for?" I had known exactly which titles we had in stock and I had been interested to see whether she knew any of the less famous titles or she would opt for something more popular; only an avid reader, such as me, would recognize obscure works by certain authors.

"Actually, I was really looking for *Moses from an Old Manse*. It's his collection of –"

"Yes, I know," I had interrupted boldly, not caring if she took offense. "I've read it cover to cover. A collection of some of his best short stories published in '46."

"Well, you certainly know your books," she had remarked.

I had simply shrugged. "I do work in a bookstore."

"I would never have guessed that anyone who works here

would have read anything remotely popular. I thought this place was now selling as many books as possible, since you obviously needed someone like Mr. Hutchinson to save you from debt." That's when it had occurred to me that this woman knew too much about Mr. Hutchinson's contract for her to be just a woman from town and I had to push further to figure out who she really was.

I had been put-off by her backhanded comment and angered that she would condemn us over Mr. Hutchinson's aid. "Actually, Mr. Hutchinson is only helping us get through the winter. Once the spring weather comes, we'll be all right on our own. And I do read a lot, all the time in fact."

"My beau also reads entirely too much," she had feigned annoyance. "Every time I go over for tea, he has his nose in a book! I can't even have a simple conversation without him quoting from something he's read!"

"I think quoting from a novel is a sign of great intellect," I had argued, remembering how Will would quote to me by the tree, kissing me softly as he accented every line.

"Well, it's downright unnatural, if you ask me," she had countered. "He says he wishes I'd read more of what he reads so we can have conversations but my father would never approve of that."

"Approve of what?"

"A woman speaking to a man in an intellectual manner. We're not supposed to have minds of our own." She had giggled at her own remark. I had to keep myself from rolling my eyes at her.

"I've been educated at a very good school in the city. I believe *my* father wants me to be as intellectual as the man I will meet," I had replied, wishing she would leave our store forever.

"Well, you're not of society the way I am," she had stated so matter-of-factly. "*We* aren't bred that way."

"I'm glad I'm not a part of *that* society then. I tend to be more outspoken than most."

"Well, you'd be a perfect match for my beau! He seems to need that from a woman. Now, can you tell me if you have that collection? I'd really like to clear his mind of all things Shakespeare."

I had immediately become defensive. "What's wrong with Shakespeare?"

"I just don't have the stomach for him reciting sonnets to me by some old tree anymore."

As soon as she had made that final comment, I had been able to piece everything together and realized that her *beau* had been Will all along and the woman standing in front of me was none other than Miss Annabelle-Lynn! Everything she had been saying about Mr. Hutchinson and his contract with my father had been a first-hand account and she had come into the store that day to specifically torment me! Could she have known about Will and me prior to this first encounter?

What had hurt more was her distaste for what Will loved best about reading. Will and I had on several occasions met by the tree to read or discuss not just Shakespeare but Poe, Alcott, Austin, and others. We had loved bantering about the characters and their flaws and I remembered how his eyes would light up when I disagreed with how he felt about certain pieces of poetry or prose. I could sit in his lap and let him recite Browning or Dickenson or even Longfellow for hours, even though we never seemed to have hours to spare. It had been such a shame she never appreciated him for any of that.

"I'm afraid I have our copy of *Moses from an Old Manse* in my room. But if you'd be interested, we do have his short stories in separate books or perhaps you'd prefer his more famous works?"

She had scoffed at me. "You *steal* from Mr. Hutchinson's bookstore?"

"It is *not* Mr. Hutchinson's bookstore and no, my father purchases books specifically so that I can read them and be more of an intellect in conversation."

"And you only have *one* copy of *Moses from an Old Manse*?"

"Just as there is only one Romeo for one Juliet," I had hinted.

"What does that mean?" she had questioned, unaware of my double-meaning.

"You wouldn't understand. You should ask your *beau* to interpret it for you."

"I don't need him to interpret anything when his eyes are distracted by my natural beauty. He has often referred to me as the Great Queen Cleopatra because of her stunning beauty and alluring sensuality."

I had smirked at her, knowing the truth, and simply walked past her to the bookcase behind her. When he had called me Cleopatra and then found out who she really was, the adulteress who brought down the empires of both Egypt and Rome, he had chosen to search a thousand literary works just to find someone to compare to me. Pointing up to a shelf, I averted her eyes there instead of on me.

"Here are Hawthorne's books. I hope you find something to take his mind off of Shakespeare for a while. I'm sure if you ask him to though, he'd read you the soliloquies of Beatrice and Benedick. I cannot recommend them enough!"

"He has never had a reason to read anything to me like that," she had sneered.

I had simply shaken my head and looked at her. "How much do you really know about him?"

"His father owns a large wheat plantation that he is going to eventually take over and when he does, this little bookstore will be gone, so I'd be careful with your words if I were you."

"*My* father still owns this bookstore!"

"Mr. Hutchinson is prepared to make a very large purchase of this store once William and I are married. The books will be sold to other stores and this building will be turned into a clothing shop thanks to *my* convincing," she had blurted out.

"*Your* convincing?" Now it had been my turn to look at her angrily.

"With the war going on, much of our trade with the North has stopped, in case you haven't noticed. So by opening up a clothing shop we can better our trade with Europe." She had bounced on her heels as she spoke.

"This bookstore is our livelihood! We won't just sell it away!" I had fought back harshly, determined to understand why she so vehemently wanted *my* store.

She had brazenly taken a book from the shelf. I had noticed the title – *Egoism; or the Bosom-Serpent* – and laughed at how apropos it had been for the likes of her and *her* kind. Perhaps if she had actually read the book, she would also see the humor in her choice. She had clutched the book to her chest and spoke venomously to me.

"Mr. Hutchinson is willing to pay whatever your father needs to survive. Rest assured, this little store of yours will be history the minute William and I say 'I do'! Now, this will be a perfect gift for him, don't you think?" She had waltzed out of the store without paying for the book.

William

12

Winter had been cold and my heart had been longing for the opportunity to see Maddie again. Since Christmas, we had been corresponding secretly by letter every few days, relying on the gentleman who ran the Postal Service to keep our letters away from prying eyes. Father had still been sour over Gracie not coming home for Christmas and Mother had been too preoccupied entertaining the Marques. I had begun spending more time with Annabelle-Lynn but it was becoming more difficult to hold her attention. She had no tolerance for sitting by the tree in the cold, so we had opted to sit and talk in the parlor room away from our mothers in the tea room.

"I received an unusual letter from my sister this week," I had tried desperately to begin a conversation.

"Oh? And where is she now?" I could almost hear the sarcasm in her tone and it had insulted me that she was not more concerned about my sister's whereabouts or that she was not home.

"She's been stationed in Baltimore since Christmas. Apparently there is more of a need for her nursing training there, with all the skirmishes close by in Virginia."

She had turned to face me and with all seriousness in her voice said, "I wish we wouldn't talk about the war so much. There are other, less dismal, things we can talk about."

My heart sank. Maddie would never have said such a thing, especially since her brother was out there fighting in it, making it more difficult for me to find something *other* than the war to talk about. Here had been a woman so set in her selfish ways she couldn't even bear to talk about what had been ailing me and what had been on the minds and mouths of everyone in town as of late. I had been sadly running out of things to say to her and I knew our mothers' tea time hadn't ended yet. I also believe she had been impatiently waiting for me to ask for her hand, but I had refused to do so, my mother's words still rolling in my head.

"I think I may retire to my room before supper." I had faked a yawn to sound more convincing. "I'm sorry I couldn't be more entertaining this afternoon."

"Do you want company?" she had asked so sweetly, yet there was a devious look in her eyes.

I had looked at her wide-eyed at what she had been implying. Even though I had been seeing her weekly, I had never shared anything more than conversation and meals with her. My bed had not been for her and I hoped she understood that. "You wish to sleep as well?" I had feigned innocence to her inquiry.

The gleam in her eyes had been almost catlike as she replied. "We don't have to necessarily sleep."

The words escaped me at that moment and a lump had formed in my throat. My body had begun to sweat and when I finally was able to speak, the words had squeaked out of my mouth. "I think I just need to retire alone!"

Before I could allow her to reply, I had exited the room and rushed up to my bedroom, hoping she would not try to follow. As soon as I had shut and locked the door, I collapsed onto my bed, attempting to push all thoughts of Annabelle-Lynn out of my head. It had been time to be honest with my parents about Maddie and I needed to find the right words to make them understand their plan to marry me to the Marques' daughter would never work. Just when I had thought I could lie down quietly and collect my thoughts, there had been a knock at my door. I hesitated until I had heard a familiar voice.

"William, Annabelle-Lynn said you weren't feeling well. They have left for the evening but I need to speak to you about something of importance," my father's stern voice had said from the other side of the door.

"Can it wait until tomorrow?" I had groaned, not in the mood for business talk or anything else he wished to discuss. Between the wheat's failure to produce a hearty harvest, Gracie being kept to the north, and my reluctance to accept my responsibilities to society and marry Annabelle-Lynn, my father's temper had not been something I cared for very often. This time had been no exception.

"No, please let me in," his had voice bellowed.

Sighing and realizing a headache had already formed in my temples, I pulled open the door. My father had stormed in and seated himself down at my desk, pulling out a piece of paper and picking up the dip pen that lay there. Without saying a word, he had expertly dipped the pen in the ink well and scribbled words I couldn't see onto the paper. After a few seconds of writing, he put the pen down and handed me the paper to look over. It was a written bill of sale for the full purchase of the entire McCall's Books store!

"What is this for?" I had clambered, not particularly sure I had wanted to know the truth.

"Exactly what it says. Once the winter weather thaws and your mother begins work on your wedding, I am purchasing that lot for Annabelle-Lynn. She's very business-savvy, that girl of yours."

"What are you talking about? We're not even involved enough to consider planning any wedding! I can't even hold a conversation with her!"

"You don't have to William! Conversations are made for men over brandy and cigars. Women aren't there for conversations!"

"Why are you buying the whole bookstore?" I had quickly switched the conversation, not wishing to argue my point about relationships further. "He only wanted us to help them get through the winter. That's why I agreed to it!"

"Your bride-to-be convinced me that books are not selling as well as garments these days and with sales of everything being cut to the North, it's better to trade with Europe."

"Europe? How do we still have ties to Europe?" This had been the first time I had ever heard anything like this before.

"Apparently textiles, apparel, and tobacco are being traded with England and France now."

"What does *she* want with that store?" My anger had been starting to rise and I felt my headache growing worse.

"She would like to convert it to a European-style clothing store." He had smiled proudly, as if he thought of the idea himself. "We would make a lot more money for this little town if we sell products more people would buy."

"That bookstore is everything they have!" I had argued, unable to believe my ears.

"And I will make sure they are provided for. Once we sell all the books –"

"Sell all the books?!" I had exclaimed.

"Yes, once we sell all the books to other stores in larger cities, we can give them that money to survive on." He had been so proud of himself and it killed me to even look at him.

"We're not buying that bookstore!" I had said sternly, holding my own against my father and his idiotic ideas.

"We are, as soon as two things happen: you sign this contract and you ask Annabelle-Lynn to be your wife!"

"I will do neither one!" I had screamed, slamming my hand down onto the desk to drive home my point.

"Your stubbornness is going to cost me everything, boy! First it was your reluctance to buy John's property, then that damn tree and your negligence to this plantation! I should have cut that thing down when I had the chance! Now you still won't do as you are told! This is for the greater good of this town!"

"Have you forgotten Gracie is *still* not home? Shouldn't you be more focused on getting her back than killing this town with your contracts?! In case you haven't noticed, their sons have gone off to war!"

"Gracie is fine. Her letters say she will come back when she is released from school. And you are taking too much of an interest in this war. As long as *we* survive, that's all that matters! Now sign the papers, William!" He had brushed off every one of my fears as if they were nothing at all. Even his nonchalance towards the war, a war that Maddie's brother had been fighting in, caused the hairs on my neck to stand on end.

"No! Don't you care about anyone else but yourself? Did you even know that the McCalls' son is in the Army? If we take their bookstore they will have nothing left for him to come home to!"

"You, my boy, care too much for that family. *If* the boy returns, he'll have a lot more money to come home to instead of taking over a business that is obviously failing in this town!"

"You are heartless! I'm not signing that paper, I'm not marrying Annabelle-Lynn, and I'm not going to let you ruin that family!"

~~*

I had received another cryptic letter from my sister but it had spoken volumes about a war that I never knew our country had been capable of producing. She had had to slip the letter to a friend because the North was now blocking all mail to and from the South to deter infiltrators. The letter spoke of soldiers pouring in to her Baltimore clinic needing immediate medical attention, or as she had put it, "many who flocked to the races, in need of seeing the horses do their best." I could almost feel the pain in her heart as she wrote about the numbers who came only to have them "lose their bets on the winning horse." She had also spoken about the smell of "horse manure" and how the "stench often made her leave the stables just to get a breath of fresh air into her lungs."

I had become too claustrophobic in the house after reading that letter and I had nowhere to go. The winter chill had hindered me from going for a ride, which I hadn't done since Christmas. I had often glanced out my window, constantly eyeing the old Yellowwood, as if its bare branches could give me some solace. But even the tree had brought nothing but memories and thoughts of a woman I couldn't fully have.

Ever since that day my father had demanded me to sign the paper for the full sale of the property, I had thought of no one but her. I had even thwarted Annabelle-Lynn whenever they came for tea, always feigning illness or headache, not wishing to be a part of her plans to rid the McCalls of their store. I had thought of her brother, Austin, as I read my sister's letters and hoped for Maddie's sake he was still alive. I had often felt compelled to see her and to confirm he was okay, but I dared not saddle a horse on a blustery day such as that – the ride into town alone would give the horse frostbite. So I had sat in the comfort and warmth of my room and reread Gracie's letter, hoping for a miracle.

A light tap at my window had caused me to jump slightly, thinking a small bird had mistakenly flown into it. I had sauntered over and peered out, seeing a delicate woman in an oversized coat, taking aim with pebbles at my window. I had been thankful that our house was quite large and no one could hear the tapping, for they would surely report the woman to the authorities. Carefully throwing open the window I had been unexpectedly hit with a blast of cold air.

"Why don't you come to the front door and knock like any other person?" I had asked the woman. When she had looked up at me and when we had locked eyes, I instantly knew it was her and regretted even asking that question. I had been very glad my window faced east and not north or someone from the road could have seen and heard her.

Slamming the window shut, I had run out of my bedroom and down the stairs that led to the rear of the house. Without grabbing my coat and gloves, since they were inconveniently located by the front door, I had raced to the side of the house where she had still be standing, practically shivering in her overcoat. Tears had frozen on her cheeks and when she gazed up at me, she had looked so broken and worn.

"Maddie?" was all I had a chance to say before she threw her arms around me and cried. "What's wrong? What happened?" Instantly I had become concerned and worried, my sister's letter still fresh on my mind.

"He's hurt," she had sobbed into my chest.

Instinctively, I had wrapped my arms around her and held onto her as tight as she'd allow me to. I had wanted nothing more than to bring her inside out of the cold, give her tea and sit her by the fire to warm up, but I knew it would be near impossible with the issues between our families already. When she had loosened her grip around my neck, I loosened my arms around her back and held onto her waist, still not willing to let go of her entirely.

"Austin is hurt," she had finally breathed out, confirming my fears and forming a knot in my stomach.

"How do you know?" Perhaps she had been mistaken. I could only hope it had just been a rumor and nothing more.

"They sent a telegram today." Letters had been sent by Postal Service and could take weeks to be delivered, as I had noted on my sister's correspondences to me. Telegrams though were of higher priority and only took a few days to a week to send, so if she had received a telegram, it definitely meant something was wrong.

"Tell me what has happened," I had pressed further, wanting to correlate my sister's words with Maddie's.

She had shaken her head in response. "Don't know. It just said that he was wounded and being sent to a clinic in Roanoke."

I could do nothing to take away her pain and it had killed me that day. I had hated seeing her so frail and heartbroken at the thought of losing her brother to this godforsaken war. Voices by the front of the house had stirred me out of our embrace and my thoughts and I had silently led her to the back of the house by the staircase I had used to meet her. She had been reluctant to go but I pulled her anyway, only able to reassure her with my eyes until we were able to speak in private again.

"We can't stay out here; it's much too cold. I'm not leaving you alone. If we go up the back entrance, no one will see us, I promise."

Leading her through a doorway that slightly creaked when it opened, we had raced up a steep flight of stairs that I knew would empty us on the second floor of the house and the long hallway leading to my bedroom. This staircase was mainly used by our servants and slaves to deliver linens and things and to take care of the second floor rooms, but I had often used it as an easy escape route to get to the stables and the plantation faster than going out the front door with the possibility of running into my parents along the way. Closing the bedroom door behind us and without saying a word, I had seated her down on the bed and then sat next to her.

"I'm sure he's fine," I had tried to reassure her. She didn't answer. Instead she had just stared out into my room, not saying nor doing anything. "Maddie, please talk to me," I had pleaded.

"What if he's hurt badly? What if he's lost an eye or an ear or worse, a limb? What if he's too frail to be moved and can't come home? What if –"

"Shh, listen to me." I had pulled on her hands so she'd finally look at me and stop fidgeting. "Your brother is just as strong as you and he'll come home alive and well."

"How do you know?" she had sniffled, not wanting to believe my words.

I had taken the liberty of gingerly brushing some hair out of her face so I could see her beautiful dark eyes better and speak clearly to them. "My sister is a nurse up in Baltimore. They've trained them well and I'm sure they are just as capable in Roanoke."

"But you're not sure!" she had exclaimed. "He could be lying on a bed dying and his family doesn't even know!"

"Maddie, you need to calm down, please," I had again pleaded with her, wanting to console her but keep her calm and quiet at the same time. "I need you to take a few deep breaths for me."

"I... can't!"

She had begun to hyperventilate and I knew I had to get her to calm down somehow before she fell unconscious on my bed. Remembering my mother's teachings about how to treat an upset woman, I had rubbed her back tenderly, encouraging her softly to breathe slower and I had kept my other hand on hers, reassuring her that I was not going to leave her side. Eventually her breathing had gone back to normal but then she threw her arms around my neck and started to sob uncontrollably. All I could do was hold her and allow her cry – until the door of my room flew open, startling us both.

Maddie had jumped back and attempted to compose herself, wiping the tears quickly from her eyes and cheeks. I had glanced up and saw my mother standing in the doorway, holding the doorknob to keep herself upright in her shock, unable to handle catching me with a girl in my room, a girl who had not been Miss Annabelle-Lynn Marques. Peering around the hallway, she had then slipped into the room further and shut the door quietly behind her. Glaring straight into my eyes, she had spoken softly but sternly to me directly.

"I'm not going to tell your father about any of this. Who is she, William?"

"I'm Madeline Rose McCall, ma'am," she had replied to my mother before I could answer.

"McCall? I didn't know the bookstore owner had a daughter. I was under the impression he only had a son." Maddie had burst into tears again and my mother had been caught off-guard, not knowing what to say or do. "Did I say something wrong?"

"Her brother is in the Army but they received a telegram that he was wounded. They won't tell her family how bad he is," I had supplied the missing piece of information for her.

"Oh. Well, is there a reason why is she here with you and not with her family instead?"

"Mother!" I had shouted, taken aback by my mother's unusual abrasiveness.

"It's all right, Will, I'll go back home. I can tell when I'm an unwanted guest." Her voice had been different then – softer maybe, but definitely weaker – and I had not been about to let her go so easily as she got up to leave.

"No, Maddie, stay," I had demanded, putting my hand up to stop her movements. "Mother, may I speak to you outside?" My tone had been anything but pleasant and she recognized it immediately, catching her breath as I spoke.

She had followed me out of my room, shutting the door behind us. As soon as we were out of the room, she had attacked me with her concerns. "William, what on earth is the McCall girl doing here? I can't believe you would sneak her into this house, let alone your room! Your father is preparing to purchase their store and you're here with her! Is she the reason you're so reluctant to marry Annabelle-Lynn?"

"Mother, stop! I'm not going to stand outside my own bedroom door and be accused this way, especially from you! Maddie's brother joined the Army of his own free will and is now lying on a cot somewhere, possibly dying! Have some decency! As for the purchase of their property, I did *not* sign the bill of sale! I'm not choosing to marry Annabelle-Lynn because we have nothing in common besides our plantations! It was you who said I should marry for love and I can't love her!"

"So if you cannot love Annabelle-Lynn, perhaps you can tell me how you feel for the McCalls' daughter, as you clearly have the need to hide her in your room without the rest of the family knowing!"

I had been caught between Scylla and Charybdis, just like Odysseus in Homer's Odyssey. My mother had just uncovered the truth of my love affair with a woman far greater than any they could ever shove my way. The worst of it was knowing that behind the door, Maddie had heard the entire argument, up to and including my admission of my lack of love for the woman my parents had slated me to marry.

Madeline

13

I had overheard their whole confrontation from inside his room, even as I had desperately glanced around the room to distract myself, but their voices were too loud. His mother had been angry at him for bringing me into their house, as if I did not belong there. Truth be told, I had been uncomfortable there and did not feel like I belonged there either. I had been quite surprised when he pulled me into the house and up the stairs. I had felt like such an intruder.

When I had first arrived there, there had been a need for his comfort, but upon hearing him defend my family to his mother, I had needed him in a different way. His father and the woman his parents wanted him to marry had an ulterior motive for purchasing part of our store and Will had refused to be a part of it. For that I had been so grateful. In his refusal though, he had gone against his father, their family name, and everything we had ever been taught about Southern expectations. In our world, if your business could not hold its own in harsh times, it was usually bought by a wealthy plantation owner to use as he pleased – usually converting it into a business that would bring in more money for the town. I had forgotten this to be so even after they had begun the process of taking over our business right under our noses!

When Will had admitted to his mother that he couldn't marry Annabelle-Lynn, my heart had skipped a beat in anticipation to the question why. When he had blurted out that he couldn't love her, my insecurities made my mind begin to race – was there another woman that had caught his eye? Was all of our time shared at the tree in vain because there was someone he had been courting besides me? What if his words to me were untrue? My breath had caught when I heard his mother ask if it was me and I had strained against the door to hear his answer.

No answer had come. Instead I had heard their muffled voices and footsteps moving away from the door. Leaping back and away when the door had swung open, I let out the breath I had been holding and jumped into his arms, wrapping my arms around his neck. I had felt his body sigh heavily as he pulled me into him tighter.

"I'm so sorry," he had breathed out.

I had pulled back slightly so I could see his eyes. Gently caressing his cheek I said, "It's okay."

"No, it's not! They're going to force this marriage anyway; I know they will!"

"What do you mean?"

I had pulled myself far enough away from him and out of his reach that he would have to take steps forward to touch me. He had sighed again and seated himself on the bed, motioning for me to join him but I simply stood in front of him, not willing to give him a reason to hold me. Taking my hands in his, I could feel him trembling before he had spoken.

"My parents had no idea about us until today. I had planned on telling both of them the truth but my father threw his plans for the purchase of your store into the pot. I had refused to sign the paperwork because I knew it was unfair to your father to rip that store out from under him completely. I also did not want Annabelle-Lynn to get her hands on something that obviously didn't belong to her."

I had gazed into his eyes then and seen the double meaning behind his words. Annabelle-Lynn's threat to me had not been idle and his father was proceeding with the whole affair, while Will could do nothing to stop any of it. I had not spoken to my father about anything I knew because I thought it would resolve on its own accord. Hearing Will now only made the threat more real.

"What is your father's reasoning for agreeing to buy the other half of our store for her?" I had asked angrily.

He had squeezed my hands before replying. "He claims it would be better for our town if we sold something a bit more practical than books."

"And you obviously don't agree." It had been a statement more than a question.

"Maddie, I want your store to survive! I only agreed with your father to pay for half the store so that you had money enough for the winter. But with my father plotting with Annabelle-Lynn and my mother unsure which side she should be taking in all this, it's going to be more difficult for us to be together from now on."

"I have to go!" I had quickly yanked my hands away and grabbed my coat from the bed. When I had my hand on the doorknob, he had rushed over and held onto my arm.

"No, wait, please. There's more I need to tell you."

I had stood there, hand still poised on the doorknob, willing myself to stay calm but my anger had slowly crept in to my bones. The fact that I believed he cared about me when he was already promised to someone else, the fact that his father was preparing to strip us of everything, in spite of my brother being wounded in the war, had made leaving him in that moment more justifiable. That day, I had left his house through the front door, knowing full well his parents had seen me leave. I had heard his footsteps behind me but when I heard his father call out to him before I slammed the door shut behind me I knew he would not be able to follow.

I hadn't run home though because I knew what had awaited me there. Austin had been wounded and my parents had been worried that no one was giving us all of the information. My mother had been in tears when I had left the house earlier that day and my father had gone out to the store, claiming he had a lot of "work" to do. So instead of returning to the "house of sadness," I had raced towards the only place that I had left to go.

The tree had been all bare on its branches and the sparse grass around its base was brown and crunched under the weight of my feet. As I sat down between its exposed roots, I had exhaled and watched my breath in the cool afternoon air. Shivering as I huddled closer to the tree, I had wished its branches could wrap around me and keep me warm, but this time of year and with everything going on, I knew even the tree could bring me no solace. Before I could stop them from coming, the tears of exhaustion and helplessness had streamed down my face, making my eyes blurry and my cheeks wet and cold.

Everything had been so confusing and I had no idea how to stop it all from spiraling out of control. Will had confirmed his father was preparing to purchase the bookstore, our bookstore, *my* bookstore. He had been that cruel of a man that he would put another out of business completely and I was not going to let him take it all away from us or from me. If it had meant not seeing Will ever again then I would fight his father to ensure our own livelihood would survive, especially so Austin had something to be proud to fight for.

Unfortunately, my memory becomes hazy at this point. I knew I had been cold, so very cold, and with everything spiraling in my head to the point of panic, I must have gone unconscious because when I had woken, I wasn't outside anymore. It hadn't looked like my room and I quickly remembered I never went home. It had scared me enough to sit up abruptly, causing my head to spin. When someone had entered the room, I felt my whole body stiffen and I had held my breath, anticipating who it was.

"Oh, thank heavens yer awake! Master William was so worried 'bout you bein' out dere in da cold all by ya'self!" A dark-skinned woman had come into the room carrying several blankets in her hands.

"Where... am... I?" I had asked slowly, placing a hand on my head to try to make it stop spinning.

"This here be the Hutchinson house, ma'am," she had smiled proudly, placing the blankets at the edge of the bed and unfolding the top one to place over me.

My eyes had practically fallen out of their sockets as I stared her down. I had attempted to scramble out of the bed but was pushed back down by her gentle but firm hands on my shoulders. The house slave had smiled at me and was gone from the room before I could protest. Again, I panicked, the air in my lungs catching in my throat and not allowing me the ability to breathe properly. Still not fully warm from being outside by the tree and still exhausted from worry, the room had grown dark and my eyes had closed for the second time that day.

"Maddie, please wake up." I had heard the words coming from somewhere above me. I wasn't sure if I had been dreaming or the voice had been real but I couldn't open my eyes – they felt too heavy. "Maddie, please," the voice had begged again.

I had tried my best not to allow the panic to grip me as I slowly opened my eyes and came face-to-face with Will's worried stare. "I shouldn't be here," I had whispered the first thing that came to my mind.

Ignoring my protest, he had shaken his head and spoke calmly to me. "They found you practically frozen by the tree. What were you doing out there? I tried to go after you but I was called back inside by my father. I'm sorry."

Before I could answer his question properly though, Mr. Hutchinson's voice had interrupted, bellowing through the halls, most likely speaking to anyone who would listen. "I will not be responsible for his daughter as well as his business! She leaves immediately and we set the wedding for as soon as possible! The sooner we purchase that store, the sooner Miss Marques will have her clothing business and the McCalls will be out of our lives for good!"

As he had barged into the room, Will jumped up to confront him, but Mr. Hutchinson addressed me directly, ignoring his son's presence in the room entirely. "You have been nothing but a nuisance since I first chased you away from that tree! You will not sabotage my plans by getting involved with my son! I want you out of my house immediately!"

Will had glared at him straight in the eyes before combating him with his own words, which surprised me since I had doubted any of his attempts to thwart his father before. "Have you no compassion at all?! Her father's business is failing because of the war! Her brother is wounded because of the war! She was found nearly frost-bitten to death by that tree and you accuse her of being a nuisance?!"

"You stay out of this, boy, and leave this problem to me! As for you young lady, your family will have to find someplace else to live because we are officially purchasing that store! Go home and tell your father to prepare himself to move!"

He had stormed out of the room, leaving me at Will's mercy for some support, but instead I found none. "I'm sorry," he had whispered, lowering his head in defeat. "I should take you home."

I had to blink to realize what he had been saying without actually saying it. He had given up on me, on us, and for that I would not forgive him. With all the strength I had left in me, I had stood up from the bed and solemnly faced him, clutching my coat tightly around me.

"I can find my way home alone. I don't need you anymore."

I had vacated his house, again through the front door, thankful that at least his house slaves had the decency to assist me with a lantern to find my way home. Looking back several times before his house was no longer in my line of vision, I had almost wished he would come after me and tell me truthfully how he felt but he never came. Instead, I had proceeded home and added to the sadness that was already there.

~~*

"I'm not selling our store, Jackson! You can't threaten me on this!"

I had tried to ignore the argument between my father and Mr. Hutchinson as I cleared away space in the storeroom for what I had hoped would be more shipments. As spring was fast approaching, there had still been a chill in the air, as word had spread that we were selling our *entire* store to Mr. Hutchinson. My father had been furious with the accusation, but even more so after Mr. Hutchinson had come barging into our store waving a piece of paper that clearly stated it was a bill of sale for the property that *was* McCall's Books.

"Robert, this is for the security of your company. I can keep this place going much more efficiently if the business was in my name." Mr. Hutchinson had been such a fool. He had honestly thought that I hadn't told my father the truth of his plot with Miss Annabelle-Lynn Marques.

"I don't think after running this business for thirty years you have any right to tell me about company security! For the last time, I'm not selling!"

"You don't have a choice! As owner of half this company, I am legally taking the other half over. My son has already signed the agreement and the bank has approved the bill of sale. Now just hand over the business quietly and everything will be fine!"

"Fine?! I've lost my son because of this war! My daughter has been almost arrested by the authorities for trespassing at a tree that not only isn't on your property but was planted by my family long before your plantation was ever there! My family has been broken apart by you and your family and you come in here demanding I sell the one thing holding us together?! No, Jackson, everything is *not* fine!"

Hearing the desperation in my father's voice had made it so difficult to ignore their quarrel.   Mr. Hutchinson had made everything sound so easy and simple but Daddy had been right – he would be taking away everything we had left. What had hurt even more was hearing that Will had betrayed me by signing that agreement and sealing our fate, when he had promised that he had only wanted to help us through the winter. I had known in my heart that when I left their house the day we had been "discovered", I had been saying goodbye to the fairy-tale romance we never should have begun in the first place.

"I'm not leaving until you sign the papers!" Mr. Hutchinson's voice had vibrated the walls.

"And I'm not signing any papers so you'll be here for a while!" had been my father's reply. I had smiled proudly at my father's response but I was numbed by the circumstances, making it difficult for me to keep the smile for long.

We still had not heard any news from Roanoke about Austin and we had no way of knowing if he was dead or alive. Mama had still believed in her heart he was alive but Daddy had grown too used to the idea of him not surviving and that had bothered us all. For a man who had wished for his only son to take over the business and run the store, I could not understand how he could give up on that son completely. I had no idea what Austin had been going through since his personal letters to me had stopped as soon as we had received notice that he had been wounded. My father had still been very angry with me for my illicit affair with Will and had a difficult time asking for my assistance in the store when he had needed it most. I had felt like I had betrayed my family and my heart had betrayed me and for that I would never forgive myself. Mr. Hutchinson's insistence on buying the entire store outright had just been another cruel addition to my father's pain.

"Have you no heart?!" I had heard my father's voice slice through the silence of the store.

"Robert, I'm sorry about your son, really I am. But we all have to survive this war too and your business just isn't going to without the necessary push."

That had been when I had had enough. I had quickly entered the storefront and stood directly in Mr. Hutchinson's line of vision defiantly. "Our store will survive without your help! I think it's time for you to leave!"

He had picked up my chin with his fingers. "Quite the defiant one, isn't she, Robert? I'd watch who you are addressing, young lady. If it weren't for you, I might have reconsidered this contract."

"Leave her out of this, Jackson! She's just a girl with no legal binding to this store. This is between you and me!" my father had interjected, hurting me with his words.

"She involved herself! I told her to stay away from my plantation; I told her to stay away from anyone who might try to talk to her; and I told her to stay away from my son! If you can't keep your daughter on a tighter rein, then it is not my fault you lose your store!"

Coming into the store at that exact moment and stepping behind Mr. Hutchinson, had been Will. It had taken everything I had in me not to run to him for comfort, but upon remembering his betrayal I had stood my ground alongside my father. He had stood there with *his* father – a clash between two families. In that moment I had felt like I was reliving a scene from Romeo and Juliet. I could see the pain in his eyes as he had glanced from me to his father, confused by which side to adhere to, but in the end, he would take his father's side, not mine.

"The deed has been written. You need to sign it." I could not believe my ears as Will had spoken those words to my father.

"No!" I had shouted stubbornly, not allowing his eyes to leave mine, forcing him to see the hurt and betrayal in them.

"I'm sorry," he had whispered, dropping his eyes.

"No, you're not! Is this my punishment then for loving you?" I had admitted outright, not caring if our fathers knew the truth. "Now you have chosen sides and intend to ruin us by buying our store completely and allowing your *fiancée* to build her clothing empire?"

I had actually seen Will cringe at my words but it was his father who spoke first. "My dear, I have no clue what you're talking about. I am simply taking over the *finances* of the business to enhance the quality of sales. I have no idea where you would get such a thought like that into your head."

I had glared at him venomously, attempting to challenge his word against mine. "You never intended to give us back the store! You took half of it, convinced us it was only temporary, and now you plan to take it all away from us to turn it into something this town doesn't even need!"

"Madeline, this is not your fight!" My father had stepped between me and Mr. Hutchinson but that did not stop me from keeping a stern eye on Will.

Tears had already begun to stream down my face as I glanced from Will to his father and back to Will. He could not even bring himself to look at me. Stiffening and squaring my shoulders, I had pushed my way past them both and out of the store. My heart had felt heavy and my head had begun to throb but I did not dare stop running. I had turned around only once to see if anyone had cared enough to follow me but when no one had, I proceeded home.

My mother had been there waiting for me, sitting on a sofa-chair in the tea room. Her eyes had been just as red and puffy as I'm sure mine had been and she did not try to hide the fact that she had been crying this time. Without a word, she had patted the seat next to her, silently asking me to join her in her sorrows. Upon sitting, I had been immediately engulfed into her arms, allowing both of us to weep openly and without reservation. When I had glanced up from her shoulder, my eyes had caught sight of a paper on the table next to us.

"What is that?" I had asked her.

My mother had released me and picked up the paper to hand to me. It had already been tear-stained, so I assumed she had already read it and that was what had made her so upset. "It's a letter from Austin. He had one of the nurses pen it for him." I had grabbed it from her and began to read it to myself.

Dear Mama, Daddy, and Maddie,

This will probably be the last letter you receive from me for a short while. I am being looked after by a wonderful nurse in Roanoke and the Corporal says I may be honorably discharged from the Army. Yet, with the stories about the war and its effect on the South I've heard, I'm afraid to come home. I've failed you all miserably. I wanted to join the Army to make a difference for the South and become a man and both of those plans have failed. I have weighed my options carefully and I have decided not to come home. I do not want to be a burden to you as I am too weak to take over the responsibilities of the store for Daddy. Once I am well enough, I will be joining up with Lee and the Army of the Potomac to finish what we started. I love you all so much and I hope to send news once I receive my new orders.

Love,

Austin

I had wished that what Austin had said was true and that his letter had been his last for the time being. I had wished more than anything that Austin joined General Lee's army in Virginia to fight for the South, but it wasn't to be. About a week after receiving his letter, we had received another, more formal, correspondence from the Secretary of the Confederacy. Austin had never made it to the

Army of the Potomac. His body had not been able to handle the wounds he had sustained and even with his extensive care, he had taken his last breath on 15 March 1862.

They never sent his remains home, just a letter and his journal he had kept while he was away, and to this day we still have no body to bury. I had held onto that book and kept it in my room to read every night, wary that neither of my parents could have handled reading all his private thoughts while he had been fighting for our rights. I had also found it so profound and apropos that he had died, like Caesar, betrayed by the very country that had given him his birthright and civil liberties as a free-born Southern man.

William

14

With the coming of spring, changes had begun to happen all around us. Plans to take over McCall's Books had been halted when we received another letter from Gracie. She had claimed she was okay and had been moved down to Richmond from Baltimore, but my mother's upset from the letter had preoccupied my father away from his plans. She had been so close to us, only a state away, but the North wouldn't let her leave their side, not for a second. It had been as if she was a prisoner, being held captive and forced to help those who were nothing more than casualties of war. I wished I could have left everything behind and taken a train to ride out to meet her but with Northern soldiers infiltrating the South at every juncture, it had been too risky.

Our small southern town had been ripped apart further by the war when Union soldiers marched through in April, only a few short months ago but seems like longer. I had learned from the talk in town that they had been on their way to Nashville to meet up with Sherman's men coming up from Georgia. Everyone in town had seemed on edge as the troop of 600 men came through our streets. No one had spoken to them and no one had given them any reason to stay and I could not believe how Southern hospitality had changed since the war had begun. We had always been known for our welcoming nature but now it seemed we were uncharacteristically antagonistic and completely suspicious of strangers who might pay our humble town a visit.

One day in mid-April, after another troop of about 350 men had come into town, I spied one going into the bookstore and my heart had stopped in my chest. I had had visions of this soldier, who could very well have been younger than me, hurting Maddie in her own store. When I had seen him lingering in the doorway and then spied her on the other side, my whole body had been gripped with – fear, anger, jealousy – everything I could muster to feel in that moment. As soon as he had left the store, I locked eyes with her and she had looked happy for the first time in what seemed like forever.

I had gathered myself and briskly walked over to the bookstore. Staring her straight in the eyes, I had demanded, "Who is he?" as if I had any right to question.

"It is really not of your concern," she had replied harshly and walked back into the store, busying herself with organizing some books. I had simply stood next to her, wishing for her to talk to me but it had been obvious she was still sour with me for everything I had done. "If you're going to stand there and brood, you might as well be useful and help."

If she was going to talk to me, at least she had been asking for assistance. I had picked up the first book I had seen and examined it in my hands, scrutinizing it so that I had time to compose myself and find the right words to say. Her voice had broken my concentration.

"If you're going to look at each one, we'll be here all day and I need to be getting home early for an engagement this afternoon."

I had finally glanced up at her in surprise when I realized why the soldier had been at the bookstore in the first place. "The soldier?"

"Yes," she had confirmed with a smile. "I've been asked to accompany him to tea this afternoon. As I stated before, it is not of your concern."

I had been angry with her. It was as if everything I had ever said to her, all those times by the tree, the letters I had sent to her privately, had meant nothing. I had still felt the need to argue further. "But he's a Yankee!" I had shouted causing her to cower at the hostility in my voice she had never heard. "He's one of them! He'll break your heart!"

"Like *Southern* men haven't already?!" she had countered, shooting me a glare that went straight to my heart. "I will take my chances with a Northern man, if you don't mind!"

"But, you can't!" I had stammered, dropping the book I had been holding, not caring if I had broken the spine. She had picked it up, dusted it off, and placed it in its spot on the shelf.

"*He* is a perfect gentleman. I have every right to see him if I choose to. Besides, I'm going to be taking over this business soon and I'm going to need a *worthy* partner to run it."

Her words had stung me to the core and I had sucked in my breath at the very thought that she would consider a Northern soldier as a companion. "I'm sorry, for everything. If I could take it back –"

"But you can't, Will! You can't take any of it back! Your father, the tree, your involvement with another woman!" she had spat angrily. "You can't change anything! And I have to move on, from everything!"

Tears had begun to form in her eyes and when I reached out to wipe them away instinctively, she had pulled back out of my reach. "Maddie…"

"No! You can't do anything to take away the pain, so please don't try! Just go home to your plantation and your life. I don't belong there anyway!"

It had pained me to see her like this – so rigid towards me. The woman that stood before me had not been the girl I had grown fond of the previous year. She had matured, not just as a woman in stature, but as a person who is changed by what she has experienced in the world. In that moment, staring at her fully, taking her all in, I had realized something that I had refused to say or even acknowledge. My mother had been the only other person who knew how deeply I cared about Maddie, as she had asked me outright for an answer. I had never thought or uttered the word love but the emotion had always been there.

"Please, don't go to him this afternoon. I'm... I'm..." I had been at a loss for words and looking back on it, it had been ironic that the language of love had escaped me.

"Nothing you can say will stop me from seeing him later!" she had challenged.

Like a fool, I had accepted the challenge and said the first thing that had come to mind. "I love you."

I truly deserved what had come next. Her hand had come in contact with my cheek and I'm sure the reddened print stayed there for a while after. Clutching my cheek with my own hand, I had felt a mix of surprise and admiration, for only a strong woman would have dared to strike out at me, especially for the admittance I had just made.

"You don't love me, so don't say it! How could you possibly love someone you've betrayed in so many ways?"

"But I –"

"This whole time you were getting close to me to get to my store! You never cared when we sat at that tree or when our store closed for winter or even when my brother was wounded!" she had accused, pointing a finger defensively towards me. Every word had hurt more than the next.

"Maddie, please." I had tried again to get her attention to tell her she was wrong.

"Go home, Will. Go back to your rich plantation life, your family and your fiancée! You've done enough damage here!"

I was not one for dismissals, as I had always stood my ground when I was being accused of something I did not do. After just admitting to her that I loved her, after finally admitting it to myself,

I had to redeem myself in her eyes. My brain had been clouded with emotions but still I attempted to stay where I was.

"I'm not leaving until you give me a chance to talk to you and explain everything."

"You've had so many chances, Will, more than enough, but you allowed your father to take away the one thing I loved more than anything – this store. Now it seems I will have to combat him myself, since I refuse to let my father sign anything. After Austin died, he was ready and willing to hand it over without as much as a fight."

"Austin's dead? When did that happen? Why didn't you tell me?"

"It happened a few days after your father demanded we give up the store. With your fiancée coming in here almost every day to take measurements or demand we leave faster, it makes all of this," she had splayed her hand around and gestured towards the books, "seem trivial."

"I never asked her to marry me and I never signed that contract!" I had defended uselessly.

"How can you stand there and lie to me, even now?! You came into our store and swore your allegiance to your father!"

"It had all been an act for my father's benefit, I swear to you! If you had looked at the paper my father had in his hands that day, you would see that it did not have my signature on it! I had found the original bill of sale on the desk in my father's study, torn it up and burned it all the pieces!"

"Why would you play a part in front of your father? Are you that afraid of what he would do to you that you would break any bonds between us and deny me any true feelings?"

She had deserved to know the truth and I had to give it to her. "He threatened me with the whip!" I had stammered out and I had heard her gasp in surprise. "He's angry, furious even, with me for following my heart instead of my head and threatened to beat it out of me if I didn't comply. So to answer your question, yes, I am afraid of my father. That man's temper has a way of making you obey when he gives you an order."

"And Annabelle-Lynn? What is your sad excuse for the way she comes into *my* store and torments *me* about the bond you share with *her*? What am I to think about you professing your love to me here and now when you have not done anything to keep her at bay?"

"I have no feelings for her, I swear to you. Please believe me," I had begged again, hoping my expression had been enough for her to see the truth in my words.

"I'm sorry, I can't. If you had fought harder I may have believed your words as true. But Annabelle-Lynn is still here, ready and willing to push my entire family out to get what she wants from these vacant four walls. Your father is still demanding we legally sign the papers to give him the rights to everything we own and everything we have worked so hard to maintain. While you stand there and pretend to be the good son, the good fiancé, and then have the audacity to admit you love me! No, it is up to me now to hold fast to the one thing I *can* believe in – myself."

"Maddie," I had begun, feeling the weight of her words.

"Will, please, just leave."

~~*

As the days became longer with the waning of April, my heart had begun to grow colder and I had barely left my room. I had received one last personal letter from my sister when the winter chill had finally receded for the year. Her words were few and not at all the way she normally would write to me. Even the cryptic words had been truncated so that I had to reread the letter several times to fully understand what she was trying to say.

Where before she had spoken of the wounded coming in to the clinic for medical treatment, now she only spoke of the great numbers dead or dying. She had been shipped once again, this time further into Virginia, where more of the actual combat had been going on. I had assumed they were forced to extricate the bodies on the field from her simple words of "too many spectators losing their bets before the race could begin."

I had wanted her back at the plantation again, to balance out all the chaos that surrounded me, but she wasn't coming home. More troops of men had marched through our town, this time colored troops made of Freemen or escapees. They had made us all wary of what our slaves and servants would do – try to run, try to join the Union troops, try to escape to the north? They had worn a sense of pride on their lips and it was then that I realized this war was being fought for many different reasons, not just the ones I had read about in the papers. And as the local papers printed up their stories, the list of names had grown longer – boys ages twelve to fourteen, men ages twenty to twenty-two, and women of various ages – all dead because of a war started by a struggle of economic disproportion.

It had been on a particularly sunny day on the cusp of May that I sat in my room with the window opened and one of the last letters I had received from Maddie in my hands. I had not seen her since that day at the bookstore when she had told me to leave, not because I hadn't tried, but because her father had been visibly cautious and kept her at bay. All I had to occupy my mind were her letters, expressing emotions she had recently discarded for the attention of a *Northern* man.

Over the chatter of the birds and the rustling of the trees, I had heard a scuffle near the stables, which were not far from where my bedroom window stood. Quickly dropping her letter on the bed, I had thrown open my door and raced down the back stairs just in time to see two men in blue uniforms riding off on two of our horses. There had been no way to stop them and as I got closer to the stables I had realized our stable hands had been stabbed.

Shouting for assistance from anyone who could hear me, I had tried everything I could to stop their wounds from bleeding, but they were cut too deep and the blood quickly stained my shirt and hands. I did what any good man would have done – I had gone back to my room, grabbed my pistol from my desk drawer, and made my way back down to the stables. Firing two shots, one in each of them, I had watched them take their last raged breaths.

Standing there in shock, unable to move a muscle, my mind had raced with unanswered questions: How could they be dead? How could someone be so heartless to stab another man for his horse? How come I couldn't stop it from happening? Why was there so much blood? What had soldiers been doing around our plantation? I had been so swept up in my thoughts that I hadn't heard anyone come outside until the demanding tone in my father's voice behind me caused me to jolt out of my skin.

"William, what did you do?"

I had turned around slowly, imagining how the scene had looked to him, especially since I still had my pistol in my hand. "I didn't... I mean, I saw..."

"I heard the gunshots! Their blood is on your hands! Our horses are gone! Don't tell me you didn't do this! Just tell me why!"

"I saw them – two Union soldiers came and took our horses! They stabbed the stable hands!"

"Enough excuses William! Union soldiers haven't been on this side of town since they first marched through almost a month ago! Now tell me the truth or so help me God I *will* take the whip to you!"

"You wouldn't!"

"Don't test me, boy! You have tried to stop me from every plan I've made for your benefit and this is just another attempt of yours to stand in my way!"

I had looked down at my hands, noting the blood still on them. "I put them out of their misery, but I did not cause this! Don't expect me to stand here while you accuse me of something those

Yankees did or take the whip for it! More often than not I've felt more like your slaves out in the field than your own flesh and blood!"

My father had turned to his left and proceeded towards the small tool shed. Immediately, I had been gripped with fear, the same fear I'm sure our slaves had felt time after time whenever he grabbed the whip from the shed. "Turn around boy and make this easy!"

"No!" I had been set on being defiant, but when he thrust his fist into my stomach and I doubled over in pain, he had been able to turn me around enough to strike at me once with the whip.

Nothing had prepared me for the sting I felt the first time his whip cracked across my back – the skin breaking underneath my shirt. The second crack had hit my back and I cried out as it tore my skin apart. He had only given me five lashings but in the end I was reduced to tears, my legs giving out from under me, and I fell to the floor of the stables with a hard thud.

"Now go in the house and get a clean shirt! And spare your mother the agony by not telling her!" was all he had said to me before walking away.

Instead of heading inside the house though, I had slowly and painfully made my way past the plantation to the old Yellowwood, standing tall and beginning to bloom. Weakening with every step, I had finally collapsed onto my stomach at its roots, allowing myself to be swept up in its fragrant white flowers. When I had heard voices coming towards the tree, I attempted to sit up but the movement had reopened the wounds on my back, causing me to cry out again in pain. The voices stopped immediately.

"Oh my God, Will!" I had heard my name screamed from nearby. "Are you okay? What happened?"

Trying to focus on the voice, I thought I had recognized it but it had been so long since I had heard it, I hadn't been sure. "Maddie?"

"It's me, Will, I'm here. Tell me what happened?" With even the slightest touch of her hand on my back, I had flinched and whimpered.

"Don't, please," I had whispered through gritted teeth.

"Please tell me what happened," she had repeated, her voice dripping with concern and worry.

A male voice had interrupted before I could answer her. "Madeline, we should get going. He obviously doesn't want to tell you."

Had I enough strength to move, I would have punched him just for being there with her. Instead I had focused what little strength I had left on the girl between us. Sighing, I had weakly lifted my head to better see her face, and glimpse the angel who had come to my aid. I had stretched out my hand to hers, taking hold and not letting go until I was able to tell her what had happened.

"Two Yankees stole our horses... stabbed our stable hands. I tried to stop them but I was too late. Father caught me with their blood on my hands... blamed me for all of it. Took the whip to me – gave me five lashes."

I had heard her gasp as I felt her other hand come up and gently caress my face. Slowly I had turned my head and looked up into her eyes. "I can't believe your father would do that!" she had spat angrily.

"It's my fault, he said. Ruined all his plans and used them Yankees as an excuse for what he thought I did. He left me in the stables but I was able to get myself out here."

"Madeline, I'm sorry, but we have to go. We have dinner arrangements that will not hold if we are late." There had been that voice again – a strong, young, male voice, unlike any that I had heard in town.

"Who are you?" I had demanded, shielding my eyes from the late afternoon sun.

"The name's Bradley." I had known from the accent that he

wasn't from any part of Kentucky and after catching a glimpse of his blue pants and jacket, the anger rose through my entire body.

"Well, Bradley, it's nice to see that Miss Madeline has introduced you to our town, but you see, this here tree is on my property and both of you are trespassing." Maddie had inhaled sharply and I knew she had been caught off-guard by my words, but after everything that had happened to me that day, there was nothing she could have said to change my growing anger.

"Will, please let me help you!" I could hear the desperation in her voice but I had refused to give in, knowing that our last meeting at her bookstore ended with her dismissing me.

"You need to leave now and take him with you."

"But –"

"Go, Maddie. I'll be fine. The wounds will heal in a few days and by then you'll have forgotten all about me." I knew my words had stung, but it had only been fair, considering.

"You heard what he said, Madeline, come on. We're trespassing and I for one would not like to endure the same fate as he."

As their footsteps grew fainter, I had laid my head against the trunk of the tree, careful not to press my wounded back against it. By the dress and accent, Bradley had definitely been the same Yankee soldier who had met her at the bookstore and now it seemed they had grown fairly close too quickly for my liking. At that moment, the whipping had become the least of my worries.

My mind had flooded with a thousand thoughts of regret. I had become a disgrace to my father, disloyal to Madeline, and a deceiver to myself. I had lost the opportunity to run the plantation strategically, I had lost the unconditional love of an extraordinary woman, and I had lost my pride as a man the very second that whip hit my back.

Madeline

15

All through our quiet supper, my mind had been driven back to the thought of Will – beaten, tortured, and humiliated by his father – his eyes telling me everything his words could not. I could not understand how his father, a man you are supposed to respect and learn from, had the audacity to be so cruel as to take the whip to his own son. I had wanted to help him, to fix him, but I couldn't do anything, knowing what had transpired between us and around us. Seeing Will that way, so helpless and in pain, had brought all of the old feelings back into my heart more than they had before.

"Madeline, are you okay?" Bradley's voice had cut through my thoughts and I almost scolded myself for not being present in the moment. I had shaken my head in response.

"I'm sorry. With everything going on lately, I have a lot on my mind." I had attempted to smile as sweetly as possible to hide the true feeling in my heart.

"You should smile more often. It makes you that much more beautiful." His gentle words hadn't reached me as deeply as Will's words had in the past and I knew taking Bradley to the tree had been a terrible idea.

"I'm sorry about the tree. I thought it would be a safe place to go."

"It's all right. You didn't know we'd be trespassing. And I for one really didn't want to be subjected to the same torture. I've heard about people like that – they'll take the whip to just about anyone!"

Bradley had been compelled to be concerned for my safety after hearing Will's threat, but I had known the truth. With everything that had happened between us, Will would never have told his father about me being there, especially after just being whipped. Just the very thought of bringing Bradley to the tree though was enough to betray Will and everything we felt for each other.

"You seem distracted."

"I just hope he's okay, that's all."

"I'm sure he's fine. You shouldn't worry so much. He looked like a man who could take care of himself." I had nodded my head but I hated how he was brushing off my fear.

"It's getting late. I should get you home before your father worries."

He had gotten up and come over to my chair to help me stand. After paying for our meal and helping me with my coat, he had laced his fingers with my own as we walked out of the establishment together. It had been one of the only places left in the town square that had remained opened since the war began, yet we all knew that the main clientele had been the Yankee soldiers as they marched through.

Reflecting back on it now, the feel of his hand on mine had been pleasant, but it hadn't been completely desirable. As we had walked out into the cool evening air, his fingers began to feel foreign to me. They hadn't felt the same as when Will grabbed my hand and interlaced our fingers together while reciting lines from whatever book we had chosen to read. Where Will's were smooth and comforting, Bradley's were rough and calloused. After seeing Will earlier that day, Bradley's hand had felt even colder than usual.

Although Bradley was incredibly handsome with light wavy hair, bright blue eyes, and a body that was obviously well-built due to the regime of the Army, his accent had shown through far more than his other features, casting an unwanted intruder shadow all around him. He had never told me his age but I assumed he was in his twenties from the hair that had grown on his face. Walking with him then, it had made me shiver as I began to feel guiltier for betraying the feelings I had in my heart.

"You cold?" he had asked, shaking me from my thoughts again.

"No; I was just thinking." It was all I could say without blurting out what had really been on my mind that evening. Will had been shamed, the victim of a vicious act by his father, and I could do nothing to take away his pain. Not only that, he had dismissed me as if I had been a trespasser on his property, just as his father had done to me two years ago.

"Well I was thinking how beautiful you look tonight." He had kept cutting through my ranting mind and inwardly I cursed myself for continuously thinking of Will while I had been with Bradley but it had been too easy to slip into the memories.

Bradley's hand had suddenly slipped from mine and he moved around to face me. Cupping my face and lightly running his fingers in my hair, he had leaned down closer before I had a chance to pull back. When his lips brushed mine, they had been tentative at first, seeing how I would respond. It hadn't been the first time in the last month we had kissed, but it felt different. It felt as if he was kissing me for the first time, chaste and unsure. Before I could respond completely, he had pulled away, waiting for me to open my eyes.

"Our troop is moving out tomorrow. I don't want to go."

I had pulled myself out of his hold, unwilling to stay in his arms a moment longer. Looking into his eyes in that moment, I had wanting nothing more than to just walk away. All I had wanted to do was run away from him and that moment and everything that had happened between us for the last month. When I had tried to run though, he held onto me even tighter.

"Madeline, please. This is so hard for me, don't make it harder," he had pleaded.

"What do you want me to say?"

"Say we can still be together. Say you'll wait for me. I'll write you every day."

That had been the end for me. Remembering my brother's letters, as well as his journal, had made what Bradley was saying even more wounding. Just like my brother, this man would leave me and could meet the same fate. Thoughts of the war had kept coming back into my mind like the throbbing of my blood through my veins and the reality of what was staring me in the face was becoming clearer to my eyes.

"I can't," I had stated weakly.

"Please tell me you feel the same way; that you'll wait for me to return."

As sweet and gentlemanly as Bradley was, he was still a Yankee soldier. When my brother was mortally wounded in battle it was because Union soldiers did it to him. My brother was dead because of men like Bradley! I had jerked back even more, feeling the tears in my eyes forming before I could even speak.

"No! I can't! I can't betray my brother!"

"How would waiting for me to return be betraying your brother? I didn't even know you had a brother."

"I have to go; I'm sorry." I had turned away, satisfied that I had done what needed to be done. An eye for an eye, as they say?

He had gently placed his hands on either side of my shoulders and sighed. "I'd like to meet your brother before I leave, if I could. Maybe deter you from the feeling of betrayal." He had sounded so sincere but he just didn't understand.

"What does this war mean to you?"

I had not turned around to face him when I asked him that question but I assumed he had been shocked by my forwardness to talk about the war, since it never came up in conversation until now. He knew nothing about me, not the way Will had known. He hadn't even bothered to look around him and see how his troop of soldiers had affected our town while they were here. Sliding his hands down my arms to around my waist before he answered, I had closed my eyes and waited for the moment to be over.

"It means ending a fight between two halves of a country so that I can come back to you," he had answered truthfully, trying to kiss my neck in the process.

He truly had not understood and I had to make him understand. I had pulled away and out of his grasp but refused to turn around to look him in the eyes. "My brother is dead because of this senseless war! The same way you feel obligated to push our divided country together, is the same way he felt about why we needed to separate! His body is lying somewhere in Virginia because the North doesn't care about the treatment of our brothers!"

Tears had streamed down my cheeks by that point, the thought of my brother too much for my heart to handle, and as he moved around me to face me, I looked away, ashamed to be so vulnerable in his presence. "I'm sorry about your brother; really I am. But you can't blame the Union for what happened. We are obligated to put an end to a war the South started. And please don't blame me for commands my comrades had to carry out."

"So you're saying it was *our* fault that he's dead?!" I had stammered out, taken aback by his skewed view on what had been going on. I had known the truth, having read my brothers journal as well as heard stories from others in town.

"I'm saying it was his choice to go against the laws of the federal government and join up with an army that has no chance of winning."

"How dare you! He fought for what he believed in and now he's dead because of it! *Your* factories and corporations are putting places like mine out of business and all he wanted was to fight to stop *them* from encroaching on our lives! That bookstore has been in our family for at least three generations and now it will be sold off to be converted into a clothing store if I don't do something about it! This is what happens when you run us out of business!"

"I'm sorry. I had no idea." He had tried to touch my cheek but I pulled away quickly, too angry to let him come near me.

"Did your officers tell you the *real* reason why you're fighting? Did they tell you that our rights as southern citizens are being taken away by *your* president? Did they tell you that as free citizens of the South, we are allowed to keep slaves and servants because it is the *only* way our businesses will run? Did they tell you that every time colored troops come through our streets more revolts occur, innocent people die, and crops fail? No, I'm sure they didn't! We are not the enemy here and yet we are treated as if it is your sole responsibility to put us in our place and ignore a way of life that has been followed for over a century!"

"I... I never knew," he had said solemnly, bowing his head in defeat.

"Of course you didn't! I have to go. I'm sorry."

"So am I," he had growled, obviously bothered by my outburst.

"Goodbye, Bradley."

"Bye, Madeline."

My heart had been as heavy and full of pent up anger as a summer thunderstorm in Kentucky when I left him standing there that day. It had finally become clear to me what my brother's reasoning for joining the Army really was. As the sun set that day, I had made my way over to the town cemetery, to a small plot of land they set aside for "casualties of war" as the sign that was posted read. I remember kneeling down at the marker with my brother's name on it – an unoccupied, shallow grave for a young man who died fighting for what he believed in.

~~*

My birthday is something I wish I could forget, but unfortunately it will be a day I will remember forever, locked away in my mind with all the other memories of the War time. Mr. Hutchinson had discovered exactly what day I had turned twenty, no doubt harassing my father into admitting it. Since we had still been trying to keep the store open, much to Miss Annabelle-Lynn's dismay, Mr. Hutchinson had convinced my father to close in honor of my "special day" and then had the audacity to ask my mother to find my best Sunday dress. According to his declaration, there was going to be a cotillion in my honor. I truly hated for Mr. Hutchinson to go through all that trouble since I had no desire to be presented to any of his friends in society.

I will never forget how humiliating an event it had been for me and my parents. He had pretended my father was his best friend and that he had known our family for years instead of the man who had been trying to ruin our lives completely. Knowing what he had done to Will sent fear through my entire body and I was anxious to see how Will would react to this type of fanfare, especially since I had discovered that not only Annabelle-Lynn had been invited but her parents as well.

We had arrived in early afternoon to the Hutchinsons' mansion – a massive two-story grand house with at least five bedrooms, three vanity rooms, a parlor, a reading room, a formal dining area *and* a study! It was intriguing that I never noticed these details before, but at that moment I had been able to scrutinize the reason behind Mr. Hutchinson's abrasive behavior towards us – the house put ours to shame and he had looked at us condescendingly, almost as if we were unworthy of comparison. As we were escorted into the parlor room by a young slave girl, my eyes had quickly darted around the room, taking in all the ornate decorations and colorful patterns, things that I knew we would never afford. Several other families that I did not know had already been milling around the room and talking amongst themselves. All eyes had turned to us as we entered the room and I had felt them burning holes into us with their stares.

How I had wanted to be taken away from this place and be rescued by Will but he was nowhere to be found! My mind had begun racing with any and all thoughts of what could be keeping him away, including another whipping from his father. Had Mr. Hutchinson seen us by the tree together? Had Will finally revealed to his father his feelings for me and *this* was Mr. Hutchinson's way of belittling him more? I had no time to seek answers as Mr. Hutchinson himself came directly over to me, his arms wide and inviting, his smile deceiving and arrogant.

"Happy birthday, my dear!" he had exclaimed as he leaned over to kiss my cheek. He then whispered into my ear, "Don't do or say anything foolish to embarrass me in front of my guests." I had wanted to glare at him for his patronizing behavior but just as he pulled back some of his guests began to come over to wish me a happy birthday as well and I had no time to be disgruntled at the man who was again making a mockery of me and my family.

Before long, my parents had abandoned me to talk with other guests, no doubt another ploy of Mr. Hutchinson to ensure we would not cause a scene. I had felt extremely underdressed and out of place as I was soon surrounded by young women my age. Where they were all clothed in beautifully laced and satin gowns with gloves and shoes to match, my dark green cotton dress had no lace accents or accessories at all. Some of them had dared to show their shoulders and neck as the ruffles dipped down too low and the skirts were large, making it difficult to stand too close to them, whereas mine had no wire hoop at all and laid much flatter against my legs.

They had begun their talk about things I didn't care to understand but when the topic switched to the war, I felt compelled to listen and cringed at what they said and the tone they had used. I was never told their names and I really hadn't wanted to remember them after that day.

"Personally, I think it's a waste of time, this war is," one girl had spoken up over the others.

"I agree. My father is more upset that it's disrupting the natural order of things with our crop this season," another had interjected, clearly not understanding the ramifications of the war on everyone else's businesses.

"I hear the trains have been stopped and our shipments from overseas are being detoured to the North. How will I ever get my coat Father ordered from London? It goes through New York now, you know," a third had whined, her priorities certainly different from my own.

"What do you think, Madeline? Is this war even necessary?" the first girl had pressured me to answer.

All of a sudden I had been put on the spot, stuttering to find the right words. "I... um... well..."

"Oh, you wouldn't really know much about the war, would you? Only the plantations are hurting with the constant threat of slave revolts and crop failure," I had been interrupted.

I had wanted to cry or scream at them for being so ignorant but I had to be on my "best behavior" for Mr. Hutchinson. Cursing him for his rules, I had taken a deep breath and chose my words carefully. "I think that if we want all of our businesses to survive, it's necessary to combat the expansion of the North and if that means a war, then so be it." I had smiled victoriously as I glanced at their stunned faces.

"Well, I for one think war is disgusting! All those men fighting each other! It's very barbaric and not at all suited for *real* gentlemen!" the second girl had replied, scrunching up her face in disgust.

I had not been able to hide the roll of my eyes and I was about to make another controversial comment when I had been interrupted yet again. "Oh, speaking of real gentlemen, there's one fine specimen of a man!" I had turned around to see where they were all staring and spied Will entering the room, with Annabelle-Lynn on his arm.

"It's such a shame he has her. I'd definitely like to be on his arm."

"Or in his bed!" The girls had laughed at their own insinuation but I had shuddered as I listened to the way they talked about him, as if he was there for their entertainment.

I hadn't been able to take my eyes off of him as they made their way around the room, shaking hands with everyone they knew. To them, he had been William Hutchinson, Jackson Hutchinson's son and future plantation master and that day that was all he had appeared to be. Gone was the hope in his eyes for the day he would see his sister again, gone was the anger towards *this* way of life, and gone was the desire to fight for anything he had believed in, including my heart. I remember watching him and wondering how he had been reduced to nothing more than a puppet on *their* strings.

By the time they had reached us, I noticed his eyes more clearly and they looked tired and weak, clouded by numbness and submission. Addressing the group as a whole, his voice had been staged and rigid, as if rehearsed. "Afternoon, ladies." They had all giggled and blushed and I watched Annabelle-Lynn tighten her grip on his arm, as if claiming him for all to see.

I had wanted nothing more than to kiss him right there for all to see, but I dared not, since he did not appear to be even the slightest entertained by my presence in the room. So it had come as a surprise when he gazed into my eyes for the first time that evening and smiled. "Happy birthday, Maddie." Leaning over, he had kissed my cheek and then whispered in my ear, "You were right; I should have fought harder for you."

When he had pulled back, I saw truth in his eyes and all at once the fluttering came back into my stomach, making it more difficult for me to breathe. It had been the reassurance that I needed, to know that everything he had said to me that day at the bookstore was genuine. My eyes never left him as he walked away and I had watched with growing anger as Annabelle-Lynn took her position again attached to his arm. As soon as they had been far enough away not to hear them, the girls had begun to swoon excessively and overtly about the kiss.

"Oh my, if he'd kiss my cheek, I'd never wash it again!"

"But he'd never kiss your cheek if he was too busy kissing mine!"

"He won't be kissing either of you so long as he has *her* around!"

All the girls had glared after their retreating backs, sending invisible daggers toward Annabelle-Lynn. I had sighed, secretly knowing what it had been like to *really* kiss Will and remembering all those stolen kisses by the tree. I couldn't stand to be there for another minute, so I had finally excused myself from the group. I hadn't been able to get very far before Mr. Hutchinson came over and grabbed my elbow, ensuring I wouldn't try to run.

"Come, my dear, we must have cake and presents." Before I could protest, he had pulled me along, the group of giggling girls following close behind.

He had led me into the dining hall where a long rectangular cake was displayed in the center. The words "Happy Birthday Madeline Rose" had been scrawled in the most beautiful script. As soon as they had seen it, the girls snickered behind me, obviously not caring if I heard them or not. Mr. Hutchinson had paraded me around the table as someone lit tiny wicked candles around the outside of the cake, careful not to get wax on their precious memorial to a girl they didn't really care about. What I thought was going to be words of celebration from my father, like I remembered from birthdays past, had turned into a well-planned speech by Mr. Hutchinson.

"Madeline, today is a very special day for you and your family. Today you are no longer a little girl and as you come into adulthood, know that with it comes self-respect and responsibility. Madeline Rose, welcome to this new life and all the happiness it will bring." He had kissed the air next to my cheek and it took everything in me not to wipe the invisible kiss away. Everyone had clapped and I was directed to blow out the candles, each in turn and away from the cake.

Numb by this point, I had been pushed into a sitting position on a large cushioned chair in the room adjacent to the dining hall as gift after gift was presented to me by everyone in the room. I had unwrapped each, smiling weakly at the expensive jewelry, garments and handbags that I would never wear or use for any occasion. My parents had stood beside me, taken aback by everything I was receiving, and Mama was nudged several times by the ladies as *their* gifts were being opened, each one trying to outdo the other with their style and lavishness. When there were two more presents left to open, a house slave had come in to tell us that dessert was being served and everyone filed back into the dining hall – everyone except me, Will, and Annabelle-Lynn.

"We couldn't decide on one gift together so we each got you our own," she had smiled brightly at me, playing the role of socialite a little too well for my liking.

"Thank you," I had replied softly.

Opening Will's gift first, I had been speechless. "I hope you like it," he had all but whispered, seeing the awe in my expression.

From the box, I had pulled out a first printing of Lord Byron's *Hebrew Melodies* and smiled up at him, remembering the way he looked at me when he had first read *She Walks in Beauty* to me by the tree, as if it had been written just for me. "I love it, thank you!"

Leaning down close to my ear, he then whispered, "I stole it from my father's collection. You deserve it more than he." That one subtle gesture, stealing from his own father's library, had been enough of a confirmation for me to know where his heart belonged and to know that even with everything he had to endure, he was still willing to find a way to fight for us.

"Open mine, open mine!" Annabelle-Lynn had interrupted our intimate moment.

I had opened the small box and slightly frowned, perplexed by the nature of the gift. "This card entitles the holder to 20% off any one item at the opening of 'Lynn's Boutique'?" I had read aloud, not looking at Annabelle-Lynn but at Will, who had been equally confused by the gift.

"Yes! As soon as we are married, Mr. Hutchinson will graciously hand over the keys to what *used* to be your little bookstore!"

"But my father never signed that contract! I made sure of it!" I had protested, feeling the anger welling up inside me as I realized it was not just Mr. Hutchinson I would be battling, but Annabelle-Lynn as well.

Before Will could say anything to me, his father had come into the room and addressed us all. "You will miss cake and dessert if you don't come along. Madeline, why so glum? This is a day for celebration!" I had watched painfully as father put an arm around both son and soon-to-be daughter-in-law and led them out of the room.

William

16

Now that my story has come full circle, we are back here, at the beginning of summer 1862. Even though my back has healed nicely and there is no visible scarring, inside I am angrier than I was before at my father. To think that he would lower himself to whip his own son into submission just to be right! My mother still has no idea what he has done and he intends to keep it that way and there's not much else I can do about it, lest I want to be whipped again. For an entire month I had woken up in the dead of night from the nightmares of that day, sweat pouring down my back and chest. After he had made a mockery of Maddie and her family for her birthday and after realizing that Annabelle-Lynn had no intention of backing down her advancement on their business, I knew I had to continue to ensure Maddie knew that I still loved her in my heart.

Unfortunately, there isn't much time for rides into town to the bookstore or even walks out to the tree – Father has made sure of that. The crop is beginning to grow stronger, with his commitment to holding onto that extra five acres, working the slaves we have harder instead of wasting money trying to buy more. He has put me in charge of running the plantation for the remainder of the season, claiming he has more important things on his mind, and I know he means forging ahead with plans for the union of the Hutchinsons and Marques as well as the taking over of McCall's Books.

Around our town, there is quiet chatter about the war. The troops have all moved on but the remnants of their presence still remains – there's heaviness in the air that we just can't shake. The grave markers are a constant reminder of what we have all lost in their wake. We have yet to receive another letter informing us when we can expect Gracie to come home, since we all assume the worst of the war is over.

It is a perfect June day outside and my mother has taken it upon herself to open every window in the house, including mine. The warm breeze gently blows papers across my desk and one falls to the floor. I pick it up but choose to keep it in my hand instead of replacing it back on the desk to be blown around again. I notice it's not from my sister, like all the others that are there, as I turn it over in my hand to examine the paper used. The handwriting of my name doesn't match my sister's either and I quickly open it to see who it is from – the name at the bottom simply written as "Rose."

It is much longer than Gracie's usual letters and the first thought to run through my mind is that she has been injured and another nurse has had to pen the letter instead. As I begin to read it more word for word, my breath catches in my throat and my heart starts racing as I realize who this "Rose" girl really is. It's an apology letter from Maddie, complete with references to Shakespeare's best-loved tragedy *Romeo and Juliet*. I can't stop smiling at the irony behind her words – two star-crossed lovers destined for death because their families despise each other.

Wondering how she had gotten the letter to me without anyone in the house seeing her, I carry it to my parents' room down the hall to find my mother and ask her. I find her sitting in a chair, perusing through a box of what looks like letters, tears in her eyes yet refusing to drop. She motions for me to join her and I move an arm chair to sit next to her. As she passes me the box, I slowly fan through it, page by page, taking note that each is a letter from my sister, beginning with the very first letter she had ever written as a young girl and ending with the last letter they had received from the frontlines.

"I'm so sorry I couldn't keep her here," she sobs, bringing my attention away from the letters and back onto her. My initial reason for being there is lost when I see the sorrow in her eyes and hear the shakiness in her voice.

"You had no way of knowing any of this was going to happen," I try to soothe, although my bitterness for my father's refusal to send for Gracie is coming to light. "It's not your fault."

"Your father insisted she go north to study because they have better schools. I wanted to keep her closer to home, sending her to Raleigh or Richmond instead. I should have listened to my instincts and told him no!"

"He's an incorrigible man who won't listen to reason, from anyone."

"I know what he's doing to you is wrong," she attempts to deflect.

"Then you know we have to stop him."

"I don't know how you expect to do that, William. He always seems to get what he wants."

I shake my head in response, not wanting my mother to give in to him. Then I remember the letter in my hand. "I need to ask you about a letter I received."

She looks at me puzzled and then hope returns to her eyes. "From your sister?"

"No, but it made its way to my desk and I'd like to know if you happen to know how."

I hand her the letter and she reads every word before handing it back to me. "I... er... I may have seen it before..." She looks away and I notice her avoidance of my eyes.

"Mother? Please, if you know anything about this, tell me." I hope if Maddie had hand-delivered it, no one had seen her.

"Annabelle-Lynn gave it to me the other day when she was here for tea. She said she found it lying on the counter in the bookstore when she had gone in. It was addressed to you and she said it was the final contract for the store."

I sigh heavily when I realize Annabelle-Lynn is behind this and again, the anger rises inside me. "As you can see it's not a contract from Mr. McCall, Mother. It's a letter from his daughter, addressed to me and no one else! Annabelle-Lynn had no right to take this letter or even be in that store! If Maddie had wanted me to have it, she would have given it to me herself!"

"What business does that girl have contacting you privately?"

"She has every right to contact me if she chooses! And what right do you have questioning who I have contact with? You are beginning to sound like Father!"

I can tell she is taken aback by my words, as I have never raised my voice to my mother this way. "Are you still in love with her?" she asks pointedly.

"And what if I am? Father and Annabelle-Lynn made a mockery out of her at that birthday disaster and you could do nothing to stop it!"

"Your father planned that as a nice gesture. Why be mad at him for that?"

My mother was, and probably still is, too accepting in regards to my father. She tries so much to be the good wife but I know when she is conflicted in her heart; I can see it in her eyes. She has often said to me that I shouldn't marry if there is no love, since her own marriage was arranged, yet in the years she has been married to the man, her love for him has overshadowed her instincts about certain things. My affection for Maddie and my concern for her family is but one instance.

"Mother, please tell me Annabelle-Lynn did not read the letter before delivering it?"

"If she read it before giving it to me, she made no mention."

"Then she has lied to you as well! The letter had a seal on it and the seal was broken before I had the opportunity to open it! Mother, please, if you love your children, convince Father to call off this union and please tell him that I will be disappointing him once again!"

As I stand up, she places her hand on my arm. "Please don't do whatever you have set your mind to doing, William. Your father just wants what's best for you and your sister."

"And that's why he never sent for her to come home before the war started? That's why he's taking away the business of a man who's done nothing to him? That's why he's forcing a marriage between two people who don't love each other?"

I can see that my words have reached her heart. "What are you going to do?"

I put my hand up to silence her. "I'm going to make this right."

That's all I say; it's all I can say. After reading Maddie's letter, it's clearer to me what I have to do. I no longer have to convince her that I love her; I have to convince her that she is worth fighting for. I have to stop feeling woeful over my broken family and my broken pride. Between my father's insistence on marrying me off for the convenience of uniting assets, Annabelle-Lynn's determination in ruining Maddie's family business, and the whipping I received, I have the most ammunition I need to build a defense against that man – a man I used to respect and revere.

My mother is becoming another casualty in my father's quest for power and I want to take her away from her sorrows, but I can't. She believes that my sister's fate is her fault and he has done nothing to take the blame away from her – to be a real man and take the blame himself. Because she knows how I feel about Maddie, and she knows how determined I am to see justice served, I hear her sigh heavily, conceding to my argument.

As I make my way downstairs, hoping to find Maddie this day and do whatever it may take to prove where my heart remains loyal, my father's voice slices through the quiet house. "Son, may I speak with you?"

I cringe at the thought of what he could be plotting now, but join him in his study anyway. He is sitting there as he always does whenever he's pondering his next move – a snifter of brandy in one hand, a cigar in the other. "I'm going for a ride so make this quick!" My tone is anything but submissive and I don't care how I am perceived.

"Where are you going now? Your mother and I have invited the Marques for tea. We need to begin discussing the details of your wedding."

"Then do it without me! I haven't even asked her to be my wife and I don't intend to! You simply can't dictate the way things ought to be!"

"Boy, you hold your tongue! We plan the wedding ahead of schedule so that when you finally get your head out of your backside, it can be done quickly and smoothly."

"Why such a rush? Is she having a child; because if she is, it's certainly not mine!"

"No, she's not, but your sister is!" He catches me off-guard by his sudden outburst.

"What?! You've heard from her and you didn't tell me?! Did you tell Mother?" Now I'm angrier than I was before I had set out to leave.

"I was going to tell you both, but not until we had discussed the plans for your wedding."

"When did you receive the letter? How long have you been hiding this from us? What did it say?" I demand.

"Last week it came to the post station, but it was marked for almost a month ago. She's... she apparently 'fell in love' with a soldier and is awaiting his return. A *Yankee* soldier to be more specific!" he grumbles out his disgust.

My fists clench and unclench as I hear the news and wonder why she hadn't written to me personally about the situation. "Are you going to send for her now?" I ask cautiously.

"There's no reason to!"

"You are a heartless man!" I scold him viciously. "She's your *daughter*, who is expecting a child, obviously out of wedlock, and you act like you don't care!"

"If she is going to disgrace this family's name by fraternizing with the enemy then she has made her own choice!"

"*You* sent her up there to study! *You* put her into their hands and did nothing to get her home before the war started! *You* gave her the choice to complete her studies while you stood here and forced my hand to make up for the child you couldn't control!" I walk away with more bitterness than my body can physically contain.

~~*

Determined as I am to change the outcome of my father's deceit, I saddle a horse quickly and ride into town. I do not find her in the store, where I hoped she would be. I finally find her where I least expect her to be, kneeling in the cemetery. Not wanting to startle her, I leave my horse tied to the gate and take my time approaching her. A branch snaps under my feet and I see her body stiffen but she makes no effort to turn her head. I quietly kneel next to her and don't make a sound until she acknowledges my presence by glancing over at me, giving me the signal to speak.

"I received your letter," I say quietly to her.

"What letter?"

"This one." I pull it out of my pocket and show her, making sure to turn it over so she can see the broken seal.

She grabs it from my hand and jumps to her feet. "You weren't supposed to find this! How did you get it?"

I also stand but I choose not to tell her the truth. "I've been trying to talk to you at the store but whenever I go, you aren't there. The last time I went to look for you it was on the floor. It had my name on it so I assumed it was okay to take it." She pockets the letter and I shake my head.

"I've already read it. What does it matter to keep it from me now?"

"I wrote it for my eyes only!" she attempts to defend, wiping her eyes with the back of her hand.

"Fine, then keep it if you want to! I was only going to tell you I agree with every word anyway!" I start to walk away, knowing it's useless to talk to her while I'm bitter and she's upset and unyielding.

"Wait!" I hear her soft voice and it stops me but I do not to turn around. I feel her delicate fingers closing around mine and I'm lost in the scent of her perfume, reminding me instantly of the Yellowwood's summer flowers. "I'm sorry," she says after a moment of silence.

I take a deep breath and let it out slowly before I take our joined hands and lift them up to my lips, kissing hers lightly before finally gazing into her eyes. They are puffy and red and her cheeks are tear-stained. I move around to face her, not letting go of her hand, and slip my other hand up to her neck, wiping at any tears still left on her cheek with my thumb. What I said to my mother is more apparent now – I have to make this right.

"I shouldn't have taken the letter without asking first. I'm sorry." Telling her the truth about Annabelle-Lynn would exacerbate the situation, so I choose to let it go and deal with her myself.

"Everything I said in that letter is true. I can't fight them without you."

Groaning in disgust, I gently run my fingers along her cheek. "I can't keep hurting you like this."

"Come here," she says, pulling me over to where I had found her before. "This is all I have left of him," she sobs, leaning over and fingering the wooden cross with Austin's name on it used as a marker. "It's all they'd *let* us have! They never told us what happened to him; never bothered to send his remains home! All the church could muster was to give us this!"

I watch in silence at how fragile she is standing there. Here I am thinking of myself and my own family issues and I don't even see how everything about this war has affected her. She lets go of my hand suddenly, catching me by surprise, brushes off the leaves that have adhered to her dress, and starts to walk away, without saying another word. I have to stop her; I have to find a way to make her see that I will not fail her again.

"Maddie!" I call out to her. She stops and only turns her head back towards me. "Meet me at the tree in an hour." She nods and continues to walk away. I am left standing in the cemetery, staring at not only Austin's grave marker, but hundreds around him, wondering if any of this is worth it anymore.

An hour later finds me leaning up against the large trunk of our Yellowwood, waiting for her arrival. The sweet smell of its white flowers permeates my nostrils as I fight not to let my emotions consume me. Between our childhood experiences here and those that Maddie has shared with me, it truly lives up to its namesake – "Crann grá" or "Tree of Love" – a name given to it by her great grandmother in her native Gaelic language. From what Maddie has told me, this tree was planted by her great grandfather as a wedding present for his beloved when they came here from England.

When I hear her footsteps on the dirt path, I lift my head and catch my breath – she's like an angel floating towards me. Her dark tendrils lay loosely on her shoulders and her eyes gleam whenever in my presence. To me, she is strong enough in her convictions to conquer anything and she gives me hope that together there will be nothing to stand in our way.

"Hi," she whispers as she comes closer.

"Hi," I repeat her whispered salutation.

"I'm sorry about earlier today. It's just that –"

"I know; I know," I cut her off, pulling her closer and into my arms.

"He's gone! And this war took him away!" she sobs into my chest. I pull her in tighter, allowing her to release everything she is feeling.

"This war took a lot of things away," I reply and she looks up at me through her watery eyes.

"What do you mean?"

"My sister's not coming home," I announce. "At all," I add solemnly.

"What? Why? What happened? Is she all right?"

I lean my head against the tree, closing my eyes and not wanting to recall the conversation I had earlier with my father, but Maddie is the only one who seems to understand. "She wrote a letter to my parents and claimed to have fallen in love with a damn *Yankee* soldier! Father won't let her come home!"

"There's something else that's bothering you; I can tell." She knows me too well and I smile weakly.

"I wish I hadn't been such a coward," I reply, lifting my head from the tree and looking down at her.

"You're not a coward, by any sense of the word!" she protests.

"If I had been man enough to join the Army with your brother, I could have done something to protect him!" I explain. "If I had been man enough, I could have stood up to my father and forced him to bring Gracie home at the first sign of war! I wouldn't have allowed him to whip me like a slave, I wouldn't have tolerated Annabelle-Lynn coming between us, and I wouldn't have needed a letter of admittance from you to give me the strength to fight them!"

"You had no way of knowing any of this would happen. I blame our fathers more than anyone for all of this."

"Our fathers?"

She nods and continues with her clarification. "If my father hadn't pushed Austin to take over the bookstore when he was old enough, then he wouldn't have been so eager to join the Army and wouldn't have been murdered by those vicious soldiers. If *your* father had sent for your sister as soon as trouble had begun with the North, maybe she wouldn't have fallen in love with a soldier at all. And if our fathers weren't so blinded by their animosity towards one another, they'd see that we're still here together, at the very place they forbade us to be!"

Her rationalization is so simple yet it is only a fraction of the complications and circumstances we are forced to endure. I sigh again and she gently leans up and brushes her fingers on my cheek, causing my eyes to close at her touch. It is then that I realize there is no greater gift in this world than the heart of another. If my sister has disgraced my family by falling in love with a Union soldier than I too have become a disgrace because of my love for Maddie. In that one moment, I know I have to prove not only to myself but to her, that I will no longer be weak or a coward. I have to show her that her strength is what keeps me going.

Taking her hand, I silently lead her along the dirt path until it forks towards my parents' house. A slight tug causes me to stop walking. When I gaze back at her, I simply nod my head to reassure her that everything will be okay. Upon reaching the back of the house, I lead her up the small staircase to the second floor, keeping a close watch for prying eyes or anyone who would dare to speak about her being there with me. When we are safely in my room, I shut and lock the door, then quickly close the distance between us with a fierce kiss, which she returns fully. Nothing else matters to me anymore except being there in that moment with her.

My hands slowly trail down her arms and sides and she doesn't realize I have moved us across the room until her legs are stopped by the side of the bed. Gently taking hold of her hips, I lift her easily up and onto the bed, moving her up until she is lying on the down-feathered pillows. I lean back just enough to glimpse the angel that has graced me with her presence and all I see is love radiating from her eyes. Leaning over her, I kiss her softly once, twice, three times, and then pull back again until she opens her eyes and is looking directly at me.

"You asked me in your letter to prove to you that I love you. *You* are the last woman who will be with me here in this bed. No one else will occupy it, no one will share it, no one will be loved in it, but you." Her nod is her only reply before she leans up and seals both of our fates with a kiss.

Madeline

17

Our society is created by the hard-working men who for generations have seen the fruits of their labors flourish. As a woman in this society, I have my place and my abilities to run a business such as our bookstore are quickly overlooked and frowned upon. This is reason enough to fight to keep our bookstore in our family since it appears I am the only one who remains strong in my convictions. It is becoming more difficult to combat the advances of Mr. Hutchinson and Miss Annabelle-Lynn Marques but I give it my all. What makes it even worse is the fact that my father has all but given up his claim to the store and Mr. Hutchinson is hoping a large amount of money will ensure a signed contract. What he fails to see is the woman that stands behind her father ready to run the business without being in his shadow anymore.

He also fails to realize how our whole town has now been emotionally struck by the war. Several more marked and empty grave sites have been added to Austin's in the corner of the cemetery and several more businesses have closed due in part because there are no men to run them, including the smith, the printer, and the town accountant. With the printer out of business, we are now isolated from the rest of the world, not knowing what is going on with the war until we receive letters through the Postal Service. What began as a campaign to fight for our rights has now become a campaign to bring our sons and brothers home. It is now a plea to make sure no more grave markers are erected in our small cemetery.

The last news we receive has come from other southern cities telling us that New Orleans and Savannah have fallen. Sherman, a man worthy of Northern recognition, has begun to march from there to meet up with Grant to the north in Virginia, squeezing the Confederate Army in between. A part of me feels for his men – boys no older than me, all marching on foot northward, some meeting the same fate as my brother. It is a senseless way for innocent people to die and if the government would just let us live our own way instead of forcing us to conform to the changes of industrial expansion, none of this would be happening.

Mr. Hutchinson has not ceased his campaign to rid the town of our bookstore, and it bewilders me that he's not more concerned about his own daughter's fate while she is directly in the line of fire. Under the laws of our town, Mr. Hutchinson cannot legally purchase our business unless we claim monetary hardship and ask the bank for assistance. Once the bank forecloses on the business, then Mr. Hutchinson would have the *privilege* to purchase it outright. Since we only asked Will to financially help us through the winter months, we are now able to hold our own – the money he provided us is enough to pay for the shipment of some of the less popular titles to Frankfurt. Recently, I have begun to learn how to promote our business better, where we focus our attention on the ladies of the town who would be more willing to spend their money on our books. I have also created space for a small "used books" section where, for a slight discount, townsfolk can purchase read books, slightly worn. They can also exchange pre-read books they no longer want for ones of equal value.

My father fought me on the idea at first but does not care enough now to argue. He hardly comes into the store at all, except to balance the accounting or to place an order for shipment, and refuses to speak to me while he is there, still upset with my insistence in keeping the store going. I attend to customers, sales and now making the store more pleasing to the eye. Mama agrees with Daddy and says not to bother because by Christmas the store will be Mr. Hutchinson's but I don't care for her despondency. If we can make enough money over the summer and fall, we can close the store for winter and not have to rely on someone else to see us through again.

I only get to see Will once a week but it's enough for me. He promises every time to do whatever it takes to fight his father more than before and this time I believe him. I don't know if in the future I'll be with him beyond our clandestine meetings but for now I know his feelings for me are stronger than any feelings his parents would like him to have for Annabelle-Lynn. Last week he told me he loved me again and this time I did not slap him for it. Each time we leave the tree or his room, it becomes more difficult to walk away when it's time to say goodbye.

As my mind flashes from scene to scene of the times I have spent with him, the times he has given his heart to me unconditionally, I am easily distracted away from the reason I am in the bookstore. The bells above the door signal the entrance of a new customer and I quickly move out from around a bookcase, shaken from my amorous thoughts. I am not prepared for who I see standing in the doorway and it takes me a moment to compose myself. Bradley's hair is longer, his features a bit older and worn, but it is definitely the same man that I left without care about a month and a half ago.

"I didn't think I'd see you again, but I thought I'd give this place a try." He definitely still has the same smile and it doesn't have the same effect on me as it had when I first met him.

"It's my store; of course I'd be here." I find my voice but in my own ears I don't recognize it. It seems older, more mature, less of the infatuated girl I had been.

"So you waited for me after all!" His smile becomes a smirk and his voice becomes that of a very smug and shallow man. I scoff at his new attitude.

"I don't think I was clear when I said goodbye. I meant forever, not temporarily." Now I can hear my own voice growing stronger, angrier, and more authoritative.

"So you're with someone then," he states more than questions.

I can't and I won't explain myself to him. It's not his business what happens between me and anyone else. Instead, I change the subject. "Why are you here? Is your troop passing through again?"

"I had permission to leave. I told my commanding officer I needed to return to the woman who was having my child here in this town."

"So you lied."

"It was the only way I could come back to you." He goes to grab for my arm but I pull back, not willing to allow him to touch me. "Come, come, now Madeline. I left the Army to be with you. You can't tell me you're not happy to see me."

I can't breathe. My throat feels like it is closing up, but I have to speak and tell him to leave me alone. Just his presence in my store makes me infuriated and knowing that he had lied to his officer to get here also means he's capable of lying to me about how he feels. Everything about this man reminds me of what I've lost from the war, especially as he stands in front of me in full blue uniform. He's not just a soldier; he's a *Yankee* soldier!

"You have to leave *now*! You can't be seen here, ever!"

"I left my troop and my comrades to come back to you. I thought you'd be grateful."

That is it for me. "Grateful?! Why would I be grateful? Your *comrades* and others like your troop killed my brother! They also deliberately snatched women from their homes, forcing them to be their wives! I know what has happened; I've read all about it!"

"Where did you hear that nonsense from? We've never done anything like that!" he counters.

"*Your* troop may not have, but others have! I've heard story after story of Southern women, respectable ladies, educated women, being charmed by Northern soldiers like you!" The only story I have to use as my argument is the one Will had told me of his sister.

"Now that's not fair! You can't use the idle talk you've heard to distrust me!"

"It's not just the stories, Bradley! My brother died fighting *your* comrades and you can't just ignore that fact like it never happened!"

"I'm not trying to ignore it and I'm sorry for you loss, really I am, but when this war is over and our country is put back to normal, you'll see things in a different and better light."

"Are you mad?! My brother is dead and we don't even have his remains to give him a proper burial! Our lives have been tainted forever and there's no bringing him back! When this war finally ends, whoever wins or loses, we've already lost! And every family in this town who has an empty grave marker in the cemetery will have lost as well!"

I want my eyes to tear, but I have none to cry anymore. I spent every day for a month straight crying at the grave marker and now there is nothing left. Bradley just wants the war to be over; he doesn't care about me or the fact that my brother and so many others are dead. I want him to leave before I am forced to go and get the authorities to have him arrested.

The bells on the door sound again, distracting me from exasperated thoughts. I look up at who is coming in the door and my heart nearly thumps out of my chest. Miss Annabelle-Lynn Marques comes bouncing into the store, waving a piece of paper above her head. All at once my mind races with the fear that it is a contract for the store, signed by my father in my absence but she suddenly stops and stares at Bradley, noticing him for the first time. The smirk that forms on her face makes me believe truthfully that she is up to something and I'm afraid to find out what it is.

"Soldier, you're new here." He nods his answer. "You're

staying in town?"

"I suppose if Madeline doesn't want me to stay, I have no other reason to." He is trying to guilt me into keeping him around, but there's no reason for him to be here and the fact that he lied to his commanding officer just to be here with me makes me want him to leave even more.

"Oh, you must stay and be Madeline's escort to my wedding!"

"Wedding?!" I scream out loud, unnerved by the thought.

How can this be? Will promised! He promised he'd fight his father for me, for us! He promised he loved me and no one else! Why would he throw his life away marrying her when he doesn't love her?

"Yes, wedding! Mr. Hutchinson has been so gracious to me over the last few months it would be rude not to marry his son. Besides, once the marriage contract is signed, William will have no choice but to agree to our plans to convert this store. He's thwarted me long enough!" she growls viciously.

"What are you converting it to?" Bradley questions her, not understanding the extent of the situation.

"It will be turned into a European clothing store since people obviously buy more clothes than books! And with the war going on, we have to make money the most efficient way. You understand I'm sure. Besides, with everyone preparing for winter soon, warmer clothes will be in high demand!"

"Does she have a say in what you do with this store?" Bradley is trying to defend me and that makes me even more upset with him, since I'm perfectly capable of defending myself.

"William's father owns half this store. It's only natural that he'd want a better investment into its future after his son marries me. *She* has no say in the matter and her father would be foolish not to take the monetary offer Mr. Hutchinson plans on giving him. Here, this is for you; it would also be rude of *you* not to come to our special day!" She thrusts the paper towards my face and I reluctantly take it from her. "The ceremony is going to be a private affair but you are invited to the reception ball!"

She leaves the bookstore with a jaunt in her step and a slam of the door. I am left standing there, confused as to why Will would agree to marry her and I almost forget Bradley is standing there until I bump into him. Instead of trying to answer the myriad of questions I know are running through his mind, I look down at the paper in my hand. Squaring my shoulders, I stay strong long enough to make the decision to appear at the reception. It is time to put an end to Annabelle-Lynn and Mr. Hutchinson once and for all.

Going behind the counter and locking the money drawer, I address him firmly and without reservation. "Bradley, I'm sorry, but I have to go. There is someone I have to see."

I leave him standing in my bookstore, aghast at the confrontation that has just occurred. I head straight for Sally's Saloon, a place I know I will find the person I am looking for. With talk in town easily flowing through the streets about the war, it has become difficult to ignore the gossip, even about Miss Annabelle-Lynn Marques. The someone I have to meet is right where I knew he would be, sitting at the bar, sipping a dark brown liquor. It is time to show Miss Annabelle-Lynn that I am not going to give up my store, my pride, or my love so easily.

~~*

The time for me to put my plan into action comes on a beautifully warm, mid-summer afternoon. I have not been able to speak to Will to find out what had happened but he would see me soon enough and even he will be caught by surprise when he sees who I have decided to bring as my escort. I had wanted to wear black, but Mama insisted that I wear pale green to bring out the color of my eyes, and even gave me one of the dresses from her own collection, saying she would never wear it again.

My father steps into the vanity room as Mama finishes the last touches on my hair. "You look beautiful. I remember the first time I saw your mother wearing that dress." My mother visibly blushes.

I look up at him and smile. It's the first time I've seen him smile in months. "Thank you."

"You can change your mind if you want to. It doesn't have to always be us bowing to their demands."

"I have to go. I need to be there to show him that I am not giving up our store without a fight," I answer him with determination in my voice.

"We should just let him have all of it. It's too much to keep going on our own."

"I'm not giving up on it!" I shout. "Austin wouldn't want us to give up on it!"

He grumbles something about Austin being dead and storms out of the room. I hate what he's been reduced to since we learned of Austin's death, but that is no excuse to give up on everything. And now that Will has left me with no explanation and no ally I have to fight even more on my own to keep our store from falling into *their* hands. A knock at the door disrupts the determination in my head and Mama looks at me questioningly – I had forgotten to tell her about my escort to the reception.

He is standing in the foyer dressed in a full suit, complete with a pale green flower at the breast of the jacket. The smirk he wears on his face is returned once I catch his eye and the look on their faces today will be priceless! My mother looks at me skeptically and clears her throat, disengaging our stare.

"Mama, this is Rex Parker, my escort to the reception."

My mother stretches out her hand to shake his and he brings it to his lips. "It is a pleasure to meet you. My father speaks highly of your family." She looks at me quizzically and I shrug my shoulders, not sure what to say.

Noticing my uneasiness with the silence that follows, Rex comes over, tucks my arm under his, and says, "We should get going. We don't want to be late. I have a carriage outside waiting for us."

"Carriage?" I am stunned by the gesture, not sure if it is really necessary. I thought for sure we'd be walking there today.

"Yes. I didn't want you ruining your shoes walking across town. My sister *has* taught me a few things about women-folk. Shall we?"

I have no reply for him. Instead, my mind questions why Annabelle-Lynn would insist on marrying Will when there are so many other eligible men in town. Although Rex seems like a gentleman, he is a mere substitution and a ploy for the *real* reason I am going to the reception ball at all. As he helps me up into the carriage and follows suit next to me, I sigh heavily, knowing this afternoon will be one of the many challenges I am going to face if I am to win this battle with Mr. Hutchinson and Miss Marques.

My thoughts seem far away from Rex but I subconsciously lean into him as we approach the house, the anticipation of seeing the look on their faces leaving me apprehensive and anxious at the same time. His body is comfortable but I know my heart truly belongs to the man who lives in the plantation house and I know he has to have an explanation as to why he chose to marry her, he just has to. As we get closer and even after the carriage stops, my heart beats faster and my breath becomes shallower. Every time I come to this house something goes wrong and today I feel is going to be no exception.

Rex exits the carriage first, then assists me in stepping out before telling the carriage driver that we are to be picked up later this evening at the same location. I look up and the mansion appears ten times larger than it ever has before. He smiles down at me, reassuring me that my plan will work and that he understands. Taking a deep breath, I put one foot in front of the other until we are standing in the foyer of the house, waiting for a house slave to take our invitation cards and bring us into the dining hall.

"I'll follow your lead," Rex replies close to my ear as he notices my unease. I nod in response and try to act less fearful of what is to come as we are escorted down the hall.

I glance around the room, as if I am looking for someone I know, and the married couple that we both came to see catches my eye. I have never seen Will look as handsome as he does in that moment. All thoughts of my plan, Rex, even Annabelle-Lynn are lost as he chooses that exact moment to glance my way. I am rooted in my place, unable to move, unable to run, unable to speak and I need to find my footing and my tongue quickly because both of them are approaching too fast from across the room. I am relieved when they are snared by a few more congratulators and I have the opportunity to compose myself and find my voice again. I know in my heart he has only married her for appearances only but I need to speak to him privately in order to be sure of the truth.

Rex tightens his grip around my waist, finally aware of the couple in the center of the room and I can feel his anger in his arm. "Don't they look happy?" he mocks.

"Don't make a scene. Remember, follow my lead," I remind him.

He growls and mumbles a response but before I can comment further, both Will and Annabelle-Lynn approach. She is the first to speak and I take notice to the fact that she ignores Rex standing next to me. "Madeline, dear, it's so nice that you could make it! You look radiant!"

"Thank you. This gown was made for my mother by her aunt. I thought it was very fitting for this event. You remember Dr. Parker's son, Rex?"

When she finally acknowledges the man standing next to me with his arm around my waist, she visibly pales and I know my plan has already begun. "What happened to that soldier-boy I saw you with at the bookstore?"

I can see the type of game she wants to play and I continue to hand her the same cards she deals. "He only came in that day as his troop was passing through. He's long gone by now. Besides, Rex was invited as an extension of his father, who must have been invited by Mr. Hutchinson. When he asked me to accompany him, I just couldn't say no."

Will simply nods, but his apparent disapproval of my choice of escort does not go unnoticed by my watchful eye. Annabelle-Lynn, on the other hand, makes it very clear from her facial expression that she is not happy in the slightest and it confirms for me that the gossip I had been hearing in town is very true. With my chin poised and my mannerism as proper as I can stand to be, I glance over at Rex next to me.

"Rex, can you please find us some champagne? I'm afraid the dryness in the room has made my throat a bit hoarse." Rex lets go of my waist and brushes past the couple. Annabelle-Lynn fixes me with a withering stare, turns on her heels, and follows Rex, no doubt to get an explanation from him as to why he had the audacity to choose me to accompany him today.

I glance up at Will, who has been left standing in front of me. "Is there somewhere we can talk?"

Nodding, he leads the way out onto the veranda, where the doors have been opened to let the summer breeze through the house. I can see that his composure is beginning to wane but I have to keep to my plan and not fall victim to his anger about the situation. At one of our meetings by the tree once, he had mentioned that after hearing about his sister falling in love with a Northern soldier, he actually would have preferred Rex be there with her, even after their argument at the saloon. Seeing him with me today most likely does not sit well with him but I cannot be concerned with his disappointments.

"You married her anyway." My voice is not my own as a glance up at him, catching the regret in his eyes. I want, I need an explanation but the anger inside me is on the verge of explosion.

"I didn't want to."

I shake my head, not willing to hear his excuses. Right now, I want reasons. "You promised, Will. You promised me you would fight your father and yet, here you are, *married* to the woman you swore you did not love," I seethe, trying to keep my voice low so guests do not suspect.

"I still do not love her and I had no choice! Maddie, you know how I feel about you."

"I gave you my heart, my body, and my soul and you took it all for granted! I loved you, Will, but being in your father's good graces was more important to you!"

"He found the letters!" he blurts out, a little too loudly for my liking and I look around us to see several guests glancing our way.

Quickly, I pull him around the corner of the veranda, to where no one is standing and address him again. "What letters?"

"The letters you wrote me – he found them! I had them in a box in my desk and he must have found them!"

"What did he say to you, Will?" I can hear my heart beating hard in my ears and I have to strain them to hear what he says next.

"He said he'd make me a deal. He didn't want to lose both of his children to their wandering hearts. He stipulated that if I agree to the marriage he would withdraw from taking your store!"

William

18

She is taken aback when I tell her the truth of my father's attempt at blackmail. "So you thought by saving my store I would forgive the fact that you married her anyway? How could you have let him find my letters? Now he has even more of a reason to keep us apart!"

Before I can answer her Annabelle-Lynn comes out onto the veranda, looping her arms around mine, her smirk towards Maddie unbearably snide. "I'm sorry to pull you away from your conversation but your father wants to make a speech." She takes me away from Maddie and all I can do is mouth the words "I'm sorry" to her, knowing it is not enough.

The dining hall has been redecorated to house two chairs at the far end, like thrones fit for a king and his queen, yet *my* queen stands in the backdrop of everyone else in the room, instead of with me where she belongs. Annabelle-Lynn is the favored queen and I know she is seated next to me because of lies and deceit instead of love and respect. My father stands to my left, waiting for the undivided attention of the room, and holds his glass up in front of him. As he begins his well-prepared speech, I scan the room for Maddie, catching her eye. It takes everything in me not to race towards her and cause a scene, but I have made a promise to my father to obey my place in order to save her business. If that is all I can give her now, then so be it.

"Thank you all for coming on this momentous occasion," he

begins. "I am so proud of my son for taking over the business and making it better than it already was. In this time of uncertainty and war, we have lost a lot, but with this union we hope to gain even more. I'd like to officially raise my glass to introduce the new Mr. and Mrs. Hutchinson – William Jacob and Annabelle-Lynn!"

Applause comes from everywhere as they all raise their glasses in our honor. I glance to my right and she leans over to kiss me, as everyone cheers even louder. I want nothing more than to pull away and run to Maddie but I have to keep to this pomp and circumstance for everyone who is there, including my mother, who knew the truth and did nothing to help me. When I pull back and sigh, Annabelle-Lynn lets out her best giggle and I realize how fake everything is about her, more so than I had before.

"Dance with me?" she whispers.

Standing, I follow as if I am no longer in control of my own body and she takes my hand in hers, leading me to the middle of the room, where everyone has parted to give us space to dance. My mind is blurry, perhaps because of the atmosphere, perhaps because of the weight that grows heavy on my shoulders, but I begin to waltz the way I had learned when I was young. Annabelle-Lynn holds my eyes, making sure we keep up the charade to hide the truth of our lack of affection towards each other. Her smile is not genuine, but reveals she is plotting something that I'm afraid is worse than anything my father could conjure.

"You need to smile, William. People will notice you're not happy."

"I'm not. You and I both know this is all an act to placate my father."

"Yes, but no one else does. Play the part or that little bookstore is history," she threatens and I look at her astounded. I had no idea she even knew about the reason I signed the marriage contract.

I glance around us at all of our guests – people just like us – plantation owners, large company associates such as bankers, publishers, and politicians. I notice ladies and gentlemen all dressed in suits and fine-silk hooped dresses, all watching us without even knowing what had taken place to get here. My mother even fakes a smile as I look her way and I close my eyes, feeling the betrayal all around me.

"You are dancing too stiffly. People will start to notice," Annabelle-Lynn breaks into my thoughts.

"I'm sorry. I can't do this now. I need a drink."

It is more than just thirst that draws me into the parlor room, where I know our stronger liquor is hidden. The way Annabelle-Lynn looks at me is troubling to me – she has this conniving gleam in her eyes that makes her untrustworthy and it scares me to know she could be plotting something at any moment. After pouring myself a snifter of brandy, I turn around and notice several younger gentlemen in the room with me that I seem to have missed before. I have forgotten that at events such as these, it is quite common for young men to disengage themselves from the familial party and form their own in other rooms of the house.

"Compliments to the groom." One smiles politely up at me, raising his glass to me. I'm not sure whether to be angry at them for finding our more expensive lot of liquor or thankful for their company.

"Thank you," I reply without expression, taking the brandy to my lips.

"Your bride is beautiful," he states. It is common knowledge that Annabelle-Lynn is quite attractive but I have no stomach for idle talk at the moment.

"That she is."

"We couldn't help but notice your attention left her for most of your father's speech."

"Running a plantation does take your mind away from certain other duties," I defend quickly.

"It's all right sir, we can keep a secret. You're not in love with your wife. Most of them never are." He nods toward the crowd of people in the other room and I understand I've become one of them.

I gulp down the remainder of my drink and place it on the liquor cabinet, ready to pour myself another. "You want to be inebriated for your wedding night?" He smirks up at me as he reaches for the bottle to pour another drink for himself and his friends.

"I don't want a wedding night," I mumble before taking another long sip.

The thought of consummating the marriage churns my stomach, especially since I've made at least one promise to Maddie that I intend to keep. Annabelle-Lynn may have gotten her wish this day but I will not allow her to come near my room this night. I should be spending my wedding night with the woman I love, not the one I was forced to marry because of a deal made out of blackmail. The wife I did marry comes bouncing into the room just as I polish off my drink and I watch every young gentleman turn their eyes toward her, wishing they were me for just one evening. If it was up to me, I'd let any one of them have her.

"It's time for cake, William!" She beams, blocking any view I may have had of Maddie, who is still pre-occupied with Rex in the other room. I cannot believe she had the audacity to be escorted here with him and it unnerves me to see them together.

Placing the glass hard on the liquor cabinet, I have no time to react before Annabelle-Lynn grabs for my hand. I feel numb to her touch – there's nothing to make me want to follow. Reluctantly I let her lead me back into the dining hall, where a white cake with four tiers sits atop the table. Everyone is standing around it, poised and waiting for us to feed each other from a cake I have no stomach for. To everyone in the room, we are a happy couple, married by the bonds of love, and yet as I stand there in front of Annabelle-Lynn, all I see is the woman who would dare to come between me and my love.

"Now please don't do anything rash, like smash it into my face. You wouldn't want me to ruin my lovely makeup," she whispers as she picks up the knife to cut a piece off the bottom tier. I chuckle at the thought of how ruining her makeup is the only worry she has. What she really should be worried about is how I'm going to ruin her once this affair is over and I can think with a clear head.

As if I have been reciting this moment since birth though, I place my hand over hers as we cut the cake and place a piece on a plate. Each of us takes a forkful and slowly feeds each other. Everyone around us claps and the house slaves begin to cut the cake to be distributed to our guests. We take our seats again as king and queen of the day and immediately my eyes scan the room for Maddie. I watch as her retreating back disappears out of the room with Rex following soon after her. If he touches her, I will not let him live this time and no authority will be able to separate us from our quarrel.

Quickly excusing myself from the festivities and not able to hear Annabelle-Lynn's protests behind me through the pulsing of my blood in my ears, I follow them out to the veranda. Maddie is staring up at the stars; Rex is approaching from behind and places a hand on her shoulder. She brushes him off and I can see that she's been crying. Rex immediately attempts to console her and at that point I have had enough of his presence there in my house.

"Excuse me, is everything all right?"

She glances over at me and shakes her head despite the tears in her eyes. "I'm fine. Go back inside and be with your wife."

Her words cut deep. "Can I speak to you alone?" I make sure she sees the sincerity in my eyes; a small nod her only answer.

As soon as Rex leaves us, I can't stop myself from bombarding her with questions of concern. "What's going on? What's wrong? Are you all right? Did he do something to you?"

"*Rex* has nothing to do with this. In fact, he's been a perfect gentleman all evening. But why, Will? Why did you let your father force your hand when you knew I was already willing to fight him for the store? Did you think I was incapable of it? Did you think giving in to him would hurt less than knowing I will forever be branded as your mistress now?"

"You don't understand," I try to argue.

"Then make me understand! Annabelle-Lynn is your *wife* and I may hold your heart but she still holds the marriage contract that is legal and binding! Emotions be damned!"

"You don't know what it's like to look in the face of the man you've become a disappointment to! You don't know what it's like to not even be a child he can be proud of!"

"Listen to yourself! He held all the cards and you stood by and watched him play his hand right in front of your eyes! So he found my letters, all of them, and used them as his gaming piece to get you to do his bidding. It was never about the store, Will; it was about merging your family with Annabelle-Lynn's! Taking over my store was never going to happen so long as we never allowed the bank to foreclose on the business! It was about using my letters, my deepest emotions for you, to manipulate you to get what he wanted out of the deal – a wedding ceremony between the two families!"

From her lips to my ears and my father's deal is painted in a different light. I allow myself to be fooled by his treachery time and time again and all for the simple reason that he is still my father. As much as I loathe his manipulation and his methodical manner, there is still that underlying respect that he has now taken advantage of. Dropping to my knees and encircling her waist with my arms, I can do nothing more than beg for her forgiveness.

~~*

As the evening comes to a close, my mind is once again flooded with thoughts I can't control. Annabelle-Lynn expects to continue the charade long after the reception has ended and our guests have gone home but I intend to distance myself from her as much as possible. I stealthily walk her to one of the guest rooms upstairs and usher her inside. I dare not bring her into my own room because I don't want her presence tainting my memories of Maddie.

"Why are we here? Shouldn't we be in *your* room, consummating our wedding night?"

"You are just a wife on paper; remember that. And I will not consummate anything that will ultimately be nullified."

"You can't abolish something when you have no power to do so," she smirks, taking my hand in hers. "Your father never signs a contract without first reading the entire document. I'm sorry you neglected to read the part that said he wouldn't back out of his plan before we made it official."

"What plan?"

"To let me have the store once we were married."

"What?!" I am astounded at what I am hearing.

"It looks like your father has a business mind after all! You are such a fool, William, and I am still going to get everything I want, including that store!"

"I won't let him take it away from them; I won't!"

"It's over, William. He's already won. With you taking over the plantation and with my new clothing venture, we could very well be the wealthiest couple in this town!"

"But they can't lose that store! They will have nothing left!"

"You worry too much. I've already drawn up the paperwork to employ the girl in my store. I'll ensure she makes enough money to provide for her parents. Unless she decides to marry Rex, of course. With his father's money I'm sure he'll be more than happy to provide for her."

She can see my composure waning and I can feel myself getting angrier just standing in the room with her. "If he wants her, he can have her!" I growl out.

"I know you better than that, William. You tried everything you could to get out of this marriage, but the minute your father agreed to let go of her precious store, you obliged. You are so weak and I knew it from the moment I asked you whether you would use the whip! You feel for her and *her* kind, but you forget who you are and your place in society! *We* control whether their businesses continue to exist!"

My eyes burn down on hers and I feel the bile rising up inside me. "I will make sure you never get that store, one way or another, I promise you!"

"I don't see how that's going to be possible with your father on my side. This war has woken him up to the possibilities of economic revolution. One man's destruction becomes another man's gain. In this case, your father and I have made a pact to benefit this little town in its time of hardship."

Her eyes gleam brightly as she continues to unfold a plan that obviously she has already discussed with my father. I am nauseous as the truth of their deception comes to light. I had thought that by giving in to my father, he would respect me as his son but after hearing her confession, it is becoming clearer that he didn't care if his children became disappointments, as long as he was able to keep control.

"How is a clothing store going to benefit anyone is this town other than the wealthy?"

"It will benefit more than that insignificant bookstore! It's taking up space – valuable space I need for *my* store!"

"Stop being selfish and take a look around you, Annabelle! Many stores have closed already and that's just in our town. Larger cities like Savannah are being burned and destroyed by Union troops every time they march through. How many soldiers have you already seen come this way? What do you think happens when colored troops march through? Do you think our slaves will care about the duties they have to uphold by law when there are freemen out there fighting for their own civil liberties?"

"Can we please stop talking about this war? This is our

wedding night and there are other things I wish to be doing." Her smirk is insufferable and I wish she wasn't as blind as my father about the *real* ramifications of the war – the empty grave markers, the boarded up shops and businesses, slaves running away, innocent people losing their lives and their loved ones.

"This war is everything; it's everywhere! You can't possibly be able to close your eyes and ignore it! Those people out there are losing everything they have and all you do is stand there making pacts with men who want to destroy their lives even further!"

"I'm building a new lifestyle for us and our future!"

"At what cost, though? If I lose the plantation, I lose everything! If this town goes out of business, what good is a clothing store without the people to buy the clothes?"

Her smirk creeps across her face again, this time from ear to ear, and it is beginning to terrify me. "I already discussed that with your father as well. I plan to make sure the clothes are sold to other cities."

"And how will you ship it there?" I challenge.

"Manual labor," she states matter-of-factly.

"My father won't buy more slaves for you."

"I wasn't referring to slaves, William. I plan on employing those less fortunate than us, namely the townsfolk."

"Are you mad?!" I jump back and away from her, as if being too close to her would infect me with some unseen disease.

"It's a good way to keep them in business and it's an ingenious plan! Business owners who are struggling without their sons will need a better way to survive the winter. I will employ their daughters or wives in my store and we both win! These are desperate times after all!"

"And you think this idea of yours will work? What if there are men in this town who don't want to be bought out by your greed? What if I was to stand in your way?"

"Try and stop me, William! Your father is packing up that

bookstore as we speak and you are locked into this marriage like the good little son that you are!"

"Get out of my sight!" I shout, not caring if anyone hears me from other parts of the house.

"I'm not leaving, William. You should realize that now. Even if you attempt to lock me out of this house on our wedding night, the entire town will be spreading gossip about it by tomorrow and I highly doubt your father would take kindly to a tainted family name."

I leave the guest room with a slam of the door and head straight for the stairs leading to the back of the house. There is no possible way I will be able to sleep in my own room knowing she is across the hallway, plotting her next move against me. Everything I want for my life, for the plantation I was intended to take over, for Maddie and me, is now being destroyed right before my eyes. Ever since her family came to call, Annabelle-Lynn has been calculating my every motion and my father has been the wall standing behind her, holding her up as they both ripped my life out from under me. What they both fail to realize is that I have something even bigger planned, something that will catch them all by surprise. Just as Maddie's great grandfather planted the tree that would eventually bring us together, *my* grandfather planted an estate in my name and I plan on using it to *keep* us together.

After hearing Will confess what his father has done, I know I have to do whatever it takes to win this battle against Mr. Hutchinson. There is no possible way that I can allow such an evil man to take over a business that has been in my family for generations. I am now the only one in my family that is willing to fight – my mother hardly comes out of the house except to get food from the General Store and my father has suffered a collapse and has been confined to bed. I go into the store every day, making sure it stays open, making sure we sell enough books to make a profit, and I teach myself how to balance our accounting. The summer is almost over and I want to make sure we won't need any assistance to get us through the winter this time, or Mr. Hutchinson will surely make my father a deal.

At times I feel like I am one of our soldiers, a mere boy in the face of political opposition. If Mr. Hutchinson and Miss Annabelle-Lynn are the Union, then I most certainly am the Confederacy, wanting nothing more than to hold onto my family's fortune and namesake while they try to rip it out from under me. The only reprieve I get is that the gossip continues to sour around her in town. Some say she has had relations with the master of the plantation in order to better her chances of providing him with an heir, since Will has made a mockery of his father's plantation life; others say that she has been seen with Dr. Parker's son, Rex, which I have more reason to believe is the truth. After watching Rex's display of aggression at the wedding reception, I do believe that Rex has developed feelings for her.

As the summer wanes, I am overcome with the feeling of loneliness as I open the store one morning. I have not spoken to Will since the day of the reception and I have to trust that he now sees the truth in his father's deception. My father's health is declining rapidly and with the possibility of another collapse looming, it is imperative that I make enough money for our family's survival, to prove that I can win on my own.

My plans are thwarted though when the head of the gossip committee in town waltzes through the front door. "I'm so sorry, Miss Madeline," Mrs. Parker says as she comes over and immediately embraces me into an awkward hug. "How is your mother dealing?"

"She's doing as best as she can under the circumstances," I reply with little emotion.

"You tell her we are here for her if she needs us. Such a shame it is. And he is fairly young too."

My mother still refuses to believe that my father is dying and I have already accepted the feeling of being alone in my sorrow. The one person I may have had to console me through this hasn't come to the store or sent word to me privately or even met me at the tree, which I still go to from time to time. And I know Mrs. Parker has not come into the store to pass along her condolences, but to find out more gossip for her ladies. I refuse to give her any but when the door opens again and Bradley is standing there, Mrs. Parker eyes my suspiciously and leaves with a smile. Just what I need – the ladies in town thinking I've gone to the other side and allowed a *Northerner* to court me.

"I heard about your father. I wanted to give –"

"I don't need your sympathy or your condolences or anything else. He's dying, he's not dead yet, and I would appreciate being left alone." I don't mean to sound harsh, but I'm in no mood for his comfort.

"Are you ever going to let me in?" he practically begs. He'll never understand me so I choose not to give in to his pleas.

"I can't and I have my reasons. Please, just leave."

"But I want to help you get past all this."

I'm not sure whether he means my father's impending death, the war, or the ongoing battle with Mr. Hutchinson, but as I look around and see empty boxes, I know I have to press on by myself. Not long after the marriage, Mr. Hutchinson came into the store and demanded we begin packing up everything, much to my surprise since Will had told me his father would give up if he gave in to the wedding agreement. Obviously, Will had been wrong. My father's health is giving Mr. Hutchinson all the incentive he needs to proceed with his vile takeover.

Bradley grabs my hand and holds it close to his body. I am trapped there and I don't like the feeling. "You still blame me, don't you? You still blame me for your brother and for what is happening to your store and your town! You just can't get past the fact that I'm from the North, that my birth certificate says Pennsylvania instead of Kentucky!"

"That's not it at all!" I protest, trying to wretch my hand free of his grasp. "My father and my brother should both still be alive, this store should still be a thriving bookstore, our town should still be self-sufficient, and I'm still in love with Will!" That last one slips out and I notice him cringe. "I mean... that's not what I meant to say."

"From what I hear he's married now." His smirk unnerves me and makes me nervous.

"How did you...?"

"I've been in this town longer than you think. I've heard so many things it would make your head spiral off your body! Now, all I see here for you is heartache and loss. It's time you changed that and moved on."

"Moved on to what? Where?" I challenge.

"Go north where things are better than they are here. You have nothing left here."

I am rendered speechless. He wants me to leave the life I am working so hard to fight for and move to a place I know nothing about except what they have done to us. And to leave my mother and my dying father before his cold body is even in the ground is heartless and cruel and I won't do it. Leaving this bookstore, this town, this life, means giving in to the North and everything they are trying to do to take away our livelihood and make it better for them.

"I'm sorry, but you're asking me to give up everything and I won't."

"You're just like all the others! You're not willing to give up your own lifestyle but you expect others to give up theirs for you!"

"You sound like you're speaking from experience."

"I am!"

Before I have the opportunity to argue further, the door opens yet again, the bells ringing loudly in my ears, and Will is standing there staring back at me. His body is sagging and drained and his eyes are red and puffy, so I know instantly that he's been upset. It is the first time I am seeing him since the wedding and I can tell that this marriage has taken its toll on him, but something else in his eyes tells me it's more than just she who has made him this way. I push Bradley away from me as Will steps deliberately over to me and wraps his arms tightly around me. I feel him sigh against me.

"I can't do this without you," he whispers into my ear.

"Do what?"

"I can't deal with my father and Annabelle and now my sister without you."

I pull back slightly and look into his eyes, seeking the truth in them. "It's been weeks and you've done nothing; why?"

"It was so long but my sister finally sent me a letter."

I know by the look in his eyes the letter does not contain good news. "What happened?"

"She... she lost the baby and needs to come home, but my father refuses to allow her back in the house for disgracing him. Now her *soldier* has abandoned her, she has no one to turn to and I... I didn't know who to go to so I came here, hoping to find you."

Everything that I have been dealing with in my own life seems insignificant in comparison and my arms instinctively snake around his waist, pulling him as close to me as possible. I seem to always forget that along with my own family crises, others in town are suffering far greater than me. Hearing that Will's sister has lost the child growing inside her as well as the solider that aided in its conception, there is so little I can say that will bring him comfort.

"I'm so sorry, Will. I'm here. I'm always here."

I completely forget Bradley is there in the store until I hear him clear his throat behind me. I turn around slightly in Will's arms and I know there is going to be problems. Bradley seems unabashed and stands firmly with his arms crossed over his chest, as if challenging Will's presence there. To my surprise, it is Will who speaks first.

"What is he doing here, Maddie? Has he hurt you? Get out of this store, now! Your kind is not wanted in this town!"

"I was making sure Miss Madeline was okay. After hearing about her father, I came to console her." Bradley is more than willing to combat Will and I know I have to step in.

"Actually, Bradley, you were just leaving. I'm sorry that you had to come all the way out to the bookstore for no reason. As you can see, I'm fine."

Bradley gives me a condescending glare, grabs his soldier's cap from the counter, and storms out of the store. The minute he's gone, I let go of Will completely and back away. I need to know the truth and now that we are alone, the emotions inside me are coming too quickly for me to avoid. My eyes water instantly when I think of all that we have both endured over the past few weeks and I need to know the one thing that has held true is the way he feels in his heart.

"Do you still love me?" I demand.

He takes a step towards me and I don't move. "I've never stopped, not for a second!"

~~*

Sitting under the Yellowwood together again feels so perfect. His arms wrap protectively around me and I feel safe and comfortable. As I lean my head back against his chest, he kisses the top of my head, causing me to sigh. With the sun warm on my face, my eyes close, and I want to stay like this forever, not wanting to think about anything else out there. But the truth of everything seeps through the comfort I feel sitting there and I know we are in danger if we are seen together.

"There has to be another way to fix this. I don't have my father anymore and the bank will foreclose on the store as soon as your father gives them a reason to."

"I can't argue with him anymore. It's like I'm dead to him. He sits in his study with Annabelle for hours and I can't do anything about it. She has every legal right to be in that house."

"Have you tried to contact your sister?"

"I've tried but I have nowhere to send my letters. Her last letter had no return address and I have no idea what state she's been moved to by now. My father dismisses my worry and refuses to send for her, but I feel like he knows where the North is keeping her!"

"What if we looked through your father's letters the same way he looked through mine? There's sure to be a return address on the envelopes right?"

Will sighs heavily. "My mother has their letters in a box in their room, but there are no envelopes with them." I can feel him lean back against the tree behind him.

"What about the Postal Service? Perhaps they know where the letters came from? If we asked them I'm sure they would –"

"There's nothing they can do about it! Besides, whatever letters we try to send in that direction will just be confiscated by the North. There's no point in wasting our time!"

"Are you giving up?" I demand, turning around in his arms to face him properly. I don't mean to sound abrasive but I don't want to hear any more excuses from him.

"What? No! Maddie, it's not as simple as going to the post station and asking where the letters from my sister came from. The last time I had received anything from her, she told me she was in Richmond, Virginia. There's no telling where she is now. And without having a soldier taking care of her, she could very well be lost somewhere and no one would know she's even gone!"

"What if we rode up there ourselves?"

"Maddie, listen to yourself for one minute! Richmond is a long ride away and it could take days to get there! I'm not leaving you alone in this town while men like *Bradley* still creep around the bookstore and I'm certainly not going to leave my father and Annabelle alone to continue with their scheme! You need me here and I'm not going to leave you and I'm not going to ask you to ride with me! With Northern soldiers around every turn, I will not risk your life trying to cross enemy lines!"

"But you need to get your sister back! If they're holding her there, then we need some way to bring her home!"

"Maddie, please, there's nothing I can do but sit and wait for her return! Right now my concern is making sure my father doesn't get a hold of your store. I refuse to let him win on *all* accounts!"

He wraps his arms tightly around me and kisses my forehead, reassuring me that he's now on my side completely. I lean into him again and do not say another word, but allow the feeling of being with him in silence to take over. A light summer breeze rustles the trees around us and I can feel the winds shifting. Off in the distance, the faint rumble of thunder sounds and I know our time together is going to be short-lived.

"What are you going to do about your father then?"

"If I know my father well enough, he's gone to Frankfurt to file a complaint to the governor about your store being an obstruction of war-time profits. He'll personally ask for a letter addressed to the bank to foreclose on your store."

"He wouldn't dare! What are we going to do?"

"I know a thing or two about business. He forgets that he was the one who taught me." Another boom of thunder, this time a bit closer than before, tells us it's time to leave the sanctuary of the tree. "I should get you home before the storm hits," he concludes without telling me further of his plans.

I am reluctant to leave but my biting fear of a thunderstorm in Kentucky makes me nervous to be sitting under a tree or out in the middle of a field when it hits. Grudgingly, I lift myself from his lap and stand up. He stands next to me and takes my hand in his, lacing his fingers perfectly with mine. Another loud boom announces that the storm is getting close and small drops of rain begin to drip from the sky onto us through the trees that are now blowing harder in the wind.

"It's too late. We're going to get soaked getting me home!" I begin to panic.

"Then we can wait out the storm here," he says, pulling me along behind him as he races through the raindrops towards the mansion.

"But what if someone sees us?"

"Remember, my parents have gone to Frankfurt with Annabelle-Lynn, so there's no one in the house but the servants?"

I allow him to lead me towards the house, raindrops continuously falling on my head and shoulders. Before we can reach the back stairs though, the skies open up and it begins to pour, soaking us both through our clothes. Laughing at our own misfortune, he chooses to pull me into the stables to attempt to get out of the rain for a short while. The entire shed is lit up around us as lightning streaks across the sky and thunder vibrates the walls. Not wanting to face the storm, I jump towards him, his arms wrapping around me protectively.

"It's all right. The storm will pass soon but we really should get inside and out of these wet clothes before we catch lung fever. I'm sure I can find something for you to change into."

Not able to speak and not wanting him to see how fearful I am of thunderstorms, I allow him to grab my hand once again as we race towards the back stairs of the house. The stairs, the hallway, the rooms, are all familiar to me now and I walk with a slight confidence in my step that wasn't there before. Where before it was as if I was an intruder in the house, I am now more confident as I guide myself to his room.

"Wait here," he instructs me. "I'll get us something to dry off and I'll get you something to change into."

As soon as he leaves the room, my eyes dance around, bringing myself back to a different time when I was less cautious to be there. When my eyes land on the bed I try not to think about anyone else being there with him and I hope that he has been able to keep that one promise to me. As the door opens, I jump slightly, hoping it is him and not a servant, and I am quickly relieved when I see his smile.

"Since she doesn't share this room with me, I had no idea the amount of dresses that woman actually owns. It's no wonder she wants to own a clothing store! This is all I could find that wasn't a ball gown," he rambles as he places a yellow and blue summer dress and a cloth to dry myself with onto his bed.

I glance around the room and realize there's no changing screen and at once my face begins to blush. Another clap of thunder, very close to the house, causes me to jump once again, this time directly into him. When I look up into his eyes, I am lost in them, and it is in that moment that I can truly feel the love between us. He leans his head down to kiss me, just as another streak of lightning lights up the room and I press myself closer to him. His hands slowly move up my wet arms and cup my cheeks to deepen the kiss.

When he pulls back, I open my eyes and smile. "We should get out of these wet clothes," I hear myself say but my voice sounds deeper, more seductive, than I intend it to sound.

"Yes, we should."

I keep my eyes directly on him as I allow him to take the clinging pieces off. Shivering as the cold of the room hits my skin, I know bumps are already beginning to form, making the hair on my arms stand on end. I hear the clothes thud to the floor but still I keep my eyes directly on his. He breaks my stare though when he reaches for the towel and begins to dry my damp skin, from my feet up to my head, leaving tiny kisses in its wake. I've never known a man to be so gentle with a woman and it makes me love him even more.

"Put the sundress on now and I'll get out of these clothes as well," he tells me.

The spell between is broken as I step away from him and over to the bed where the yellow and blue sundress lay. As I am dressing, I hear the same sound of his wet clothes as they fall onto the floor and dare to peek in his direction. In the dim light from the window, his body is shadowed but I can see the curvature of his deeply defined muscles. For a second, I think back to the words of the girls at my birthday party, so long ago it seems, and I have to agree that he is a perfect specimen of a gentleman. I have to stop myself from staring as he dresses, so I busy myself with gathering up my wet clothes.

"Leave them for the servants," he orders and I quickly drop them back down on the floor. When I cast my eyes up at him, he is dressed again in dry clothes and combining our wet clothes into one pile for the house servants. "Are you warm enough?"

I nod my head in reply. He comes over and places his hands first on my arms, then my waist, before picking me up and placing me gently on the bed. When he kisses me this time, everything feels surreal – it is *our* house, *our* bedroom, and he's *my* husband. For as long as I can hold onto this feeling, nothing can take him away from me – that is until we hear the a door slam shut with a loud bang.

William

20

My heart thumps so fast in my chest when I hear the door slam closed and I cast a wary look her way. I'm afraid to find out who has braved the storm to come all the way home from Frankfort. I swiftly let go of Maddie and walk over to the window just to check the stables, but I see no signs of horses or a carriage. My eyes dart back to hers and I can see the worry starting to creep in. In three strides I'm pulling open the door to my room and peering out to see if I can catch a glimpse of anyone and footsteps on the main staircase cause me to shut the door immediately.

"Someone's coming up the stairs."

"What do we do?" she practically screams.

"Shh! I need you to stay here as quiet as can be."

She obliges reluctantly and I move to open the door again. Just as I get to the doorknob, it opens wide and a house servant is standing there, arms full of bed linens. I hear Maddie gasp from behind me but I smile and let out the breath I had been holding in my chest. Stepping out of her way, I allow her to come further into the room.

"So sorry, sir. I din't know anyone's upstairs," she apologizes, her head bowed out of respect, the way they were taught.

"It's fine, Madera. Leave the linens, take these wet clothes, and go. You can come back later to take care of the linens," I reply, my tone more commanding when I speak to *them*.

"Yes, sir."

She exits the room and I close the door gently behind her. Maddie looks even more worried than she had before, but she has nothing to fear. Our house servants have been specifically warned not to say a word to anyone. My father may use the whip to scold them, but all I have to do is threaten to go to him and they stay quiet.

"They won't say anything," I try to reassure her.

"I think I need to leave anyway. It's not safe for me to be here at all."

My eyes dart briefly to the window and not to my surprise it hasn't stopped raining at all. The sky is still gray and is being lit up every few seconds by bursts of lightning, followed by loud claps of thunder. It will be nearly impossible to get her home without both of us being soaked again and running the risk of being struck by lightning.

An exceptionally loud clap of thunder rips around us, shaking the walls of the room, and she squeaks out her surprise, pulling me closer to her. I wrap my arms around her as tightly as I can, but still she clings harder to me. As strong as she has been through everything life has thrown at her, including losing her brother and father, I find it humorous she is scared of our Southern storms. Rubbing her back, I reassure her that the storm will pass and that I'm here to protect her. Being preoccupied in each other's arms though, neither of us hears the *front* door open or footsteps on the stairs again until it's too late.

"William, are you home?" my mother calls out.

Maddie glances up at me with so much fear in her eyes and there isn't much I can say to calm her this time. "I'll take care of her," I whisper gently.

I slip out of my room just as my mother reaches the top of the stairs. "William, good, you are home. I was afraid you might have gotten stuck out there in this storm."

"What are you doing home? Weren't you supposed to stay at

Aunt Laura's tonight?"

"We were but your father is still out there making a fuss over the final sale of the bookstore so your wife can have the property. Honestly, there is no reason for a woman to own a store like she wants. Your father is wasting his money and his time and –"

"Are you alone, Mother?" My tone is anything but peaceful.

"No, Annabelle was nice enough to accompany me home so I wouldn't have to endure the ride alone. Come down and join us for some tea."

I hesitate, knowing Maddie is still in my room and I can't leave her to bear a thunderstorm alone. "Why don't you two have tea without me today? I'm not feeling all that well and I was lying down when you came up here."

As a mother always does when she's concerned about her children, she presses the back of her hand to my forehead. "You don't feel warm. Your hair is wet; were you out in the storm?"

"I... I needed to take care of a few things in town and before I knew it, it was pouring," I lie hoping she won't notice. As with every mother though, they have a way of catching you in a lie.

"Is she here, William?" she demands.

"She who?" I try to avoid her eyes.

"Don't be smart with me." She begins to lower her voice so that Annabelle-Lynn doesn't hear from downstairs. "What is she doing here?"

Sighing, I lower my voice as well. "Spending time with the man she loves, Mother! I'm sorry if that doesn't fit into my father's or your plans for me!"

"She needs to leave, William. Although I did not agree with this marriage, she is still your wife and she is waiting downstairs to spend some time with you."

"No, Mother. Not today or any other day. She's my wife on paper only and you know it! I refuse to play into her imaginary world especially when someone else holds my heart!"

"What would you have me do, then?"

"You're the only one who understands me. Please, let me have this one good thing in my life without having to worry about proper etiquette and society showmanship."

I can see in her face that her aggravation is waning. "All right, but we will call you for supper and she better be gone by then." She kisses my cheek gently and walks back downstairs. I breathe a sigh of relief as I walk back into my room.

Maddie is sitting on the bed, her knees pulled up to her chest. She looks like a frail child instead of the resilient woman I have fallen in love with. I sit down next to her and place my hand gently on her knee to get her attention.

"My mother and Annabelle have returned from Frankfurt early."

"What? Your father's not with them?"

"He's still there, working very hard to get the papers to buy your store from the bank."

She tenses and pulls back. "He won't get my store! Just because my father is dead doesn't give him the right to take it away from us!"

"I won't let him take it away, I promise."

I can see the pain in her eyes returning and in that moment I realize it was never about the books themselves, as I thought it had been all along. As much as she knew story plots and characters, it was not the books that mattered more but the store itself. Her father had entrusted her with the knowledge of running a business. She learned how to *sell* the books, not just what was on their pages and that made her a threat to someone like my father, who was now fighting to invest in his daughter-in-law's business.

Sighing, I know what I have to do to combat my father and I hope Maddie will understand. "Listen to me. I'm going to do something that will probably destroy my ties with my family but I have to do it, for you and for that store." She looks at me quizzically and I continue. "When the storm passes, and after I bring you home, I'm going to the bank to invest in your bookstore. This way my father can't possibly force you to sell it to him."

"You can do that?"

"Yes, as an investor in your store, it gives me higher rights to the finances than he would have trying to buy it from the bank. My father's plan is to make Annabelle believe that it's her store but he'll ultimately *own* it and the profits will go directly to him."

"But where will you get the money to invest in it? And why would you spend your money on it?"

I smile at her, knowing the answer will shake my entire family. "My grandfather has set aside money to be entrusted to me alone and I am allowed to do whatever I please with it. I was granted access to it the moment I turned twenty-one. I wouldn't be wasting my money in something that I truly believe in."

"You would do that for me?"

"I owe you so much more than just that, but I can start there."

~~*

"I can't believe you would defy me this way! Of all the insults you could have thrown at me!"

I knew he would be cross with me, but as I listen to my father's bellowing, I take it all in stride. I kept my promise to Maddie and invested in her bookstore, much to his chagrin. When my father told Annabelle-Lynn that it was because of me she wasn't getting the store, she locked herself in the guest room she had been living in and refused to speak to any of us. My father, on the other hand, is choosing to take his anger out on me exclusively, which I knew he would so I am prepared for his wrath.

"You ungrateful little miscreant!" he continues. "After everything I've done for you, you do something like this to me!"

"You can stop scolding me because it's not going to change anything," I interject with calmness in my voice.

"Don't you understand that you've stopped any and all work on the new business venture your wife has started?"

"Actually, I see quite clearly what I've done. I've invested in a business I believe in and I'm sorry if that hurts *your* business venture. Were you ever going to tell Annabelle that she was really working for you?"

"That's beside the point! You've ruined this family yet again! How is that going to look to everyone else?"

"How have I ruined this family? Please educate me. And you of all people should know by now that I've never entertained the idea of what others think of my behavior!"

"Annabelle's store was going to bring in money to help this family prosper during these 'tough times'."

"Tough times? Father, our family has never known what tough times really are! If you put the McCalls out of business, *they* will fall under tough times, regardless of how much you get from Frankfurt for their books! They have lost too much already and all you can think about is ruining them further!"

"Stop defending them as if you were their lawyer!"

"I am invested in their business. It's only right I defend them, especially from you!"

"Get out of my sight, boy! You will not make a mockery of our family anymore! If you choose to fight on *their* side, a fight is what you'll get!"

I expect nothing less from the man so I leave the room quickly and quietly, heading directly up to my room. Locking myself in there has become calming, the next best thing to sitting by the Yellowwood tree. As long as Annabelle-Lynn doesn't choose to come knocking on the door demanding attention, I can stay there undisturbed for hours.

After a few minutes alone though, a light tapping on the door signals I will not be that way for long. It is so low that I can barely hear it until it happens a second time. Opening my bedroom door aggressively, not wanting to be disturbed, I am taken aback and in shock at who is standing there. The only way I truly recognize my sister Gracie is the hazel eyes that were always a shade lighter than mine. The woman that stands before me though is not the sister I remember – her clothes are in rags, her hair matted and tussled, her face dirty and sallow.

As soon as I guide her into the room and shut the door, she collapses into my arms, sobbing, her tears staining my shirt. I instinctively wrap my arms around her and try to soothe her. "Shh, it's okay. You're safe here."

She clings to my arms, not willing herself to let go. She is so frail and small in my arms, even if she happens to be older by three years. I've never seen my sister this way and I wish she was able to articulate what has happened but she has been rendered mute. From her past letters, there was no indication of how she would get back to us, so by her being here with me, it puzzles me even more.

"Do Mother and Father know you're here?" She shakes her head in reply. "We should let them know you're safe." I move to guide her gently away from me but she clings to me even harder and shakes her head profusely. "Why not?"

Tears form in her eyes. "Let me stay here, please," she begs, her voice raspy at best.

I can see the pain in her eyes and I agree to keep her away from the prying eyes of anyone. "What happened to you?" She remains quiet but I need answers now. "Gracie, please tell me."

It takes her a few moments to speak but she finally does find her voice. "When I found out some troops were being sent through Kentucky, I tried to go with them. They… they wouldn't let me go, said I was needed more up there at the tents." She licks her dry lips before continuing. "They eventually put me on a train."

I've never seen my sister so broken in all my life. She leans into my shoulder and for several minutes, I rock her until I feel her body relax. I look down and she has fallen asleep. Shifting her up into my arms, I place her into a more comfortable position on the bed, and let her sleep as long as her body will allow her to.

Watching her sleep, I am torn between telling our parents she is here and keeping silent in order to find out more information from her. I can feel there's so much more she hasn't told me and I'm afraid that if I involve our parents, she will not speak a word of it. Since all communication to us has been cut off for weeks now and every railroad has been blocked by the North, I need to know how she managed to travel by herself from Virginia to Kentucky. Unless she had a horse or carriage, it would have taken her months just to walk from there to here on her own.

She is only asleep for no more than ten minutes before she sits up abruptly, her arms clutching her stomach and her neck and brow full of sweat. I move to sit next to her but she jerks back against the pillows, not wanting me to come near her. Sighing heavily, I know I need to get answers to all the questions circling around in my head.

"Did they hurt you?" I inquire rather impatiently.

She shakes her head slowly. "I pretended to still have the baby growing inside me so that I could get home," she whispers.

I remembered one of her letters to me and finally piece everything together. That bastard of a Yankee left her before she lost the baby and I will hunt him down for sure! Still I press on for answers, trying to get all the information I need from her.

"What happened to the soldier?"

Before she can answer, we both hear the footsteps on the stairs. There is no mistaking that they slow right when they get to my door. She looks petrified and slumps further into the pillows on my bed, curling her body into a ball. Reluctantly I step over to the door just as it opens from the other side.

"William, your father has asked me to bring you downstairs to discuss what he believes is an urgent matter. Something about your plans for the plantation harvest." My mother glances from me to my sister and her face blanches. "Gracie? Oh my sweet child, what has happened to you?" She approaches my sister but stops in her tracks when she sees her tense and pull back.

"William, go down and see what your father needs. I will tend to your sister."

I try to protest but she silences me immediately. Sighing, I give my sister one last look and leave the room. When I reach the bottom of the stairs, I am ambushed by our father, grabbing my arm and dragging me into the study. On the desk is the accounting book, turned to a fresh new page, ready to start working on this year's harvest count. He doesn't hesitate to pour himself a drink as his questions bombard me. They unfortunately fall on deaf ears, as all I can think about is Gracie still up in my room with our mother.

"Are you even listening to a word I've said, William?" he interrupts my thoughts.

"What? I'm sorry. I have a headache. Can we just discuss this tomorrow?" My sister's presence in the house is all but consuming my mind.

"William, please, we need to discuss this now. The end of the summer is near and you need to work on preparing for the harvest; you know that! It's bad enough you've ruined my chances of expanding both our businesses; the least you can do is work on the business that's *supposed* to be yours!"

"I'm sorry. I've had a lot on my mind today. Draw up your plan and I'll look over it later; make any changes I deem necessary."

Before he can answer or be cross with me further, I leave the study room and quickly head back up to my bedroom. Neither my mother nor my sister is in the room and my heart begins to race thinking someone will alert my father to her presence in the house. Rushing out of my room in a panic, I nearly collide with my mother, who is making her way down the hallway.

"Where is she?"

"She's fine, William. Nothing a warm bath couldn't fix."

She is smiling so brightly and it is not the reaction I thought she would have upon seeing Gracie again. With my sister quickly shying away from even me, her own brother, I was quite sure my mother would have left the room feeling heartbroken and misunderstood. I grab my mother's arm, none too lightly, and practically shake her.

"You were able to bathe her? Where is she now?"

"She's dressing in one of the guest rooms and then she's leaving."

"Leaving? But she just got back!" I protest loudly.

"Keep your voice down. There's no sense in alarming your father to her presence with the state of mind he's in at the moment."

"Are you going to tell him she's alive and home?"

"No. I told her that right now her best chance of surviving your father's wrath was to go to your aunt's in Frankfurt and you will be taking her tonight, but your father needs time to calm down before you leave with the carriage."

"What scheme have you concocted for us to leave without him knowing?"

"Wait until he has retired for the evening and then you two can leave. I'll go into town in the morning before he wakes, so he thinks I took the carriage."

I curse under my breath and walk back to my room. She's forcing my hand just as much as my father has, but there isn't much I can do. I have to wait until after we eat, without my sister present, before I can properly escort her out of town. My mother is beaming from ear to ear and it's the first time I've seen her happy since this retched war began. Her baby-girl has come home; I just hope we can get her safely to my aunt's house under cover of night.

As much as I didn't want him to keep his promise, I am glad to still have my store. Every day when I unlock the door, I know it's because of him that it still belongs to my family. Unfortunately, since he has now become an investor it means we have to keep our love even more of a secret or others will suspect he had an ulterior motive for the investment. Today though, all thoughts of investments and money and bookkeeping come to a halt when I have an unexpected customer.

"Savannah, what are you doing here?" It's unbelievable how their family cannot leave mine alone for very long. All I did was ask Rex to accompany me to the wedding reception, and then Mrs. Parker came in acting as if she wanted to comfort my mother when my father hadn't even died yet, and now this.

"I heard about your father. I wanted to come in and pay my respects." I know better than to believe her.

"Well, thank you. Is there something I can get you while you're here?"

"Actually, come to think of it, my mother told me about a soldier that was still around these parts. She said you know him."

"Why would she think I know any soldiers?" I lie, hoping she doesn't mean Bradley.

Savannah quickly approaches me and it catches me by surprise at how assertive she is compared to her brother, who is quite the opposite. I am in no mood for confrontation and I have no time for her games, since I promised my mother I would close the store early and help her prepare supper before the sun goes down. Sighing heavily, I intercept her as I walk around the counter and stop her from crossing the threshold of the store.

"I know you know him! Mother said she saw him in here!" she protests and confirms she is speaking about Bradley. When will her mother learn to stop talking about other people when the information is completely exaggerated?

"I really don't know what you're talking about. Besides, any soldiers still lingering about probably don't belong here. It's better if they were gone." I glance at the clock, knowing I only have an hour to clean the floors, organize the storeroom, and count out the money in the drawer before heading home. Savannah is just wasting my time.

"How can you say that? And yes you do!" she argues further. "I need to know where you're hiding him. I need to meet him!"

I can't understand why she would want to meet such a vile man and on principle alone, I stand my ground against her. "I'm not hiding him anywhere and why would you possibly want to meet him?"

She begins to peek around all the bookcases, behind the counter, and even attempts to walk into the storeroom before I stop her. "You can't go back there."

"He's there, isn't he? Please, let me meet him!"

"Do you hear yourself? What did your mother tell you about him that makes him so important to meet?"

"That he was in here when she came to call and send her condolences to your mother. She said he was wearing a blue cap and blue uniform and she assumed he had been calling on you for a while."

My face begins to redden with anger. How dare Mrs. Parker spread such filthy slanders about me! Now that I know Bradley can't be trusted, regardless of how charming he might have been to me at first, I will not allow him anywhere near me, my house, or my store. In fact, he should have left our town a long time ago, when I was firm with him to leave me alone, but apparently he refuses to listen.

"That's absurd!" I shout at her.   "Your mother must be mistaken!"

"No, she saw him! She said he was here, with you, and you *have* to tell me where he is!"

"What's so urgent that you *have* to meet him?"

"I need him to take me north!" she exclaims proudly.

"What?!"

"He's obviously a Northern soldier from the way my mother described him, yes? That means he'll be heading north soon. I need to go with him."

"Why would you want to go north?"

"I've heard the stories! It sounds so wonderful up there and I need to see it for myself, but my father refuses to let me go! He's stifling me and I figured the best way to get away was to find myself a Northerner to take me with him!"

"Have you lost your senses? There's nothing up there worth leaving here for! And I've heard stories too – stories about Northern soldiers leaving Southern women after they've had their way with them to fend for themselves! It's animalistic the way they treat women!"

"It's better than staying in this stiff and boring town!" she quickly spits back. "My father is the only one who cares about this place. My brother even wants to leave because there's nothing here for him. He doesn't want to become a doctor and he certainly isn't going to find a respectable lady to call a wife!"

I'm not sure whether to agree with that statement or be insulted by it. While I have no intention of ever becoming Rex's wife, I will not deny that he is attractively built. Any woman would be proud to be seen on his arm, if he had eyes for them. Whether Savannah knew the truth or not, I'm sure she has heard the gossip around town about her brother's role in Miss Annabelle-Lynn's infidelity. Even William has admitted to me on occasion that he does not trust that she has remained faithful to their vows.

She stiffens and places each hand on either hip, as if rooting herself to the spot she is standing in. Sighing heavily, she glares at me, challenging me to give in to her demands. I know from past meetings with her that she can be easily thwarted if you hold out long enough and that's what I intend to do. Even if I knew where Bradley was staying in town, I wouldn't dream of telling her, regardless of how much she wants to leave.

"You can't hide him forever. Eventually this whole town will know about your love affair and then he'll be forced to leave. When that happens, I'll make sure to introduce myself."

Smiling proudly at her proclamation, she turns on her heels and saunters out of my store. I sigh and look at the clock, realizing I should have closed already and knowing I won't be home before the sun sets. As I get the broom from the storeroom, I wonder if I will have any more obscure interruptions in my day.

~~*

The money from the day's sales has finally been locked away and the floors swept when the bells signal one last customer. I forgot to lock the door before taking care of cleaning up and after Savannah's unexpected visit; I was too flustered and angered to remember to do so. Glancing up from the counter, I am caught off-guard by the woman's appearance – her dress is too formal for every day walking about and does not fit her properly because she keeps pulling up the sleeves as they slide down her shoulders. The shoes on her feet are slightly bigger than they need to be and there is a gap by her heels. I blink twice, thinking her attire is too ill-fitting for her frame.

After everything else today, I am in no mood for any more

unusual customers, so I quickly come around the counter to address her, but she jumps back and away, as if I was to harm her. "I'm sorry, but can I help you?" I ask her as politely as possible.

"Um... well.... I..." she stutters.

"It's okay. Take your time. What can I do for you?"

"My brother...." She has a Southern voice for sure but something about her puzzles me. She's too skittish to be like any of the other sophisticated women in town, and she's not making much sense in her words.

"Your brother? Who is your brother?" Again I try to be calm and soft-spoken, inching my way towards her, but she inches back again. "I'm sorry; I don't mean to frighten you. I'm closing the store for the evening. Why don't we step outside and we can talk there."

She shakes her head profusely and her demeanor worries me. I move to gently touch her arm and she stiffens and sucks in her breath. "He... sent me here."

"Who sent you here?"

Again she shakes her head. "To say goodbye."

Her words are incoherent and don't make a lick of sense. "Do I know you?"

"My brother ... he loves you."

I stare at her blankly for a few seconds, bewildered at what I have just heard and slowly piece her words together. *This* is Grace? *This* is Will's sister he told me so much about; the woman who had endured so much pain and sorrow? He never showed me a picture of her but she looks nothing like I had imagined her to be or how Will had described her. She appears less likely to be a Hutchinson than I am!

"Have to go... we... we leave tonight."

"Leave? But you just got back! I'm sure everyone is so happy you're home!" I exclaim, taking a bold step towards her. I realize too late that it was not the right thing to say or do because she slides back closer to the door and any moment I know she will run.

"He'll be back... don't worry."

This cannot possibly be the sister that Will talked so much about. In his mind, she was so brave and strong, to have dealt with losing a child before its time and falling in love with the wrong side of the war. Standing here staring at her, I see nothing more than an empty shell; a woman who has seen too much of a war she shouldn't have been a part of. I read about this sort of thing from my brother's journal – people so troubled from what they had witnessed that they have no way of conveying what they saw and no way of calming their minds from it.

She barely whispers out, "I... I have to go," and quickly leaves the store.

I race after her just in time to see a man grab her about the waist and cover her mouth so she can't scream. I am immediately stopped in my tracks and almost lose my footing because I had been running so fast to catch up to her. He says something to her that I can't hear and I watch in agony as he lets go of her mouth and pulls a pistol out from his hip, pointing it directly into her side.

"Don't move, Madeline, or she's dead!" he growls and I recognize his voice instantly.

"Let her go, Bradley! You don't want to do this." I try to remain calm for both of us but my legs are beginning to shake and my neck is starting to sweat with fear. One wrong move and he will not hesitate to kill her.

"You don't know what I want! You know nothing about me!"

"What do you want with her then?" I challenge, hoping that if I keep him talking, Will might come to our aid but he holds her tightly about the waist, not letting her go.

"Go back into the store and pretend you saw nothing and no one will get hurt," Bradley demands, pulling her backwards, making her lose her shoes in the process.

I stand my ground though. "Bradley, please, let's discuss this rationally. What could you possibly want with her?"

"It's simple really! Grace here can't keep her mouth shut! This is just payback for what she's done to me!"

"What did she do to you?" As long as I can keep him talking, he won't hurt her.

"You almost cost me everything, you little witch!" he growls into her ear, completely ignoring me.

She is squirming in his arms but he holds her even tighter, willing to stop at nothing to make her pay for whatever she did to him. I've never seen him act this way before and it frightens me how very "Roderick" he has become. Even though he's never left this town when I've told him to, he's never been physically forceful with me, so it surprises me how very much like Poe's character he's become.

Grace speaks out against him and I wish I could do more to help her. "Didn't do anything! Said you... you loved me!"

I attempt to step closer during the diversion, but he glares up at me through piercing eyes and deliberately cocks the hammer of the pistol. I stop moving immediately and glace at her – tears are streaming down her cheeks and she looks even more petrified than when she had entered my store. For a second I forget that he's a soldier and must know exactly where to shoot to deliver the most pain. It's all weaving a giant web in my head and I'm able to piece together everything that I've learned so far about him. With Grace's declaration, I realize that *he* was the soldier that left her!

"Why does she deserve this now after so long?"

"She told them about that baby!" he snarls and I notice in the dim light from the store, he is pointing the pistol directly where the child should have been. "Almost cost me everything! Should have kept your little mouth shut!"

She whimpers in his arms. "You said... we'd be together... the three of us!"

He shoves the pistol into her stomach and again we are at an impasse. "Shut your mouth! I was just supposed to be in that camp for a short while and then we were going to head south to where all the *real* action was! They told us we would be heroes if we got those *Southerners* to come back to the Union but instead of being a hero, I get detained because *she* opens her mouth!"

I'm remembering a part of my brother that wanted to join the Confederate Army for the exact same reason. They told these soldiers, on both sides, they'd be war-heroes if they'd get the other to comply with their demands. No matter who wins or loses this war, everyone has lost because they've been lied to since the beginning – there is no glory and honor and heroes, just death and empty graves.

"You're all the same!" he accuses heatedly, positioning the pistol higher on her side, knowing exactly which organs he will hit if the pistol goes off. "Thinking you can have everything handed to you instead of working for it! *We're* supposed to be the heroes, not you, but then you destroy our chances by telling us you're expecting a child!"

"So this is retribution, then?" I ask him, keeping him focused on me instead of her, wishing that Will would somehow know to come here as the seconds tick by.

"By telling my commanding officer she was expecting *my* child, he detained me there, as I watched my fellow comrades move south to find glory without me!"

"How did you know where to find her then?" This is the only piece of the puzzle that I just can't understand. He's been here for months and she only just got home.

He smiles into the darkness around us, a menacing smirk that scares me more than a Kentucky thunderstorm. "I confiscated one of her brother's letters and knew exactly where she would run home to once I abandoned her. I left that camp as soon as I knew where I needed to be and told my men to let her leave by the railways after giving me a head-start!"

"You don't need to hurt her. She's lost the baby that stole your life away. Didn't you know that? So you can leave in peace and go back home!"

I see him squint at me through the darkness and his hand lowers the pistol, no longer pressing it against her body. I don't know if he knew this piece of information before he left Virginia but upon hearing it now, I can see him process it before he can react and there is a faint glimmer of hope that he'll let her go without hurting her. She must have felt his arm loosen around her and she pushes off of him in order to free herself of his grasp. I want to help her so I scream after her.

"Grace! Run!"

With all her might, she flees into the darkness, her bare feet kicking up dirt and dust. Faster than I can blink, a loud shot rings through my ears, echoing through the still evening air, and for a second I am stunned. As soon as I adjust my eyes, I see Grace lying on the ground only a few short feet away from where we are standing. I feel numb and I am rooted to the place I stand in as he repositions his pistol, aiming it at my heart, and cocks the hammer again. All I can think about is Will as another shot is fired.

William

22

"Maddie?" I call out her name. "Maddie!" I exclaim louder, trying to get her attention.

She opens her eyes and blinks. Shaking her head, she eyes the smoking gun in my hand and peers down at her own body, checking for wounds. Tears are streaming down her cheeks and I step towards her, attempting to hold her steady. She pulls back, fear on her face.

"Your sister," she whispers, glancing over at Gracie.

I follow her stare and look down at the ground. My sister is lying on the ground, in a pool of blood surrounding her body. For a second, I am brought back to the day the stable hands were killed and my body goes into shock. The bile begins to rise before I can clear my head and take control of the situation.

Finally able to kneel down next to my sister's body, I check for any signs that she is still alive, hoping to find anything. Her faint breath is all I need. As quickly as I can, I rip off my sleeves and place one of them over the bleeding wound in her side, keeping the other available in case I need more, applying as much pressure as possible. Even with her shallow breathing, I see her wince as I touch the wound.

"Maddie, go get help!" I scream but she remains still.

"You shot him," she breathes. "Is he...?"

"Maddie, forget him! I need you to get help! She's going to die if we don't help her!" I am not about to lose my sister now, not after just getting her back.

Maddie turns around and races off towards the small clinic building we have in our town. I know I shouldn't move Gracie's body but by the time Maddie finds Doc Parker, it could be too late. Placing one hand carefully under her back and one under her knees, I lift her up and into my arms. She groans in pain and I stop moving, applying more pressure to the wound with the hand that's around her back.

"Will?" Her voice is raspy and I can barely hear her.

"Shh, don't talk. Save your strength. We're going to get you help."

"Let me go," she breathes.

"No! Gracie, please, you have to live. I have to take you to Frankfurt so you can be with Aunt Laura and Uncle Albert!"

She slowly shakes her head. "Let me go, William."

"No!" I scream, pulling her closer to me and putting more pressure on the wound. "Gracie, please, I need you! I need you to stay with me!"

"I... can't. This is... my fault."

"No, don't say that! Please, stop talking and keep your strength!" I order her.

The moments seem to lag and I fear Maddie is taking too long retrieving Doc Parker. I'm worried Gracie will lose too much blood if I don't start moving towards the clinic to meet them there. My heart is racing so fast in my chest as I put one foot in front of the other and I cringe with every step. I hate that I'm hurting her more but I have to keep moving if there's any chance of her surviving.

"Just a bit farther and you'll be okay; I promise," I say more for my benefit than hers.

I glance down against my better judgment. Her breathing is shallower than before and her blood is staining through the shirt sleeve. A few more labored steps and I hear heavy footsteps approaching and I lift my eyes to see my father and Doc Parker on horseback, with Maddie lagging behind them on foot. *Damn her,* my mind screams. *Why is my father here with them? He had no idea Gracie was even in Kentucky and I wanted to keep it that way.*

"William, what's going on?" his voice slices through the evening air as he leaps from his horse and shakes his finger in my face.

"She's been shot; I told you already!" I hear Maddie reply behind him, completely out of breath from running to keep up.

"Did *you* do it, boy?" he accuses, completely ignoring her comment.

"Bradley did it!" Maddie answers for me again and I am unable to speak on my own accord.

He turns around and glares at her. "Who is this Bradley you keep referring to? Where is he now? Stop falsifying information to save my son's reputation here!"

She sighs and rolls her eyes at my father. "Mr. Hutchinson," I hear her start again, her breath slightly more even, "I explained this to you already. Bradley was a Northern soldier who attacked and shot her. Will then shot Bradley to protect her and me."

"Is this true, William?" I find it revolting he has to verify her story with me instead of believing the words of a woman outright.

Ignoring his disbelief, I try desperately to hand Gracie over to him but he refuses to take her. "She's bleeding badly. We need to help her! Father! Take your daughter, please!" I shout at him.

"I don't have a daughter," he says low enough for only me to hear.

"Yes you do and if you don't help her right now, she's going to die!" I exclaim.

"Let me see her, William," Doc Parker says, motioning for me to show him the wound. He surveys it closely and then adds his diagnosis. "The bullet looks like it might have hit her kidney. She's lost a lot of blood, but I may be able to remove the bullet, provided it hasn't hit any other organs."

Gracie groans and winces in pain again and I glance up at my father – a man so set in his convictions, he shows no compassion for his own flesh and blood. Without waiting for an answer from him, I nod my head at Doc Parker, giving him the permission he needs to bring her back to the clinic to perform the surgery. Someone has to care about Gracie.

"William, I would like to speak to you, in private," my father announces, rather business-like, as we watch Doc Parker and Maddie walk away with Gracie.

"Not now. She needs us more," I answer him, pointing towards my sister.

"Doc Parker has her now. She's in good hands. But what in tarnation is she doing back in Kentucky?"

"I don't know. I couldn't get her to talk to me. All I know is that soldier, Bradley, seemed to know her and I killed him before I could find out why!"

"And why is Madeline McCall here? I told you I didn't want you hanging around her anymore!"

"Enough, Father! If it weren't for her trying to find Doc Parker, your daughter would be dead right now! So don't hate her for being here to help me!" I demanded, not wanting to get into another argument. "And what are you doing here? She was just supposed to go find Doc Parker!"

"I was asked to meet with him for drinks after supper, when that girl came racing into the saloon screaming like a banshee, which by the way was extremely rude of her to do."

"Forget about Maddie for one minute and think about Gracie! If Doc Parker can't help her…"

"Doc Parker is good at what he does. But I want you to go home now, to your *wife*, and leave your sister to me."

"No!" I shout defensively.

"William, I'm not asking you, I'm telling you. Go home. Your wife would like some of your time. I will send Madeline home as well. She doesn't need to be here anymore."

"She stays and so do I!"

"I will not let any of this nonsense get pushed around town, especially the part about you being with that wretched McCall girl! Doc Parker knows he must keep this quiet, but by the way Madeline came into the saloon carrying on about Gracie being shot, it's going to be a wonder if the whole damn town won't know something by morning! When Gracie is well enough, she goes back north!"

"She has nothing to go back to! *We* are her family and she needs to stay with us!"

"She goes back north! This discussion is over, William!"

I can't take his insolence anymore and I finally do the unspeakable – as if he was just some man I have had an argument with at a saloon, my arm pulls back, my hand clenches into a fist, and I hit him square across the jaw – before storming off inside the clinic. The minute I enter the building, I am confronted with a pungent purified smell. Coughing, I attempt to fill my lungs with something else but it is too strong and overpowering. Before I am consumed by it, a hand grabs mine and I am pulled into a small room. The air is less sterile here and I can breathe a bit easier. When I adjust my eyes and have a look around, it appears to be an office room.

"I know what happened between Bradley and your sister," Maddie replies, bringing my attention back to her. "They knew each other, Will."

"What does it matter? He's dead and she's barely alive! Why did you get my father?" I accuse angrily, not intending for it to sound so harsh.

"Doc Parker wasn't here and I was told he was at the saloon. Your father was with him. After I interrupted them your father demanded I tell them both what happened!" she explains.

"He wants her to go back north when this is over," I say solemnly.

"Go back?! But she needs to be here with you and her family!

You need to know the truth!"

"I know what happened to her from here letters! She fell in love with a Yankee who left her to lose her baby on her own! Now she's fighting for her life because another damn Yankee decided to put a bullet into her side!" I shout, my anger building up again.

"Will, that Yankee soldier is one and the same! Bradley came here specifically to wait for her! I should have never invited him into my life!"

~~*

Two days after the incident with my sister, we are burying her body and my heart is shattered. We had to tell Mother and she refuses to speak to my father, blaming him for sending her North. Only our family, Doc Parker, and the minister stand in the small town cemetery and only we know the truth. Mother has forbid anyone to speak about it and if anyone asks, Gracie was hurt at a hospital tent in Virginia. Everyone says their farewells, we say our last prayers, and I am left to say goodbye to the person who died while I tried everything I could to save her.

As soon as they are all gone, I drop to my knees and peer into the hole in the ground. "I'm sorry I couldn't protect you!" The weight is so heavy on my body now and I'm having trouble breathing.

Footsteps on the path behind me cause me to turn my head and I see Maddie there, eyes swollen and red. I know she has been feeling so guilty about everything and instantly my eyes begin to water again. She races to my side, drops to her knees and holds my head to her chest as I wrap my arms around her waist. It is quite interesting to note that Annabelle-Lynn didn't bother to console me or shed a tear, but Maddie is right here where I need her to be, crying alongside me.

"It's okay. It'll be okay," she soothes, running her fingers through my hair lightly, almost the way my mother used to when I was growing up.

"I let her die! It's my fault!" I sob into her.

"No, it's not your fault at all!" she counters. "Bradley was the one who shot her and Doc Parker did everything he could to save her! This is anything but your fault!"

"But I couldn't stop him from shooting her first! I saw him there, holding the gun at you, and I didn't even know she was shot!"

"You shot him before he could shoot me. For that I owe you everything!" She pulls my head up with both of her hands and I can see the sincerity in her eyes.

"I should go. My family is waiting for me to go into mourning," I whisper, knowing right here in her arms is where I'd rather stay.

Without saying a word, she gently pushes me back so she can get up and brush off her skirt. Taking my hand, she leads me further into the cemetery and it doesn't take long for me to realize why. The amount of grave markers with empty graves is indescribable and I know now exactly how she feels in this very moment.

"Now we've both lost someone because of *them*," she replies vehemently. I've never heard her talk so bitterly towards the North.

Wrapping my arms around her from behind, I hold her close to me as she leans back against my chest, placing her hands on top of mine. "What did you mean the other day when you said that the Yankee soldier was one and the same?"

"I was able to keep him talking in order to get the truth out of him. She thought it was best to tell one of his commanding officers that she was expecting to keep him there with her. He was planning on leaving her anyway."

It all comes crashing together in my mind and I tighten my grip around her. "Why would he want to come after her the way he did though, hunting her down like a fox?"

"He wanted her to pay for telling his officers."

"I don't understand if someone you love tells you she's expecting a child, why would you be mad at her for telling your superiors?"

"Their 'love story' doesn't appear as happy as she made it out to be in her letters." I gently turn her around in my arms to finish the conversation. "By telling his commanding officers, they demanded he stay behind with her and the child. He was bitter with her for holding him back from glory as he had no intentions of starting a family with her. He also made it clear to me *we* were at fault for the entire war and the North was just trying to force us to rejoin the Union to make everything right with the country again."

"So, he leaves her expecting a child out of wedlock and goes on to fight in a war that he knows nothing about? Was he even around when she lost the baby?" I growl uncontrollably. "I don't even want to know how she managed to get home with all the railroads being held up by the North."

"He said he told his comrades to give him a head-start and then send her home with a free pass along the railways. This war is so out of hand and we've lost so much! It was just supposed to be to keep our economy going so the North didn't put us all out of business. My brother may have disobeyed my father by joining the Confederate Army but he believed that what we were fighting for was just. Now the North wants us to surrender the very livelihood this country was founded upon!"

I can feel the anger rising up in her body and I quickly move to subdue it, holding her closer to me. "There's nothing we can do anymore. We've got to let this country fight its war."

"We can't lose any more!" she argues, pushing away and out of my grasp before I have the chance to react and pull her back.

"We have to try to keep going with our lives," I retort.

"How can I go on? You have a family and a *wife* to go home to!
You were able to bury your sister's body in a grave marked by an
ornate gravestone and overturned soil! I have to go home to a
mother who cries herself to sleep every night at the loss she feels
inside and then come here to see this – a poor excuse for the fallen!"

"You still have me!   Do you hear me?   No matter what you
think, you still have me!" I defend uselessly.

"Divorce your wife and maybe I'd believe you!   Take the
investment you made on my store and turn it into something more
than just bought time with me and maybe I'd believe you!" she
challenges me defensively.

"I can't divorce her," I reply solemnly. When I see her reaction,
I quickly add, "but I'm working on the paperwork to file an
annulment with the court. Once that goes through, I am yours
completely!"

Her anger morphs into sadness and I have to stop her from
falling into despair. Lifting my hands to her cheeks, I bring my lips
down to hers, silencing both her retaliation and her gasp of surprise.
As she gains reassurance, she returns the kiss. Standing at the far
end of the cemetery, we continue to kiss until breathing properly
becomes a problem for both of us. She is gasping for air when we
finally pull away from each other.

"I love you and no matter what other circumstances are in my
life, that will never change," I say sternly, making sure she sees the
truth in my eyes. "Right now though, I have a responsibility to my
family to stay in mourning, at least with my mother."

She nods her head in understanding and slowly untangles her
arms from around me. I kiss her lightly on the lips one last time
and squeeze her hands, letting her know it's going to be all right. It
takes another minute for me to let go of her completely and walk
away. I feel helpless and my head has begun to throb. I hear her
footsteps behind me and just as I turn around, she flings herself into
my arms and buries her head onto my chest.

"I love you too," she whispers and I pull her tighter to me.

Never in all my life have those words felt so good to hear. "Let me walk you home?" I decide against my better judgment, not wanting our time together to end just yet.

She nods her head and looks up at me. I lean down to kiss her again and everything seems to disappear except us in that cemetery. When the kiss ends, I take her hand and lead her out of the cemetery through the streets of our town, not caring who might see us together. Besides, it's about time the gossipers had something else to occupy their palates with other than the war.

When we reach her home, she releases my hand. "Thank you for walking me home."

I shrug my shoulders then quote to her, "The course of true love never did run smooth."

She smiles up at me, clearly recognizing her favorite line from *A Midsummer Night's Dream*. "Meet me at the tree tomorrow afternoon. I have something I want to show you."

"I'll be there," I breathe, closing my eyes and letting her perfume consume me.

The last words I hear before walking away will forever be etched in my mind. "I love you with so much of my heart that none is left to protest." I can't believe she remembers my favorite line from *Much Ado About Nothing*!

Madeline

23

The summer months have gone and the cool breezes of the autumn days have come again. Our town is in an uproar as General Braxton Braggs has been seen in parts of Kentucky and there is fear he is stirring up trouble with the Union to the north and south of us. Our state is almost surrounded now as word has finally come that Sherman is approaching South Carolina and Grant has sent troops into parts of western Virginia and northern North Carolina. It is only a matter of time before our state becomes another casualty of war and we are left in ruins like so many others.

Every morning I visit the cemetery on my way to the bookstore and the old Yellowwood before I go home in the evening. It has become a habit for me and it helps to put my mind at ease with everything going on. All hostile takeover of the bookstore has ceased due to family altercations – Will has told me that there have been instances in which Annabelle-Lynn has violently thrown something at him. Will even had to receive a stitching when she attempted to shoot him in the leg with his own pistol – it only grazed him but was deep enough to warrant the stitching.

I have not had the pleasure of seeing her around the bookstore, but I know she has informants since I've seen both Savannah Parker and her brother Rex around, asking questions about this and that. Even though it hasn't been completely confirmed by anyone yet, I have inkling that Rex and Annabelle-Lynn have been seeing a lot more of each other than previously thought. Truth be told, I could care less who she bothers to spend her time with, since the man she married spends most of his free time with me, without caring now who sees. He has defied his family by investing in my store and if anyone asks, we spend time at the tree to discuss the future of the business.

When I see him approaching from the distance on the path to the tree, my heart begins to flutter anew. It still amazes me to this day how he has that effect on me. Whenever he speaks to me or kisses me as if I'll never see him again, my whole body reacts and makes me melt into his touch. Today, before he speaks a word to me, he picks me up and spins me around like a child.

"I've missed you today," he replies after putting me down gently.

"Soon you won't be able to do that," I laugh, anticipating his reaction to my words.

"And why is that?" He has a twinkle in his eyes that I hope will never fade.

"Will, we're expecting," I breathe out, staring straight into his eyes.

"What? Really? Are you sure?" he stutters out.

"Yes, I'm positive. I went to see Doc Parker the other day and I believe I am about two months along already." I'm smiling from ear to ear just thinking about the baby growing inside me.

Before I can protest, he lifts me into his arms and kisses me soundly. "I can't believe it! Two months already? That would mean –"

"We'll have a baby sometime in May, possibly around my birthday," I answer, unable to hide how happy I am at the prospect of having a baby to share my birthday with.

"I love you. Never forget that?"

I place my hands over my stomach instinctively and gaze into his eyes. "Yes, that's how I know everything will be all right no matter what circumstances are in our lives," I repeat his own words.

"This is the best news I've heard since this morning!" he exclaims, kissing me quickly again.

"What happened this morning?"

"My father is officially and fully handing over the business as a birthday present!" he smiles proudly.

"And this is a good thing?" I'm confused as to why he's so happy about this piece of news, given his past disdain for the plantation life and it makes repeating his words seems useless.

"It's a wonderful thing! Now I won't have pressure from him to work the plantation to his expectations and standards! I can finally do things my way!"

He is elated but I am still skeptical, knowing his father always has a secret motive. "So he's giving you the plantation, just like that, with no arguments?"

"That's what he told me! He feels I've made enough of a difference with the expansion of the plantation that it's mine if I want it!"

"That's great." Unfortunately my enthusiasm is not present in my voice.

"What's wrong?"

"I just… I want to make sure this life isn't going to make you forget about us." I pout, looking down at my stomach even though there's nothing to see. I remember my mother when she was expecting my brother and for months I kept asking how she knew there was a baby growing inside.

He pulls my chin up with his fingers. "I will never forget or neglect you or this baby. And the plantation will give me enough money to buy or build us a house."

"A house for you and the wife you're forgetting you have." I pull my chin away but he moves his body in order to face me again.

"No, a house for me and the wife I intend to marry; the one I love and who is now carrying my child."

"Will, by state law you have to divorce one wife before you can marry another."

"I've been trying desperately to get the annulment paperwork sent to me from Frankfurt but everything at the state office has been tied up because of the war. You know she won't go away quietly, but I will deal with her in due course."

"When, Will? My body will begin to show signs of this baby in a few short months and then you will be dealing with Annabelle-Lynn trying to hold onto you for dear life!" I argue emotionally.

"Did someone say my name?" we hear behind us from the path.

Will begins to slightly panic, as if she has had no idea what has been going on between us as of late. I simply smile and walk around the tree, seating myself on the swing that still hangs from its branches, knowing that she is losing her own battle. Her eyes dart from me to him and back to me before she speaks again. Her words are full of spite but I don't allow her any room to bask in the glory of them.

"Shouldn't you be working in the bookstore? I'm quite sure there are people wishing to buy books this afternoon."

"They can wait until tomorrow. One more day isn't going to change their purchases."

"But they could go to other stores and you could lose their business," she attempts to argue desperately.

"The closest bookstore to here is in Frankfurt so it would benefit anyone to wait the twenty-four hours," I counter.

She draws her attention to Will. "Shouldn't *you* be counting the money we've made from this year's harvest?" She is incredulous when it comes to his money.

"The money is all accounted for and in the bank already," he answers her, squaring his shoulders to combat her.

"Good. I was thinking of going into Frankfurt tomorrow to buy a few dresses."

"You don't have access to that account and you already spent your allowance for the month. It's time you learned what saving money is all about." I try not to laugh as he looks down at her sternly.

"That money is just as much mine as it is yours, William!" she argues as she stomps her foot like a petulant child.

"That money needs to be used for other things, such as food and supplies for the winter. It is not to be used carelessly whenever you see fit to spend it!" Sometimes, I find marriage quarrels amusing.

"I will get that money even if I have to go to your father to get it!"

"My father doesn't control the finances of the plantation anymore. Whatever I say goes now and if you don't like it, you know where you can go!"

Realizing she can't win her argument, she turns her attention back to me to try again. "You're trespassing on our property. Leave now or I will find someone to arrest you."

"You are taking a page right out of Mr. Hutchinson's book, aren't you? You have no idea what you're talking about. This tree falls directly *outside* of the plantation acreage and my great grandfather was the one who planted it as a wedding present to my great grandmother! I have more of a right to be here than you do!" I retort.

"William," she averts her attention back to him, "your mother wants you home and I am going out tonight so don't wait up for me."

As she bounces down the path, I get an idea in my head. "How badly do you want to that annulment?" I smile deviously when he finally turns to look at me instead of glaring at her retreating back.

"What are you thinking of doing?"

"The gossip around town has it you're not the one in this marriage who has found someone else."

"You mean someone in this town actually wants her?" I laugh as I get down from the swing.

"Leave everything to me." I smile again as the wheels of ideas begin to turn in my head.

~~*

Will has come into the bookstore to help me unload a new shipment of books from Memphis. "How can you be sure? They've only been seen together twice around town. They've been very discreet."

We are unpacking in the storeroom, discussing the possibility of Annabelle-Lynn's infidelity, when we hear the bells over the door chime. I glance up at him and sigh, knowing a customer means we'll get nothing productive done today or finish our conversation about Annabelle-Lynn. Walking to the front of the store, we are greeted by Mrs. Parker.

"Hello, dears. How are you doing today?" She is exceedingly giddy and that worries me greatly. I never trusted her before and I certainly do not trust her now.

"We're fine. What can we do for you today?" Will answers for me since I'm afraid to speak and say something I'd regret.

"I'd actually like to speak to you about something I've been hearing around town and I hope for your sake it's true!"

My ears instantly tune into their conversation and I'm concerned about what has been said around town. "What have you heard?" he encourages her conversation.

"Well, I heard that your wife is expecting and I wanted to see if it was true and offer my congratulations to you both!"

"I don't think you heard right, Mrs. Parker. I have not been told such news." I busy myself behind a bookcase, before she notices me catching Will's eye.

"Are you sure, dear? Because according to my son she is."

I realize very quickly how this piece of gossip spread like a wildfire in our town and it'll only be a matter of time before they begin talk of Will's affair with me, especially when my body begins to show the signs of our child. If what Mrs. Parker is saying is true, and Annabelle-Lynn *is* expecting, she will do everything she can to make the town believe the child is Will's, to keep his family name, fortune, and the appearance that they are still a happily married couple. Slowly, a plan begins to form in my head and I know what Will needs to do in order to rid his life of her for good. I walk back towards them and simply smile at Mrs. Parker, ready to give her my full attention.

"What exactly did your son say to you, Mrs. Parker?" I begin questioning, catching Will's eye for a brief second.

"Well, he told a friend, who told his mother, who naturally told me, that she was talking to Rex the other day and blurted out she was expecting. Since you're her husband, William, I wanted to congratulate you in person." I wish I could shake her for her blindness and deafness to what her own son has been doing right underneath her very nose!

"Thank you," he replies, keeping his demeanor as expressionless as possible.

"I must go, but wish her well for me!" She waves happily as she exits the store, leaving Will and me both stunned and annoyed at the interruption to our fairly productive day.

"Well, now that makes two of us that are expecting," I say sarcastically, glancing straight at him and placing my hands protectively on my stomach.

"You know I had nothing to do with hers!" he defends rather quickly, but I have to laugh.

"Yes, but the only way you're going to prove otherwise is to either get her to admit it's not yours or get the man who she's involved with to admit it's his."

"What would you suggest? We don't even know if *that* gossip is true!"

"Eavesdropping on her conversations with others always works best if you're trying to get the truth to come out." He chuckles as I smirk at the thought but his expression changes as if he's contemplating a plan of action and not just finding humor in my words.

"Can you close the bookstore early tonight? I'm sure Annabelle-Lynn isn't expecting me home early so she won't be looking for me around the house. Before I left today, she said something about having a friend over for tea."

"Of course. You are invested in the store and if you feel we should close, then we close."

Placing a few more books on their proper shelves, I go over to the counter and lock the drawer with the money. When we are about to leave, I lock the storeroom door and the front door behind us, taking his hand in mine as we head across town to the mansion together. Creeping up the back stairs and entering the second floor as quietly as possible, we are not surprised to hear talking from one of the rooms.

"Are you sure it's Rex's?" a young woman's voice asks.

We hear Annabelle-Lynn's voice reply. "I haven't been with my husband. It's definitely Rex's."

"What are you going to do?" The young woman sounds concerned for her friend and it takes everything in me not to ask Will who she is.

"I will just pretend it's William's so that no one will know the difference."

"And what about Rex? Doesn't he have a say in the raising of his own child?"

"What about him? Just because his father is a doctor doesn't mean he is as well. He doesn't have as much money as William does to take care of us."

I glance up at Will, stunned. She has just confirmed for us that not only is Rex the father of her unborn child but that she is going to use Will's money to take care of them both. Will nods his head and walks down the hallway into his room without a word, and I follow close behind. Taking a piece of paper out from his desk, he begins to dip the pen in the ink well and write furiously. Handing it over to me to read, I see that it is a document of annulment on the sole count that she is expecting a child that cannot be claimed by him.

"Are you sure this is going to work?" I ask skeptically. "She's not going to sign it willingly."

"I'm not getting *her* to sign it," he declares. "I'm going to persuade *Rex* to sign it!"

He quickly folds up the paper and grabs my hand, pulling me out the door and down the stairs. Walking briskly towards the Parkers' house, Doc Parker is hesitant to inform us that Rex is not home. As we enter the establishment that Will swears he will be in, all eyes turn to us. Will's hand grips mine and with determination in his eyes, I feel more confident as we approach the bar, where Rex always sits.

"Afternoon, Rex," Will says, voice unwavering, the way he gets when he's commanding his slaves.

Rex looks up from his drink and glares at Will, disregarding my presence completely. "What do you want?" he growls pensively.

"I want you to read this and sign it," Will states, gritting his teeth and slamming the paper onto the bar.

"I don't have to read or sign anything!" Rex retorts.

Before I can blink, Will has him pinned up against the bar and a pistol digging into his back. I didn't even see him take the gun from his drawer so I am taken aback as he continues to interrogate Rex. "I would highly suggest you read and sign it, Rex."

Rex lowers his head towards the paper and reads the words carefully. "This is madness!"

"Not as mad as it is true! Her words to my ears, Rex, and I am *not* going to take care of your bastard child for you!" Will growls low in his throat.

"She's *your* wife! What do you want me to do about it?"

"I want you to sign the paper, making me no longer legally bound to her or that unborn child!"

"But this isn't a legal document! It has no bearing on anything!" Rex tries to protest.

"Perhaps not, but I have ways of making it legal, so I wouldn't press your luck! The child she carries is yours! You know it, I know it, and Annabelle-Lynn admitted it. Now sign the paper and take responsibility for what you've done!" he demands, pressing the barrel of the gun into Rex's back.

"If you ask her again, she'll just deny it! You can't prove anything with this paper, so I can refuse to sign it!" Rex challenges.

"You'll find a bullet in your back if you don't and I'm not bluffing!"

I have never seen Will act this way and it scares me. The only other man I have ever known him to raise his voice to was his father and after gaining control of the plantation, that seems to have quieted down almost to a dull whisper. I gaze around the saloon and everyone is staring at us, making me even more nervous that someone is going to call for the authorities. Will makes one final demand with a jab in the back. Rex reluctantly sighs and asks the bartender for a pen and ink, signing the paper and sealing his fate. Will can finally get the annulment on account of infidelity of his wife and an unborn child conceived by another man.

William

24

"You must be reasonable, William!" My father is furious with me, as always it seems, but this time I have to stand my ground and make things right.

"It's not mine and I will not be accountable for someone else's mistake!" I argue tiredly. "This travesty of a marriage is annulled and I will not argue this further!"

"I'm not going to watch you mar this family even more than you already have!"

"Pardon me?" I am stunned at his accusations, especially after he was perfectly calm in handing me over the plantation for my birthday.

"Getting your marriage annulled is not the answer, boy!" he shouts at me, throwing his glass across the room and shattering it against the wall. "Think about the implications it will have on us!"

"On *us*?! She's the one who's marred this family by having another man's child! How does that look when your own son is viewed as sterile?"

"That's why you need to bring the child up as your own! No one will ever know the difference!"

"We are done with this conversation!"

I turn on my heel and practically collide with Annabelle-Lynn, who had obviously been listening in to the conversation. I disregard her as well, determined to get out of the house and away from all of them. She calls out to me but I don't waver in my step. I also hear my father call out and demand that I "return at once" but again, I have no care about either of them anymore. The plantation is mine, the annulment is final, and I can now focus on more enjoyable things in my life.

I walk down to the Yellowwood, still standing tall and wide at the far end of our plantation, and survey the work being done next to it. With the money from the sales of our crop, I was able to hire builders, keeping them in business while the war rages on all around us. A new two-story house is being built on the opposite side of the plantation to my parents' house, along with a carriage house and stables. The slave and servant house will still remain on their side of the plantation, but control has been relinquished to me.

This new house will be for my new family, which will hopefully grow in the future. I am no longer legally bound to Annabelle-Lynn but I can't force her out of my father's house; I can only keep her out of this new one. She is Rex's responsibility now and even though the bookstore will lose the Parkers' business, I think we can all use a little less gossip in our lives from now on. I'm also very fortunate to know that Savannah has found herself another man, keeping her at a fair distance as well.

"It's coming along nicely, Mr. Hutchinson," one of the young men working on the house says to me as I approach.

"You're quite right. Will it be done before winter sets in?" I'm concerned that when the winter truly sets in all building will stop until spring and I wish to have it done before the baby arrives.

"We're hoping. The framework is finished. Now it's just the inside that needs working on. Are you sure you want six bedrooms upstairs?"

"Six, yes."

"Why so many for just you?"

I smile – one bedroom for Maddie and me, one for her mother, one for a nursery, one as a child's playroom, and the last two for guests. "You just build them and I'll worry about what they're for."

"Yes, sir." He nods and heads inside the frame of the house to start work again.

When I turn around, Annabelle-Lynn is standing there, hands on her hips, ready to start an argument. I sigh, roll my eyes and prepare myself to walk away. Unfortunately, she steps in my way and glares up at me. I know she's not happy with the way things are but she did this to herself and made her own mistakes. She just doesn't understand that life doesn't work the way she wants it to all the time.

"This house is too small for us and why can't we just stay in the bigger house?" she complains.

"*This* house isn't for you at all and it would be best to leave the main house anyway," I reply.

"Well if it's not for us, then who is it for? And why are you wasting our money on it when you should be spending it on the baby?" she whines.

"That money is not *ours* and it certainly isn't a waste. I'd suggest you go back to the main house and make arrangements to have your things delivered to Doc Parker's house. I'm sure you don't want to keep him away from his grandchild."

"You know I can't expect them to take me in. Besides, I don't think Savannah likes me very much. Now be reasonable and help your expectant wife get settled for her new arrival," she demands, unabashed in her chosen words.

"Don't you understand? It's over! The annulment papers are legal, final, and binding! You are no longer a Hutchinson so stop acting as if I owe you or your bastard child anything so much as a glance!"

I storm off, leaving her standing there, clearly taken aback by my anger. Between the death of my sister, my father's anger, and Annabelle-Lynn's whining I'm at my wit's end and need to get off the plantation property for a while. I wander towards town and instead of heading towards the bookstore to tell Maddie the good news about the progress on the house, I venture out towards the cemetery behind the church instead.

Kneeling in front of Gracie's grave, I can taste the salt as my tears stream down my face before I even realize I've started to cry. "I'm sorry. You'd still be alive if it weren't for me. I know how scared you were when you found out about your baby – I've never been so afraid in all my life. I followed your advice though and my heart is so full of love. I just hope it's enough to make her happy again."

I stand up and turn around to leave the cemetery, but Rex is standing there, fuming like a bull. I'm not quite sure how he found me unless he saw me walking through town and followed me here, but I'm in no mood to fight him again, especially near my sister's grave. Yet he stands his ground, stepping in front of me, clenching and unclenching his fists. I glance down near one of his hands and there's a pistol on his right hip.

"I want you to reconsider those annulment papers," he barks sternly, his voice and his eyes not wavering.

I sidestep him but he steps in my way each time. "Get out of my way, Rex!"

"Not until you destroy the papers and take her back!"

"I'm not reversing what's been done. Please let me pass."

He pulls the pistol from its holster and aims it at my chest. "I think you better change your mind."

"Or what? You'll shoot me in cold blood on my sister's grave so you can prove a point?"

"If you were half the man you claim to be, she would never have come to me for the attention you neglected to give her!"

"If you love her that much than take care of the child you created together instead of pawning it off on me!"

"I don't love her and it was a mistake!" he growls, becoming more agitated.

"You can't be serious!"

"Take your wife back because she deserves the life you can give her! Or if you want, I can hold *you* at gunpoint so you can destroy the papers you forced *me* to sign!"

"This is ridiculous! Get out of my way, Rex!"

I shove him out of my way and that's when I hear it – the bang is so loud in my ears I don't have time to process what happened, until I feel the pain in my calf. I fall aimlessly to the ground, screaming and clawing at the grass but it feels like my whole leg is on fire. Glancing up, I see Rex hovering over me with his pistol poised and ready for another shot.

"Stay down, William, or I will not hesitate to shoot again!"

The pain is unbearable but slowly, while bracing my hands on the ground, I push my body up into a kneeling position. Every movement, every breath, is painful but I need to get up and face him like a man. His pistol is still pointed at me but it doesn't stop me from moving. I wonder what his father will say when I tell him I've been shot by his own son.

"I said stay down!" he shouts.

"You don't want to do this," I grit my teeth. "You don't want my blood on your hands!"

Another shot rings out through the cemetery as I scream, the bullet piercing my shoulder this time. He's getting too close to my heart and the next shot could hit its target. I'm lying on the ground now, clutching my shoulder and gasping for air. There's no one in the cemetery to hear the pistol go off and I'm literally there at Rex's mercy, something I refuse to beg for, even with a pistol pointed at my heart.

"I hold all the cards in my hand right now," he growls above me. "You can either do what I say or die – those are your choices. There's no one here to help you and you're losing a lot of blood."

"I'm not going to pay for your mistakes, Rex. I've told you, killing me isn't going to change the fact that you caused this! My family won't take care of her if I'm dead. They know the truth."

"You're lying!"

"I wish he was, Rex," a female voice replies.

Looking up, I see someone standing a few feet away from us. "Annabelle?" I wince in pain, my tiny movements agonizing.

"Rex, put the gun down," she speaks again, addressing him directly.

"You said this was what you wanted. You said to follow him and you said –"

"I know what I said! The plan was to injure him, not kill him, Rex! Now put the damn gun down!"

"You probably don't even know how to use that thing." I squint though the pain and that's when I see her holding *my* pistol in her hands.

A shot rings out and I watch as Rex goes down, still clutching his pistol. Glancing back at Annabelle-Lynn, I shake my head in disgust, knowing this was her plan all along. I heard every word exchanged between them and now I know she had her hand in Rex's attack on me. Did she think that getting him to attack me, I'd change my mind about the annulment and take her back? Sighing, I lean my head down on the cool ground, knowing it will be a long and painful walk to the clinic and an unfortunate explanation to Doc Parker.

~~*

The winter chill is beginning to set in and all I can do is watch the slow progress of my new house from my bedroom window in my parents' house. My arm has been in a sling, protecting the shoulder that had been shot and my leg has been tied in bandages for weeks. Doc Parker said I was lucky that my shoulder bullet didn't pierce a lung and that the leg was a through-and-through but I'll most likely walk with a limp for the rest of my life, after I stop walking with the help of a cane. Every day I am reminded by my father that Annabelle-Lynn saved my life and I now owe her everything but I still refuse to give her anything more than a glare.

She only slightly injured Rex, on account of her bad aim, but it was enough of a distraction for her to help lift me and get me to the clinic. Doc Parker was not happy with her explanation of a duel gone wrong between me and Rex and insisted on asking the authorities to keep us apart from now on whenever we were in town at the same time. He was and probably still is oblivious to the fact that *his* son was the reason Annabelle-Lynn is carrying a child.

None of this has stopped me from marrying the woman I love though. After her last visit with Doc Parker, Maddie found out about the unfortunate "duel" and made haste to find me to make sure I was all right. We were able to have the minister sanctify the marriage with only her mother as a witness, but I haven't been able to see her since, as I have been put me on bed rest, our marriage ceremony having agitated my wounds, and my father has placed me under house arrest, wanting to keep me from her even now.

"William, you should be in bed," my mother interrupts my thoughts as she comes in with that awful-tasting elixir Doc Parker has prescribed.

"I can't stand being locked up in here while I watch that house being built. I need to be out there instructing them," I whine, staring out the window.

"Well stop watching and get back in bed. You have a visitor," she smiles as she directs me back into the bed.

"Please tell me it's not the Marques. I really don't want to play nice anymore. Their daughter should be off this plantation for all the pain she's caused." I wince as I situate myself on the bed.

"No, it's someone you'll want to see."

After taking my medicine, I hand her the empty cup and watch as she walks out the door. With my free hand, I push my body further up on the bed so I can rest my head on the headboard. As the door opens again, I squint my eyes thinking about who has come to call. Just seeing her though brings a smile to my face immediately.

"I didn't think I'd see you until after winter," I tease her lightly for her reluctance to visit.

"I didn't know if I was allowed to see you," she replies sweetly.

"He has no power over me anymore. He can't control either of us now that we're legally married," I reply, motioning for her to join me on the bed.

I was lucky that Rex shot me twice on the same side of my body because it's easier for her to curl up next to me on my "good" side. Once she's situated, I wrap my arm around her and pull her in close, kissing her forehead. She leans up and gently touches my face before kissing me. I haven't felt this secure and happy in a long time. Her eyes flutter open and she stares into mine.

"How are you feeling?" she asks with concern on her face.

I shift slightly. "Better now that you're here, but going a bit batty in this room."

"They don't let you out?"

I shake my head. "They even have meals brought up to me. Doc Parker says bed rest to heal the wounds and my parents are following the doctor's orders, almost too well."

"So they treat you like a prisoner in your own home?"

I shrug my shoulders. "How are you doing?"

Instinctively, I watch her place her hands on her slightly protruding stomach. "We are both fine. Doc Parker said the baby is growing just fine."

I am elated as I pull her tighter against me. "Do you want a boy or a girl?"

"A little girl would be nice, to learn everything about the bookstore, but I want a little boy to be able to take over the plantation someday," she answers. It's the first time I've heard her speak genuinely about my business.

A knock at the door sends her scurrying away from me towards the edge of the bed. "Relax; it's probably just my mother. She knows everything."

The door flings opens and my father is standing there instead, with my mother close behind, I assume to stop him from interrupting us. Maddie looks terrified in his presence and I myself am unsure how he's going to react to her being there with me. Without so much as an angry word, he glances from me to her and back to me, and grumbles something under his breath before walking out of the room, slamming the door behind him. I hear Maddie sigh heavily and she curls back up next to me.

"What does your mother know?"

"She knows how I feel about you, about the investment in the bookstore, about our house, and she knows that the baby is mine."

She gasps but I continue. "Don't worry. She also knows my father will never understand."

"Did you see the way he came in here and looked at me, still like an outcast after all this time?"

I can see the pain rising in her face. "Hey, now, none of that. It's not good for the baby."

"What if he stops construction on the house or he forces you to dissolve the marriage or tries to keep us apart?" She is almost in tears thinking of the worst scenarios possible.

I cup her face gently in my hand. "None of that is going to happen. No one is going to keep us apart ever again."

"How can you be sure?"

"In the eyes of his peers, my father has failed to keep his family in order. A dead daughter, a son who has annulled his marriage – they have scarred him greatly. It would be foolish to do anything else."

Shouting from outside eludes our attention towards the window. Hobbling as best I can, I pry it open with her assistance. People are scurrying everywhere and the shouting is getting louder. My cane is in my hands just as my door swings open again.

My mother's face is distorted in horror. "The Yankees are here!"

"We have to stop them!" I lunge towards the door with determination but my mother's hand stops me.

"Your house, Madeline, is one of the ones they've torched. I'm sorry." I turn my head to see Maddie burst into tears.

"How? What?" she asks through her sobs.

"They're burning them down one by one and pillaging stores as we speak," she reports.

"My mother... is she all right? Is she alive?"

"We don't know."

As I look from my mother to my love, I realize all the fighting was for nothing. All of the people we both lost – her brother, her father, my sister – means nothing because *they* still came. No matter how hard we tried to keep our livelihood going and our crops from failing and our stores from closing, *they* still came. As I stand there and hold onto Maddie as she cries from the fear of losing the last remaining member of her family, I realize that no matter what we believed in and how we were taught to live, *they* still came.

THE END

ABOUT THE AUTHOR

Kimberly Belfer has been writing mainly historical fiction since she was fifteen years old. She has written novellas, as well as novels, such as this, and has dabbled in poetry for four years. One of her poems was published in an anthology created by Poetry.com, *An Awakening to Sunshine* (2000). By utilizing CreateSpace publishing, she has previously been successful in self-publishing *A Norseman's Legend* (2011), an historical fiction set in the Age of the Vikings, and *Love's Dark Embrace* (2012), a French romance combining two novellas into one saga.

She keeps a website open to all who wish to read, *Across the Ages: A Narrative Through Time* (www.ages.squarepins.org). This houses her other unpublished novellas, accessible on the website directly or by downloading to any e-reader. Also keeping up with social media, she has created an online blog about her writing experiences on Livejournal.com under the name SouthernHeart07.

When she is not writing historical fiction, Kimberly enjoys spending time outdoors, whether going for hikes in the woods or teaching by the bay. She is an Education Coordinator for marine science conservation and has also published a K-8 Teacher Resource Guide containing fun lessons about marine science. She has always been a hobbyist writer and will continue to write whenever the mood strikes.

Made in the USA
Middletown, DE
17 May 2015